BUTTERFLIES AND HURRICANES
N GRAY

By N Gray

Blaire Thorne
Ulysses Exposed
Voodoo Priest
Butterflies and Hurricanes
Salvation
Underworld Legacy

Scout Thorne
The Secret Tomb
Murder of Crows

Shifter Days, Vampire Nights, & Demons in Between
Twisted
Lady Hawk and Her Mountain Man
Hidden Shifter
Wolf
Wolf Retreat
Night Hunter
The Fixer
Kai
Lee
Flynn
Jude

Vinci Books

vinci-books.com

Published by Vinci Books Ltd in 2025

1

Copyright © N Gray 2020

The author has asserted their moral right to be identified as the author of this work in accordance with the Copyright, Designs and Patents Act 1988. This work is a work of fiction. Names, characters, places and incidents are the product of the author's imagination or are used fictitiously. Any resemblance to actual persons, living or dead, places and incidents is entirely coincidental.
All rights reserved. No part of this publication may be copied, reproduced, distributed, stored in any retrieval system, or transmitted in any form or by any means, including photocopying, recording, or other electronic or mechanical methods, nor used as a source for any form of machine learning including AI datasets, without the prior written permission of the publisher.
The publisher and the author have made every effort to obtain permissions for any third party material used in this book and to comply with copyright law. Any queries in this respect should be brought to the attention of the publisher and any omissions will be corrected in future editions.
A CIP catalogue record for this book is available from the British Library.
Paperback ISBN: 9781036702304

The EU GPSR authorised representative is Logos Europe, 9 rue Nicolas Poussion, 17000 La Rochelle, France
contact@logoseurope.eu

Life is not always fair
Nobody really seems to care
I'm too sad to think of her death
While she took her final breath
I've always tried not to cry
I never wanted to say goodbye

—Poem written by my ten-year-old daughter in memory of her grandmother

Prologue

She brushed hair out of her face. That small gesture of pretending to tuck a strand behind her ear, only to wipe a tear with the palm of her hand, brought sadness. The setting sun cast her profile in a golden hue and masked the red in her eyes. She turned in my general direction with a smile. The love in her eyes and smile shined through a world of her pain. I wanted to kiss it better, like all the times she had kissed me better, to take away all her pain.

"You're a very special little girl, Blaire. Your dad and I have done many things we're not proud of, but you're the best thing that ever happened to us," Ma said, squeezing my little hand. "But you must promise me, Blaire, no matter what happens today, you will move on. You will not look back. You will not make my mistakes. Now, no more tears. Forget the pain. Lift your head high, and move forward."

I nodded as Ma gently wiped away my tears.

I don't know how, but Ma always knew when I was sad. Even though she couldn't see the world around her, she could still *see* me. Her and Pa always wanted the best for me and did everything in their power to help me get it.

My breath caught in my chest; the hairs on my body stood on end. Glancing around, I couldn't see him but felt him. He was near.

Ma stared behind me with her clouded, damaged eyes—a faint pink circled the edges from crying, then, in an instant, panic flashed through them. She sensed his presence too.

"He's coming back, Blaire. *Run!*" Ma yelled as she rose from her chair.

I ran back inside the house with Ma trailing behind me.

"The stairs, Blaire, go up the stairs. Faster!"

We ran hand in hand, taking two steps at a time. We reached her room, and she opened her closet door. With one hand, she pushed her clothing out our way, got onto her knees and pressed hard against the wall until I heard that familiar snap sound.

"Quick! Get inside. He mustn't find you, Blaire. He can't find you today. Stay hidden, baby girl, and don't come out no matter what you hear. Stay here until someone opens for you." Ma kissed my wet cheeks, wiped away my tears and gently pushed me toward the hidden compartment—my secret hiding place—where the monsters couldn't find me.

I crawled in, turned around and sat.

Ma kissed her index and middle finger and blew me a kiss and closed the compartment door until it clicked shut.

I stared at that silver line between the compartment door and her closet wall. The light from her bedroom provided me with some comfort.

Scratching sounds alongside the walls echoed in the room, inside the closet, and in my hidden spot. I covered my mouth to muffle my whimpers. The tapping of his nails on the doorjamb felt like glass slicing down my back.

I squeezed my eyes shut. I could either block my ears or cover my mouth, but I couldn't let him know I was in here. I had to be silent. I had to disappear. I had to be a ghost. He couldn't see ghosts. I knew that. Even though he was a monster—a very bad one—luckily, some things he couldn't see.

"I waited for you, Alice. You did not come to me like you promised. You forced me to come fetch you here," he growled with a deep and commanding voice.

"I'm sorry, but I've already told you I can't go off with you. We can't be together."

"Is it because of *her*?" His words were laced with malice. He couldn't even say my name.

Ma whimpered, then she gasped—it sounded like he grabbed her.

"Please don't make me choose." Ma cried, her sobbing growing louder.

"You're the only one I care about, Alice. It means nothing to me to kill her."

"Please, don't hurt her," Ma said through tears. "I do love you."

"But not enough?" he yelled.

"I'll do whatever you need me to do. I promise. What do you need? We can go now. Come."

"No!" His yell cut through my core. "If I can't have all of you—"

I heard gasping and *gah* interjections then the sound of teeth grinding with force. After a few heartbeats, I heard a thump against the door and then another against the wall. They were struggling. But Ma wasn't calling for help. She wasn't telling him *no*. She wasn't stopping him.

I heard one last gasp and then a loud, heavy thud on the floor. I opened my eyes and blinked as I readjusted to the dark of the cupboard and the bright light in Ma's room. I saw her hand; her fingernails were ripped and bleeding—and … unmoving. She wasn't getting up. I wanted to crawl from my hiding spot and go to her, to help her. I could help her, but she told me not to leave. I had to stay here. I had to keep quiet. I had to stay hidden from him. If he found me, he would hurt me.

Someone would open for me, that's what Ma had said, someone was coming. Then they would help Ma.

I pressed my head against the side of the wall. I would rather feel pain, and it took my mind off Ma's hand, that wasn't moving. I covered my mouth with both hands to silence my cries, squeezing my eyes tight.

He was coming.

His deep breathing neared the cupboard.

He was near me.

His presence was just on the other side of the hidden compartment.

I heard his deep-chested exhales, like wind in a cave.

I smelled that strong odor I had come to hate—musk and sweat and something else I couldn't quite place; it must be his animal.

All those times he pulled me by my arms and threw me to the ground, luckily, I'd never broken anything.

The metal from the hangers clanged against the closet rods as he shoved Ma's clothing out of the way. The roughness of his actions launched her shoes against the wall. He grunted as he slammed his fist into the cupboard door, pulling it off its hinges.

"Where are you, little girl? I can smell you," he growled. "The smell of fear has a bitterness I love." He inhaled deeply, causing the hairs at the back of my neck to stand on end. He sniffed closer to the wall, near me.

My heart hammered in my chest, and my pulse thundered in my ears.

Please don't let him find me.

Please. Please. Please.

Let me be gone. Let my abilities help me hide, help me to disappear.

Someone yelled from somewhere within the house.

A smack against the bedroom door as he hit it, and then his loud footsteps moved farther from Ma, farther from me.

The front door slammed shut.

He was gone, saved by whoever had called him away.

A loud exhale escaped my mouth.

I stayed in my hiding spot for three days before someone finally opened it and rescued me. I learned a lot about myself while I sat there, slept there, and cried there. That I would get through my loss, and when I was old enough, I would find him. And I would stop at nothing to kill him.

My name is Blaire Oona Thorne. I was only eight years old when the monster my ma trusted and once loved had murdered her and took her from me.

Chapter One

I threw my gym bag on the floor in the bathroom and emptied the dirty contents into the laundry basket. Maria, a were-rat Elena had introduced me to, started keeping my house in order for me. I had no idea what I did before someone helped with housekeeping, but I was grateful to have Maria in my life.

Maria was preparing my lunch in the kitchen while I was freshening up in the bathroom. That first day she came to work for me, she walked in on me eating butter on toast. She shook her head in disapproval, saying a woman could not survive on bread alone. Since then, she would come every day to clean and cook at least one meal for me. I didn't need her every day, as it's only me, and there wasn't much for her to do, but she said I paid her enough for her to tidy up and cook. So I let her.

She's a legal immigrant from Mexico who had been bitten by a were-rat five years ago when she was still living in Chicago. She had lost her job, her husband, and her friends. Everyone thought she was disgusting, because she turned into a were-rat when the moon pulled at her once a month. Lance, their king rat, took her in and gave her a home. I suspected it was the constant reminder that her husband, family, and friends had rejected her that prompted the move to Sterling Meadow—out of sight, out of mind. Elena had arranged with her king rat, Arturo, for Maria to join their colony in Sterling Meadow. And I had provided for her by offering her a job.

I finished showering after my hectic gym session and sat at the kitchen island with my plate of food while Maria started a load of washing when a knock came on the door. I opened the door to two men standing in front of me. The one who had knocked still had his hand up mid-knock; he lowered his hand when I opened the door.

"Can I help you?" I asked, looking from one to the other.

Both men frowned.

"It's us."

I gave them my blank expression and shrugged.

"Don't you remember us?" the one who had knocked asked. He was tall, dark, and handsome. His head was shaved; he boasted dark chocolate-colored eyes and an oval-shaped face. I could see he had once been thin, but now he sported a slight paunch. The other man was just as tall, pale, with chestnut-colored hair cut short, light brown eyes, and a Vandyke beard. I could tell he went to the gym every day; his dress shirt stretched taut against his body.

"I'm sorry. No, I don't. Who are you?"

They looked at each other then back at me with wide eyes.

"We are your neighbors, Blaire." The pale one with the Vandyke beard thumbed at the house across the street. "We rent the house over there."

Butterflies and Hurricanes

I shrugged. "Sorry, but I still don't know you or what you are doing here."

"What happened?" the pale one asked.

His friend stared at me with a shocked expression.

"Were-animals attacked me six months ago, and I hit my head pretty badly. Unfortunately, I don't remember much from my life before that day. If you do know me, I would really like to know everything you know." I opened the door wider. "Would you like to come inside?"

"Perhaps you should come with us instead," the tall, dark one said. "I'm Jermaine. This is Hugh." Jermaine held onto Hugh's shoulder while Hugh held Jermaine's waist.

"You'll want to come with us, Blaire. I promise. And bring those stunning keys of yours."

"Wait, what? Are you talking about the ones with the hieroglyphics?"

They nodded as one.

"Wait here." I ran to my bedroom to grab my keys. As I closed the front door, I saw Maria shaking her head and mouthing, *No, don't go*. But I could handle myself. Plus, I'd been training with Ralph, and I was starting to do more and more. Muscle memory was working with me.

I walked behind the couple as they held hands. We crossed the street toward a single-story house with a white picket fence. Before we entered, I caught a whiff of freshly baked cookies. My mouth watered at the sweet aroma.

"Please excuse the mess," Jermaine said. "I was busy baking. Can I offer you some coffee?"

I stopped in their living room. "Yes, that would be great. Black with two sugars."

The interior resembled a show house from a catalogue for *House and Home*—modern with the latest technology, a smart television, the latest surround sound, and the electronic eyes alarm companies use for motion detection.

Jermaine activated the coffee maker, donned his navy-blue apron and removed cookies off the dry rack and into a cookie tin.

"This way." Hugh pointed to a door I assumed was the basement. "Let me show you while Jermaine gets the coffee ready."

"Uh, okay," I said reluctantly.

Hugh opened the basement door and descended the steps.

I could either go with him and trust he wouldn't hurt me, or I could bolt out the front door and call Ralph. Ever since the voodoo priest had tried to kill me, I'd started wearing my gun in the shoulder holster all day, every day. I crossed my arms and felt the hard, cold metal in my hand and followed Hugh into their basement.

"Do you want to tell me what's going on?" I asked when I reached the bottom.

Hugh stood by a door. "This is yours."

I frowned at him. "What do you mean, it's mine?"

He pointed to the lock on the door. "Where are your keys?"

I held the keychain and approached the door. The lock was ancient. I inserted the second key and turned it, and the lock shifted in place. I pulled on the handle and opened the door. I glanced at Hugh as the door swung wide. My eyes widened as my mouth opened in a surprised *O*.

Chapter Two

Framed black and white pictures hung on one side of the little bedroom. In these pictures, I was holding a baby in some, while, in others, I stood beside a man who looked like a young Mason. I recognized him from the photos Kit had shown me; he was Léon's private investigator.

A cot sat in the right-hand corner adorned with a neatly folded pink blanket and a plush elephant. A desk and a chair rested bedside the cot. A large corkboard with a map and thumbtacks securing notes scribbled on pieces of paper hung against that wall and above the desk. A bookshelf rested near the door. The first shelf housed children's nursery rhymes, and the others featured young-adult books. Lavender and cotton scented the room.

I blinked back tears, my body trembling and the back of my throat hurting. "What is this? And please don't lie to me. Was this my daughter's room?"

"The stuff is Scout's, yes."

"You knew her?"

"Of course, we know her. We are her godparents." Hugh closed the distance between us, pulling me into a hug. "It's okay, Blaire. She's safe."

His shirt smelled of cookies, and I laugh-cried. It smelled like home. Drying my eyes with the palms of my hands. The edges of my smile quivered when my face and hands were wet. "I think I need a tissue."

He chuckled, letting go. He handed me a couple of tissues from the box on the bookshelf. "You always cry when you come here, so there's always tissues for you."

I laughed and more tears fell. When the tears were gone and I could trust my voice again, I said, "Why didn't you come over sooner?"

"You only pop over on birthdays, Blaire."

The back of my throat ached when I swallowed. "Who's birthday is it today?"

"Scout's." Hugh smiled, but it didn't reach his eyes. "We all miss her. We write her letters, and you send them on our behalf."

"I know where she is?"

He nodded.

"Do you know?"

"No. It was safer for her and us that we didn't know." He eyes glistened in the light.

"Do you know why she had to leave—her and Mason?" I bit my lip. I'd rather feel pain than continue crying.

"You must've hit your head very hard not to remember, Blaire."

"I'll tell you about that later. Please just tell me about Scout." I raised my voice. "What happened that she had to leave?"

"Come upstairs, have some coffee, and we'll tell you

everything we know." Hugh approached the stairs. "It'll be better for you if you don't stay in this room alone for now."

I nodded too fast, and felt light on my feet. Hugh was already up the stairs while I scanned the room one last time. I touched the soft pink blanket from the cot and cradled the plush toy, the smell of fresh linen heavy in the air around it.

I locked the door behind me to join Hugh and Jermaine upstairs. I reached the top and found them sitting on their living room couch.

"Come, dear. Come sit by us." Jermaine tapped the seat beside him.

I sat beside Jermaine, my eyes flitting from one to the other. "Okay, tell me." I hugged the plush elephant close to my chest, and the faint smell of linen wafted in the air.

"Ah ..." Jermaine said. "It looks like you're reliving the day she had to go."

I eyed him.

Hugh continued, "We don't know exactly what happened that day to cause all the panic. Mason picked up Scout from daycare, like he did every day. You were still working. I think it was a vampire you were tracking on that ghastly mountain. When Mason came home, he ran straight to our house instead of yours, and they stayed with Jermaine until you got home."

"Is that it?"

"Mason said he couldn't tell us anything. He didn't want us to get involved. Even though he did by staying at our house. But we never found out what he was hiding from. When you got home, you shifted into overdrive and arranged for them to leave immediately. They said their good-byes, and that was the last time we saw them. This happened over ten years ago."

This was more information than Kit could find out, and I doubted he knew to visit this couple.

"Why do I have that room in your house and not in mine?" I asked, frowning.

Jermaine replied, "You used to live here. When Mason moved in across the road, you two started dating." He pointed to my current house. "When things got serious, you moved in with him, and you rented this one to us. When they had to leave, you asked if you could use the basement, and we didn't need the space, so we agreed."

Hugh added, "I think if you didn't have the room here, we would never see you. After they left, you poured your heart and soul into your work. You were always chasing all the monsters you could find. You kept saying, *Just one more monster.*"

"Jesus, I sounded awful." I squeezed the plush elephant against my chest until it hurt. My mug of coffee on the table was already getting cold, and the plate of cookies were waiting for me to eat them, but I had no appetite. I faced the couple. "Can you tell me anything more? Anything about my life?"

"We became friends after we rented your place. When Scout was born, you and Mason asked us to be godparents. We had dinner together at least once a month. But we don't know much about your or Mason's past before then, so we don't know about your parents or if either of you had any siblings. If you did, we never met any." Hugh shrugged. "You worked for Ulysses Assassin as an assassin. Jermaine almost had a heart attack when you told him." Hugh's laugh was deep and throaty, while Jermaine squeaked. Bless his heart.

I smiled at them; they were a very cute couple.

"Oh, you hated shifters. A Lot. As in you H-A-T-E-D them."

"Do you know why?"

"No. They were your pet peeves. Not sure which shifters you hated more, but you seemed to hate them all at varying degrees. Mason didn't know either, and he suspected something must've happened in your past."

A tune I recognized sounded. I pulled my cellphone from my pocket; Ralph was calling. "Excuse me," I said and stood to answer the call. "Ralph, what's up?"

"Are you still heading out tomorrow?"

"Yeah, why?"

"You feel like coming to dinner with me and Devan?"

"I already have plans."

"With Sebastian?"

Beep ... Beep ...

"Hang on. I have another call." I put Ralph on hold, pressing the green button. "Hello?"

"Where are you?"

"At home," I retorted.

"No, you're not. Sawyer is in your house, and Maria said you left with two men."

"I'm across the road, Sebastian. Tell Sawyer to walk across, and he'll find me here." I tried to sound happier, more pleasant, but I knew I was failing.

"Please don't go anywhere without him, Blaire. *Please...*"

"I'm sorry," I whispered into the cellphone. "I didn't think I would take so long. I see Sawyer walking toward me. Let me get him, and then I'll see you soon."

"Okay." He hung up without saying goodbye.

I opened the front door and motioned for Sawyer to enter.

"Hello ...?" I heard faintly.

"Sorry, Ralph, I forgot you were still on hold."

"I guess we won't see you until you're back in a few days' time."

"Yeah, sorry about that. Will everything be okay without me for a few days?"

"We'll be fine. Chat later."

He too hung up without saying bye. Men were so rude.

I greeted Sawyer and introduced him to Hugh and Jermaine.

"You ready?" Sawyer asked, heading for the front door.

"Yeah, just give me a sec." I faced the men still sitting on the couch. "Thank you for coming to fetch me and for showing me the room." I raised the plush elephant. "I'll hold onto this for a while."

"It's yours, Blaire. You can do with it as you please," Hugh said, standing from the couch.

Jermaine followed suit and hugged Hugh from the side. "Are you going away?"

"To Chicago for a day or two. I was wondering, can we meet again when I get back?"

"Of course. Jermaine is always at home. He's my little housewife." Hugh tickled Jermaine's neck, and they both chuckled.

"They're sweet," Sawyer said as we crossed the road to my house.

"Yeah, aren't they just?"

Sawyer stood on the porch while I packed. He was making me nervous dressed in his black bodyguard outfit with his weapons showing. I suspected he looked threatening to my neighbors. I saw a few glances our way as people passed my house.

Sebastian and I had a date night planned, and then I'd be going to Chicago for two days to meet the king rat. At first, I had avoided his letter when I had first gotten home over a month ago, but, after much convincing, I had agreed to go. I had been staying by Sebastian, so they could monitor me when we thought my were-leopard was about to go all furry on me, but nothing had happened after that blue moon when I had some of that blood.

For now, I was still a human.

Apart from the fact I now seemed to be collecting lycanthropy strains, so far I had were-wolf, were-lion, and were-leopard inside me. After that attack six months ago, the witches who had tended my wounds discovered I had a little secret—a talent of sorts. Apart from my aura that glowed white and like a beacon, I had a strong connection to the *other side*, the mystical and metaphysical world—the monster's world. I could absorb their power and use it against others. And, between all that, I had discovered I could heal others by using that white aura of mine. I still didn't understand how any of it worked, as I was trying to regain my memory.

Word of my saving Ivy had spread through the were-animal community, and they had invited me to attend the Were-Animal Alliance meeting. I had gone with Sebastian last week and had met a representative from Chicago who begged me to visit his king. Lance, the were-rat King of Chicago, had been injured during a challenge. At first, they had thought it was only a superficial injury, but he had been deteriorating, and of late, it had worsened. After trying everything, he was desperate, and I was his only hope. He would richly compensate me for my time and pay all travel expenses.

Sebastian had agreed, but only if I took Sawyer with— my very own personal bodyguard. He wanted me to have two, but that's where I drew the line and said, *No*. If I absolutely had to have a bodyguard, one would suffice.

Before we left, I told Maria she had the rest of the week off.

Her face paled. She thought I was letting her go. After twenty minutes of explaining I was just leaving town so she didn't have to come in, she was content. After she left, I locked up, and Sawyer drove me to the Labyrinth.

Chapter Three

I glanced at my feet and realized the blades I was strapped into were not my friend. Sebastian flew past again. I growled at him—a sound I was getting used to here in the cold.

It was his turn to pick our date's activity, and he chose ice skating. I hated ice skating, because I couldn't do it.

We were at a frozen pond, and I worried about the fish below my feet and whether I would fall through the ice and sink to the bottom with the skates as my anchor.

Sebastian glided past again, smiling from ear to ear with an outstretched hand.

I leered at him but not for too long. I smiled when he stuck out his tongue at me. "You are childish, you know that?" I shouted at him.

He circled around again, stopping behind me. He slipped his hands around my waist with his warm breath against my face. "Come, Blaire. Hold on to me."

"I can't, Sebastian."

"You can."

He spun me around, and I almost fell, but, luckily, he caught me. He hooked his arm around my waist again and guided me as we glided across the frozen pond together. I clung to him as if my life depended on it—which it did. We passed Sawyer, who stuck out like a sore thumb in his black uniform as he surveyed the area. Everyone remained on high alert. After the incident with the voodoo priest who had wanted to expel me from my body so he could put his damaged girl into mine, we couldn't trust anyone anymore.

Devan, Ulysses Assassin's touch clairvoyant, had explained to me how I could keep my shields in place so I wasn't conspicuous, like a white beacon of light, for all the bad guys to see and come running.

Désiré and Seraphine, the two witches who had been guiding me on what they could around spells and magic, were determined to teach me how to use my abilities and push them as far as I could. And so far, I had only been able to use their power against them. But it must happen immediately; I still needed to practice retaining that power so I could use it later. But it's proving to be more difficult than we had initially thought.

Also, power hurt. They burn like fire. Sting like insects. And they take away my breath or suffocates and bites. The witches power moved through my body like ice in fire as it travelled from one hand into the other. When it reaches the other hand, that's when I must push their power back into them. Now, all I needed was to find a way to garner their power for a while and use it at a later stage. Apart from what's written in their literature, they had never encountered someone like me to know exactly what to do, therefore everything was an art, which we played by ear. And made plenty of mistakes.

Sebastian's arm still kept me upright on my skates. We moved so slow that a seven-year-old had just passed us.

"If you promise not to let me go, we can go a little faster," I said, watching the kid zoom passed and squeezed Sebastian arm, so he could see what I saw. He smiled, kissed me on my temple and pushed across the ice to make us go faster. My grip on him tightened, but I felt the wind on my face. I had to keep my skates firmly on the ice and straight. I couldn't do that walking-gliding step yet and had to concentrate on not doing the splits. My hips and ankles stung, but I continued, ignoring the pain.

I had to admit, it was wonderful being in his arms. So much had happened these last six months, and it felt marvelous to let someone guide me on the ice, while it felt like I was flying—that free feeling of having nothing to worry about, not having to see which bad monster was behind me: were-animal, voodoo priest, or other. With my eyes closed and clinging onto Sebastian, I enjoyed every delicious second I was with him.

We returned my skates to the little popup station. Sebastian had brought his own skates—yeah, he was that good. He could skate backward and was a twirl-in-the-air kind of good.

"What's for dinner?" I asked as we returned to the Jeep.

"It's a surprise."

Ugh, I hated surprises.

Sawyer drove us to a large building right before the sign that read, *You Are leaving Sterling Meadow*. With about ten parking spaces out front, it sat on the edge of the forest. I couldn't recall this place, and that little voice in my head waved a red flag. I'd seen too many horror films where people got killed in places like this one.

"Um, Sebastian, what is this place?" I asked, not taking my gaze off the weathered building.

"You'll see."

I wanted to say, *No, I don't*. Instead, what came out was, "Yay." I swallowed hard as butterflies fluttered around my stomach. Sawyer entered the building with us. When I first saw it, it didn't look that big until we stepped inside. It was at least ten-stories high. On one side, they had a seated area for dining, but the rest of the place resembled a circus. A woman climbed a long metal ladder until she reached a platform big enough for one person. Someone else swung from the other side, waiting for her. A man wearing a matching shirt helped the woman grab the bar, and she swung when he told her to. The already swinging man caught her legs, and she dangled below him as she screamed with bouts of laughter.

My stomach hit the floor as I gripped Sebastian's hand harder, digging my nails into soft flesh.

"You must try it at least once," he said, pulling me into his arms.

My mouth was dry, and swallowing wasn't helping. "I don't think I can."

"Of course, you can."

I shook my head frantically.

He cupped my face in his warm hands. "Try, Blaire. Please?" His soft lips met mine, and I didn't want him to let go.

When he pulled away, I glanced at the swing again; it was so high in the air. I had to squeeze my eyes shut to avoid the dizzy spell.

"Only once?" he asked softly and sweetly against my ear, sending shivers through my body. And to top it off, he gently kissed me on my lips.

It was so unfair; all I had to do was stare into those extraordinary green eyes adorned with a sliver of gold and be held by him. I not only lost IQ points but melted in his arms. The tension in my shoulders dissolved as I stood in his embrace. He must have pushed some of his power into me, because I relaxed in the circle of his arms. I glanced at the trapeze equipment that filled the space in front of us and noticed a large safety net. You only live once, right? Or die trying.

"Okay. If I die, it's all your fault."

"Let's do it now before we eat dinner," Sebastian said, walking away from me and toward the ladder.

I giggled nervously when the man strapped me into my harness. He pulled so tight on it I almost wet my pants. The worker told me to climb, but, when I didn't move, he pushed me toward the metal stairs. I shook my head at the tiny bars of death. When I heard a rasping yowl, I recognized Sebastian's voice trying to cheer me on. He was already at the top, waiting for me, so he could swing and grab me. This man was full of surprises; was there anything he could not do? I would ask him, if I survived. I climbed one tiny death bar at a time.

The man who had helped the woman reach for the trapeze bar before me yelled, "Don't look down!"

I froze, eyeing Sebastian, and my gaze followed his metal ladder downward until I saw the ground. The people below swirled; the floor contracted in on itself; and my stomach dropped. Ice washed over my body, and I swallowed hard. Gripping the ladder tighter, I forced myself to look up again.

"Don't look down... Don't look down... Don't look down..." I chanted.

When I finally reached the top of the platform, the man

disconnected my harness from the cable that ran along the ladder and attached it to a cable connected to the ceiling and handed me the swinging bar.

Sebastian was already swinging, his arms reaching for me.

My hands cramped from gripping the bar. I dusted my hands with the chalk again, but they were too sweaty.

The man yelled, "Now!" but, before I could protest, he pushed me off the platform. Screaming as I swung and gripped the bar tighter, my stomach flew into my mouth, and then my ankles were being held.

"*Let go!*" someone yelled either above or below me; I couldn't be sure. My world was literally upside down. As if Sebastian knew I would struggle to let go after swinging more than once, he had caught my ankles on my first swing and, in effect, forced me to trust him and let go. And I did. I trusted him with my life, and I let go.

When I opened my eyes, I saw the sides of the building then the ceiling, the sides and then the floor. I laughed and cried. Tears stung my face. My arms were wide open and dangling. The feeling of flying free in the wind as Sebastian held onto my ankles was liberating. This was the equivalent to the *Do you trust me?* game, when one falls backward into someone's arms. I trusted him, even though a net stretched below. I knew he wouldn't drop me.

During these last two months, we had seen one another every day and most nights. When I was not with him, my chest ached, because I missed him and wished I were near him. I loved spending time with him. It was being apart that made me sad.

The swinging slowed, and blood rushed to my head as I giggled.

"Blaire, can you hear me? I'm going to let go," Sebastian said.

I could never grab hold of the bar again to get on the initial platform. I had to go down. I stared up the line of my body at his and said, "Okay."

The strength I had felt as he held my ankles waned, and he let go. And I fell. My stomach moved into my throat and to my toes, and then I bounced on the net. I giggled like a schoolgirl as happy tears streamed down my face again, and I was spent. I lay in the wake of the moving net, the movement easing the tension of falling. Just as the net settled, it moved again, and I almost fell off it.

Sebastian laughed deeply with an edge of his leopard growl and crawled toward me. His crawl was smooth, like liquid metal. All his muscles were supple and limber as he moved above me like he was doing a pushup and lowered for a gentle kiss.

I wrapped my arms around his neck, and the kiss grew into something wild and pining.

He pulled back, grinning. "That was awesome." His lips found mine again. "You were great, Blaire."

"I didn't think I would enjoy it, but it was fun. Thanks for making me do it. Can we eat now?" My stomach growled.

He chuckled again as we climbed off the net.

There hadn't been a peaceful moment to tell Sebastian about my neighbors until we were seated and waiting for our food. I told him about Hugh and Jermaine and the room I had unlocked in their basement and that I had used one of those keys to open the door. My heart pounded as I listed the items that belonged to Scout, my daughter, and I had to blink back tears of joy. Even though it's only her stuff, I was one step closer to finding her.

He narrowed his eyes at me. "Isn't it strange they only came to you now? Why did they wait so long, if you were supposed to be such close friends?" Forever the suspicious Sebastian.

"They said it was partly due to me being busy since Scout left. And that I only saw them on birthdays. And today was Scout's." I stared at my hands.

"I'm sorry." He smiled sincerely. "We should order cake after we've eaten and celebrate."

"I'd like that. Thank you."

"I hate that I can't join you in Chicago, but there's just too much happening here."

Sebastian was a hybrid—half vampire and half were-leopard. His father, a master vampire, had fallen in love with a were-leopard. Statistically, his birth should not have happened, but it did, and he had the best of both worlds without their weaknesses. I've yet to discover all he could do, but something told me some vampires still got under his skin. I suspected that's why he had allowed his brother Léon, Sterling Meadow's Master Vampire, to be in charge. Lately, he had become more involved in vampire politics and with his leap. Anne, the leap's alpha, was preparing to relinquish the throne to either her son Greg or Sebastian. According to leap law, someone could challenge her, or she could pass it to someone of her choosing, but only if the rest of the leap agreed to their new alpha.

"It's only two days, Sebastian," I said when our food arrived. "Besides, you're needed here." I didn't sound convincing. I would've loved it if he joined me, but I knew he had things to do for Anne and the leap. Since he had a good chance of being the next alpha, he needed to act accordingly—whatever that meant for us as a couple.

With each forkful of food, my stomach twisted and

turned. I suspected it was from all that high flying earlier; it had been too much. Luckily, I ate without any of it coming back up, but I couldn't finish my pasta dish.

A gust of wind blustered from someone opening the front door, followed by a loud bang, and then a handful of people entered *Jenny's Trapeze & Dine*. I noticed Sawyer stiffen and approach our table.

"That's him, Sebastian," Sawyer said, nodding toward the group of people who had just entered. "Corey is the one with black hair."

Sebastian and I turned at the same time, but they didn't notice us as they went straight to the trapeze area. The man Sawyer had pointed out, Corey, had jet-black hair cut short. From where I sat, even his eyes seemed dark, and he had a boyish face, like he was still trying to grow into his manhood.

"Who is he?" I asked.

"A new werewolf who joined Shawn's pack," Sawyer said through a low growl I felt vibrate through my bones.

Sawyer was a were-jackal, the only one in the city, and had joined Shawn's wolf pack a few years ago. Even though he wasn't a werewolf, they had accepted him as one of their own, and he was high in their leadership ranks—eighth, if I remembered correctly.

"He's from Vegas. Apparently, he's a new wolf and didn't like the pack there. Shawn put him on a two-month probation period, and he's halfway through it. So far, he acts above board, but something about him makes my animal want to come out and shred him alive."

I stared with wide eyes at Sawyer. He was not naturally a violent person, even though he was a bodyguard. He was there to protect, not to murder. For him to say something that gruesome, made me realize how he felt about Corey.

Sawyer added, "It could all be coincidental, but, ever since he arrived, things have been happening."

"Like what?" I asked.

"Just last week, an older wolf was missing a few items from his bag and all his money. In all the years I have been with the pack, no one has ever complained about someone stealing money. And yesterday, a wolf disappeared. She's new to the pack, so she could've returned to her hometown, but we are still investigating."

Ever since my attack, I realized we couldn't count on our police to assist with anything relating to were-animals. It was up to every one of us to figure it out by ourselves.

"What does Shawn think?" Sebastian asked, keeping his gaze on the new wolf.

"Just that we need to keep an eye on him."

"Have you asked the Vegas pack?" I asked.

"It doesn't sound like Shawn has the best relationship with their alpha. But I think he needs to have a word with him."

"This is what I suggest," Sebastian started. "I'll have a little chat with Shawn about Corey, see if the WAA can do anything about it, apart from watching him."

The were-community had created the Were-Animal Alliance so all the were-animals could congregate to discuss things such as this, in order to keep everyone safe.

"Let me know about the missing wolf and whether she returns," Sebastian added.

"Thanks, Sebastian." Sawyer nodded and resumed standing like the scary guard they paid him to be.

We finished eating, and Sebastian ordered a cupcake with a candle stuck in the middle for us to share. We sang *Happy Birthday*, and I blew out the candle. I made a wish to see Scout and soon.

When one cupcake piece remained, Sebastian raised his fork in a duel. "Fight you for it?"

"On guard!"

We did a quick sword fight with our forks. I poked him with it, and he bowed out of the competition like a gentleman. I ate the last piece, humming as I chewed slowly. I seductively licked the little fork and curled my tongue around it until it was clean. We stared at each other during my fork-cleaning display.

He tsked then chuckled. "You know how I feel when you tease me in public." His green eyes pierced my soul.

"I know." I placed the fork on the small plate, grinning. "I'm ready."

He chuckled again and shook his head. "Here ..." He placed a blue velvet box on the table.

I glanced at him in surprise. "What's this?"

"Open it and find out."

My jaw dropped when I saw a pair of glistening sapphire earrings, with tiny diamonds surrounding them. "They're beautiful."

"Put them in, and never, ever take them out. I was promised that they are comfortable during sleep."

"I promise." I removed my small loop earrings and inserted the sapphires. I kept touching them and smiling at him.

"Beautiful indeed," he gushed and kissed my knuckles. "Come. Let's go, my naughty one."

We walked toward the exit and looked back at the group when we heard laughter and someone complain as they gave the employees a hard time while they climbed the ladders.

"Don't worry, Sawyer. We'll keep an eye on him."

During the car ride home, Sebastian was curled around

me in the back seat. I sat in the middle seat and buckled in with him on my left, also buckled into his seat belt. Yes, he would survive a crash through the windscreen, but I might not, even with his vampire mark on me. I leaned against his chest with his chin resting on top of my head. Being so close to him, I could faintly smell the ocean and musk, and beneath that lay the scent of him—his leopard, a hint of leaves after it rained, and tall dry grass. My metaphysical leopard sprinted to the surface and sniffed the air. A soft growl came from her sharp teeth and then a purr; she liked his smell.

"I smell leopard," Sawyer said from the driver's seat. He turned to stare at us with wide eyes. "Are you going to finally turn?" he asked, half-panicked.

"No. She's smelling Sebastian's leopard."

A soft purr escaped his lips. I turned in his arms to face him, my lips touching his. While we kissed, his leopard sniffed the air around mine, that space where our souls lived in the real world and the metaphysical world. We weren't in leopard form, but a part of our soul was—an out-of-body experience as our leopard's scent marked one another. It was pure emotion, one full of affection, tenderness, and love.

Sebastian's leopard was black with faint rosettes, while mine was white with grey rosettes. When I stopped kissing him, our leopards retreated, and mine returned to her cave, grateful to have been out and be near Sebastian's.

"I like it when she comes out and greets mine," Sebastian said against my temple.

"Hmm, me too." I nestled into his arms, closing my eyes.

My other two animals—the wolf and lion—were in their own caves, each waiting for their turn to emerge and sniff the metaphysical space between here and there. All three animals turned to look behind them as if something was there, but I couldn't see anything else; it was only them and me. I erected stone walls around each of their caves. I couldn't have any of them fight their way out, like the leopard had tried a few months ago. She had wanted to tear me up inside to get out. That was the evening everyone had feasted on Grant—the leopard who had attacked me, and I had shot and killed. I had drank his blood, and then my leopard had wanted to claw her way out, but she didn't. And I didn't turn furry, but it was damn close. Much too close.

Sawyer's phone buzzed. He answered it, but all I heard was, *"Yeah okay,"* and *"On our way."*

Sebastian sat upright. "What is it?"

"They found the missing werewolf."

We stared at him attentively.

"Someone had poisoned her with a dart. Shawn has asked that we meet him there." Sawyer made the first right turn he could and sped until we arrived at an outlet mall.

Shawn stood on the pavement with his arms folded. His intense blue eyes watched us through a curtain of black hair as we climbed out the Jeep. "Thanks for coming, Sebastian." He then greeted me and Sawyer as we followed him around the mall. "She was a new wolf and had only been with us a few months. We realized she was missing yesterday when she failed to meet with a friend. I spoke with her friend, and he told me she wouldn't have left without saying something first. The cops don't give a fuck about us shifters, so we started our own investigation and tracked her here after we pinged her cell."

We had circled the mall toward the loading area. The kidnapper had dumped her body against the wall with boxes placed around her to keep her hidden, although not very well.

"I'm glad you're here, Blaire." Shawn stepped aside, so we could see the body. "You have some experience in solving murders. Maybe you can help us with this one."

"I'm not sure, Shawn, but I'll try." I surveyed what remained of the body. Her skin was shriveled and leathery. Her eyes bulged from the hollow sockets and were a sickly yellow. "She looks mummified." I crouched beside Sebastian, who was also trying to make sense of what we were looking at.

"We found this dart in her side, with this green-red goo inside."

We stared up at Shawn at the same time to see him holding the dart in a see-through bag.

"We should have that tested, to see what exactly we're up against," I said, focusing on the body again.

Sebastian nodded. "Mel can do it for us." He stood and took the bag from Shawn. "Sawyer told me about the new guy. Corey."

"Yeah. I feel something's off about him, but I just don't know what."

"Do you think he's the cause?" I asked, jerking my chin at the body.

"I don't know."

"We can help tail him, if you like," Sebastian said.

"Yeah. We'll need all eyes on him," Shawn said, and they shook hands.

"You guys okay to sort her out?" Sebastian asked, pointing at the body.

"My wolves will burn her body. With that poison in her, I don't think we can celebrate her life and feast on her."

I shuddered at the thought. Were-animals feasted on

their dead to ensure they continued to live with them metaphysically and to celebrate their lives. It was something I couldn't get used to.

We left Shawn and his wolves to drop off the bag with Mel. She was still at the hospital and promised to inform us the moment she knew what we were dealing with. She couldn't chitchat, as she had patients waiting on her, but promised to phone us with the results soon.

I became exhausted as my adrenaline tapered off and was relieved when I saw the Labyrinth come into view. I was shocked when the entrance to the nightclub *Kiss* had a long line snaking around the building. "It's not usually this full, is it?" I asked as we drove passed.

"It never used to be so full. But since Léon is hosting the club, now that Roland is gone, the lines are longer—much longer." Sebastian did not sound particularly pleased.

"You don't say. Look at that line. It's still going, and we're almost at the garage."

Sawyer opened the large metal door with the remote, and some women who were standing in line ran toward the car.

"Shit," Sawyer said, unlocking the car to get out.

"No. I'll handle them. Get Blaire inside now," Sebastian said, climbing out.

"What's happening?"

"They know the garage is one of the entrances into the Labyrinth. They think they can enter here and get into the club. Léon needs to move the nightclub to a bigger venue and far away from the Labyrinth."

Sebastian put his arms around the two ladies and guided them away from the Jeep. He must have said something funny, because they laughed.

I rolled my eyes.

One of the ladies lowered her hand until it rested on his backside. I wanted to climb out and permanently remove her hand.

"You don't have to worry, Blaire."

I flinched when Sawyer spoke. "What do you mean?"

"He was just trying to get them away from the garage."

"I know," I said, sounding angry.

Sawyer chortled in the driver's seat, but I knew it was directed at me.

We pulled into the garage, and the door started closing. "Wait, you can't close it. What about Sebastian?" I asked, sounding panicked.

"He'll make it."

Right before the garage door closed, a black blur slipped underneath and slammed into the Jeep so hard it rocked. Sebastian stood at the back with his hands pressed against the glass, looking like a cat that caught the bird. His kitty-cat eyes shined pure green with the gold slivers glowing. He smiled and flashed his sharp leopard teeth.

"Show off," I said, climbing out the car with my overnight bag.

Chapter Four

"Do you feel like going to the club?" Sebastian asked with his back against the wall, eyeing me like a prized steak and licking his lips.

"No. I want to stay in with you," I purred, trailing my fingers down his bare chest and tugged his belt. I unbuckled his belt, opened his pants and pulled them down, so he could climb out of them. I removed my shoulder holster and gun while he lifted my arms and pulled off my shirt. He loosened my jeans and pulled them down in one quick motion, removing my panties in the process. He chuckled seductively when he realized what he had done. His gaze swept up and down my body as his smile held heat. He picked me up and playfully threw me on the bed. I laughed as I bounced. I'd landed in such a way that my back was to him. An arm cradled my waist, his fingers running over the scars across my stomach, pulling me in closer.

Sebastian drew me into the circle of his naked body pressed against mine. He kissed me from the side then turned me so I faced him and kissed harder, like it was our last night on Earth. He was pressed hard against my thigh. Feeling naughty, I slipped my hand around the soft delicate parts of him, and he moaned into my mouth.

"I'm tired," I said, letting go.

"Tease," he replied with a lazy smile. "Turn around," he whispered near my ear. I turned in his arms and pushed my lower body against his. His hands caressed the side of my waist then lightly brushed my hips with his fingers and moved between my legs. He pushed my legs apart and found my sweet spot, slipping his fingers inside me. "Hmm, so ripe for me."

"Uh-huh," I said through a smile, my eyes half closed.

Sebastian moved my hips until I was in the right position for him. He entered me from behind, gently at first, trying to find his rhythm within that tightness. He went in as far as he could and slowly withdrew, then his rhythm of driving in and out of me hard and fast increased until I writhed beside him. He stopped while still inside me, brought me onto my hands and knees and pushed down my upper body so I opened wider for him and, with his knees, pushed my knees farther apart. He drew himself out and worked his way in again. Slowly, he pushed in and out then harder and faster until he built that pressure between my legs.

He held my hips under the strength of his hands so I couldn't move. He had all the control of pushing himself in as deep as he could until I cried out for him. He made low, deep sounds in his throat as the orgasm caught us both at the same time. It came like an overwhelming wave, engulfing me as I rode it over and over as I writhed for him. He convulsed one more time as hard as his hips could, and he screamed as he came, and I felt the heat of him pour inside me.

I was on birth control, and since he was immune to any disease, apart from death, he didn't need to use a condom. Now that we knew we didn't host any diseases, we would be safe. And Sebastian didn't think I could fall pregnant, but I didn't want to take a chance, so I started on the tiny pill.

He collapsed beside me. Between deep breaths, he kissed my temple. "I'll miss you," he whispered gruffly. His kitty-cat green eyes filled with longing.

I grinned at him. "It's only two days, Sebastian. You could always come with."

"As much as I want to be with you, I can't. And don't forget, we have that dinner with Léon."

"What's this for again? And why must we even go? It's vampire business."

He sighed. "Léon is the city's master vampire, and Shannon is the vampire running for governor. He and Léon need to stay in each other's pockets."

"I hate politics."

"Yeah, me too."

"When is it?"

"Friday. It's a fundraiser dinner. All the high-profile monsters will be there, with only a handful of humans."

"I don't have a dress."

He chuckled. "That's the easy part." He sat up. "Shower?"

We always showered together, and, as usual, it didn't take long for us to kiss and touch each other again. He was ready to go and, with force, pushed me against the cool shower tiles as he maneuvered himself between my thighs once again. He growled as he went in harder and faster.

From the corner of my eye, I saw his eyes glow, like cats do at night. His thrusting began to hurt me, and the pressure of his cold hands pinning my body against the hard tiles was painful. "Ow, Sebastian, not so hard," I cried out, trying to push him away.

I tried turning around, but I couldn't move beneath him; he was too strong.

He kept pushing hard inside me and against the cold tiles.

"Sebastian?" I cried out again with panic laced in my voice.

But he didn't stop. He carried on in the heat of the moment, like his life depended on it. He shoved himself in as deep as he could. Over and over, he rammed harder and harder. He growled near my ear as he held my body in place against the wall, thrusting his hips against mine.

I knocked my head against the wall and felt an ache blossom. He drove himself in and out until I felt the heat of him pour inside of me. I flinched when he bit my shoulder, squealing as I writhed between him and the cold tile wall. The contrast of his heat inside of me, his cold hands on my body, the hot water raining on us, and the coolness of the tiles was startling yet pleasant, and it sent shivers up my spine.

He grunted near my ear, his hot breath against my cheek.

When he finally pulled out, an ache throbbed between my legs, and I doubled over. With my hands on my knees, I glanced at my feet, and blood ran down my legs. I watched it disappear with the water down the drain.

"Blaire? Are you okay?" Sebastian asked, holding me up. His eyes weren't glowing anymore; they were back to his *human* green.

"You were rough with me, Sebastian. Didn't you hear me call out your name?" I exclaimed, holding onto my stomach.

With wide eyes, he answered, "No, I'm sorry. I didn't hear you." He raised his arm to touch me but hesitated, waiting for me to give him permission.

When my body shook from the cold, he added, "Let me get you out of here."

I nodded pensively.

He helped me from the shower, grabbed a towel and dried me. When he was satisfied I was dry enough, he wrapped the towel around my body then grabbed one for himself.

When I glanced at him, I saw pain etched on his face.

"Is it bad?" he asked.

I glanced at my feet and saw just water pooling around me; the blood had stopped. "The pain will go away. But be careful next time. You're much stronger than me, Sebastian. You can tear me apart."

He backed up from me like I had struck him. A look of horror crossed his face. We stood staring at each other for a few heart beats. He blinked, shaking his head as if he was in a daydream. "I'm sorry, Blaire, I don't know what happened. I'll be gentler next time." He extended his hand to me. "Forgive me?"

I hesitated but took it, and he led me to the bed.

Once we were under the covers, he pulled me into his body, holding me tightly, and kissed my temple. "Sorry, Blaire. You drive me nuts when your body is so close to mine. And I was so far into the moment I didn't hear you. I would never, ever hurt you like that on purpose. Never."

"I know, and it's okay." I turned my head to the side so our lips could connect.

Even though he held me in the heat of his body, I was still shivering under the blankets.

He must've felt my body shake and pushed some of his power into me, because the shaking stopped, and I drifted off to sleep.

Chapter Five

Rory and Sawyer entered the garage like muscles on waves; both were tall and large. Only one of them could walk in the hallway at a time, since their shoulders were so broad. Rory was a werewolf, had olive skin and short brown hair shaved at the sides. He had pretty brown eyes and a pleasant face. He wasn't ugly or handsome but floated somewhere in between. It was to his advantage as a guard, as I didn't think anyone would remember what he looked like if he was ever in a danger zone with witnesses.

Sawyer had tattoos covering both arms, a full black beard and short curly black hair. His dark eyes could pierce a soul, if he was allowed too close. His smile was contagious, with perfect teeth, and he had a perma-tan. Whenever we walked outside, he would get looks from wandering eyes. He had a British accent and had been born to Egyptian parents. He was a were-jackal in the werewolf pack, so teaming up with Rory was a good idea, and they got on like brothers.

I watched them approach us. "I hope someone is driving

you back from the airport," I said to Sebastian while I watched the guards.

"I'll drive myself back."

That made me turn to stare at Sebastian. "I thought only Sawyer was coming with me?"

"Please, Blaire, I want both to go with you."

Dammit, it was hard to protest when I was in his arms. It was an unfair advantage. I pushed away from him until we weren't touching anymore and frowned at him. "I can take care of myself, Sebastian."

"I know you can, Blaire. Please, I would rather have the extra manpower and have too much than wish you had him."

Dammit, that made sense too. I stood with my hands on my hips and narrowed my eyes at him.

"We're ready," Rory said when they reached us.

Once we were at the airport, I stood on my tiptoes to kiss Sebastian goodbye. I breathed in his scent and let go of his neck. "I'll see you in two days."

He kissed the top of my head, letting me go. "Be safe." He arched an eyebrow when he stared at Sawyer and Rory. "Take care of her for me, boys. I want her back in one piece."

Both bodyguards stilled with an uncomfortable stance, like Sebastian had already had a private conversation with them, threatening them with carefully chosen words. They nodded quickly and in unison. The three of us piled into Léon's private airplane, waving goodbye to Sebastian as the door closed—just one of the many perks knowing the city's master vampire.

Sawyer sat across from me. The chairs swiveled, so he was facing us, and Rory sat beside me. They were quiet bodyguards, and, as I thought about Sebastian, I wondered whether either of them had someone to share their bed with.

"Do either of you have girlfriends?" I asked, glancing from one to the other.

"No," they said at the same time.

"Why? Is it the long hours you work?"

"Yes, and besides, who wants to be tied down?" Rory said with a sly smile.

Sawyer added, "Who wants to turn down so many women who offer themselves to us to try and get closer to Léon, the Sterling Meadow Master Vampire?" They both laughed together.

"So, you don't mind being used?"

"No," they said at the same time again.

"Does it happen often?"

"Oh yeah," Rory chimed in. "Ever since Léon started to manage the show at Kiss, we've had plenty of opportunities. He only kisses two ladies an evening, or he might feed on them after the show, but he always sends them on their way. Instead of leaving, most will ask to stay the evening with whichever bodyguard is tasked to see them out. They all hope to see Léon again, but they never do. That's also why he needs to move the club, to avoid having any of them stay over, and it's becoming too small where it is. Lately, we've had to turn away a lot of the patrons."

"I had no idea his club was so popular," I said, deep in thought. "And what about Charlotte? Are they still together?"

"Not as far as I know. She's in her own room now," Sawyer said, watching me carefully.

These bodyguards were full of useful information. I would be speaking more often to them if I ever needed info on someone who lived at the Labyrinth, but I should also be careful; they might know too much about me too.

"Yeah, not sure what's going on there," Sawyer interjected. "She's been sulking a lot lately, not sure if that's the reason why though."

The captain interrupted our conversation with an announcement over the intercom. "We're ready for takeoff. Please fasten all seatbelts."

We all fastened ourselves in our seats. Sawyer swiveled his chair to face the other way, and the plane took off. The flight was only two hours long. I squeezed in a nap and a light meal, and, after I used the bathroom, we started our descend.

I was still tender from my shower with Sebastian but was sure the pain would ease in a day or two. He apologized again this morning, remorse etched on his face. I couldn't get his frightening expression from my mind and hoped it was only a onetime event. He could hurt me so easily—and in the throes of passion, he could shred me. I shuddered at the thought.

As we landed, I caught a glimpse of people standing near a black SUV. When the plane stopped and the doors opened, I slipped on my sunglasses. Sawyer walked ahead of me, then Rory came behind me, carrying my bag.

The people I had seen when we had landed approached us on the tarmac. We reached them halfway and stopped. They stood in height order—shortest to tallest; not sure if that was on purpose or by accident. I approached the one who was my height, the shortest person.

"Blaire," the man said, extending his hand. "Welcome to Chicago."

I shook his hand; it was firm and didn't linger—I liked

that. Nothing worse than when a man kept your hand in theirs for a heartbeat longer than appropriate.

"I'm Derick. This is Mandy, and that's Tyrone."

Derick seemed very young, but that could just be because of his sepia-brown complexion, dark hair, and great genes. His eyes told me a different story; he held years' worth of experience in that look, and him donning two teardrop tattoos under his right eye should have made all my red flags fly. But there were none, because he seemed charming and non-threatening.

Glancing over my shoulder at my two guards' stoic faces, I saw a glimmer in their eyes that told me they didn't trust any of them.

Mandy, who was taller than Derick and pale with sun-kissed freckles scattered over her skin, scowled at me, so I just waved and said, "Hi."

"Ignore her. I think she has her period," Tyrone said. His voice was deep, like rolling thunder, which matched his umber skin tone and brown eyes. His hair was shaved close to the skin, and I noticed a hint of tattoos on his neck but couldn't decipher what they were. But, as always, looks were deceiving. Tyrone seemed large and manic, but his smile was warm and inviting, and he shook my hand gently, as if I were made of thin glass.

I introduced my bodyguards to them, and we all piled into the black SUV. I sat in front with Tyrone driving. Sawyer and Rory sat with Mandy between them and Derick in the back. We drove downtown through a few rundown areas until we arrived at our destination. It was a ten-story red-faced brick building with a sign showing two boxers standing face to face with their gloves raised. We parked behind a luxury vehicle in the garage with a fireman's pole in the middle.

As we climbed out the vehicle, a woman slid down the pole and landed on the soft cushion on the floor with a loud thud followed by laughter. "You finally made it. Where is she? Where is she? I want to see her!" The woman ran around the SUV and almost into me. She stopped before bumping into me. "Blaire?"

"Yes." My gaze flitted from the woman to Mandy and back to the woman. "Twins?"

"Uh-huh. I'm Monique."

I gave her my hand to shake, but she hugged me. She squeezed so hard a wheezing sound escaped my lips.

"Let her go, Monique. You'll kill her before she can even help Lance," Mandy said with a sour undertone.

When Monique let go, I could breathe again.

"Come. He's waiting for you," she said, running to the elevator.

I picked up my luggage and followed her with my two guards closely behind me. The elevator stopped at the top floor, and we piled into the large entrance hall adorned with a red rectangular carpet to wipe our feet before we entered the living area.

"He's in bed. Some of his hair fell out."

"Monique, that's enough! She'll see for herself when Lance is ready for her," Mandy yelled and broke away from the group to disappear into a bedroom on our left.

Tyrone led us to a bedroom on the far right. "Through here, Blaire." He stood aside, allowing me entrance into the bedroom first.

As I entered, I saw the man. He seemed small and lost in the sizable bed. His yellowed thinning hair was damp against his face. Sweat beaded down his pale gaunt face, his skin thin enough to see the blue veins beneath. A dark-haired woman wiped his forehead and neck. Deep-set grey eyes followed me as I stepped farther into the room. He tried to smile, but the corners quivered, draining his energy further.

I didn't know this man. I had never seen him before, but I felt sorry for him and knew I had to help him. I wanted to help him. He was suffering a slow and incredibly painful death. I frowned.

"What's wrong?" he asked, his gaze flitting from me to someone behind me.

"Everyone needs to get out." I said, needing space in which to concentrate.

"No. You can't be alone with him," the person who stood behind me said. I didn't need to turn around to know it was Mandy.

Lance coughed. "Okay, everyone get out."

"Are you sure about this, Blaire?" Sawyer whispered close to my ear.

"I'll be fine. Thanks, Sawyer." I squeezed his arm, gave him my bag and went closer to the dying man in bed.

The dark-haired woman who was wiping Lance's face left with the others.

"You too, Mandy."

"But, Lance—"

"Don't make me repeat myself," Lance said, wincing.

When everyone had left and the door was closed, I surveyed the shadow of a man, a skeleton with skin. "Okay, now that it's just us, tell me. What happened to you?" I asked, my voice barely audible.

"I was challenged by someone I thought I knew and trusted. I won the fight, but he left me with a parting gift." He coughed up blood and wiped his mouth with a tissue he had in his hand. "Before he left the boxing arena, it's customary to embrace the fighter, to ensure no hard feelings. And, in that embrace, he jabbed a needle between my shoulder blades, just missing my spine."

"I'm sorry. Where is your friend now?"

"He fled, but"—he coughed again—"I have people looking for him."

"And when they catch him?"

"I want to know what this stuff is and where he got it." He winced again, and the lines between his brows deepened. He clutched his chest as if he was having a heart attack.

"Lance, I need you to understand this might not work. I've only recently come to grips with who I am and what I can do. Even then, I don't know it all. But you must know I might not be able to heal you. You may still die. Do you understand that?"

He nodded slowly. "Yes, I understand. But you saved Ivy, and she was almost dead."

I nodded. "Again, I didn't know then, and I still don't know what is possible."

"I know I might die today, or you may heal me. It doesn't matter either way. I'm ready."

I'd saved Ivy after Phillip had challenged her to a fight. They were both were-leopards, and Phillip had won, and Ivy had been dying. I couldn't sit by and watch as her light faded from her eyes until they were dark and empty. I had held onto her and had brought light back into her by using my white aura, that which could heal. And she made it. She lived.

Somehow, this white aura of mine could not only syphon other powers if used against me, but it seemed to have healing capabilities I am yet to fully understand. That's why I was here, why I had been invited to a dying man's bedside.

"Okay," I said, climbing onto the bed. I sat on my haunches next to him, pulling the sheet low around his waist, and froze. He had an eight-point star tattoo on each clavicle, with an epaulette on each shoulder with more stars. A large cross decorated his chest with the Virgin Mary on his side. His body was littered with tattoos. I swallowed hard. One had to be on the good side of a mob boss, or they might end up dead. It was good I was doing him a favor, which meant I had him in my pocket. Maybe. It would all depend on how today ended.

Once I was over the shock of all his tattoos, I took his frail hand in mine, and it was cold. He was on the edge of his grave. I closed my eyes and dropped my shields just enough so some of my light came out. I opened it up so my pure white aura could go from my hand into his, up his arm and near his heart. My white aura searched his heart for a beat. He had done bad things in his life, things no man should ever repeat and live. But with his new life as king of the were-rats in Chicago, he was trying his hardest to make amends, to do right by others and protect not only those he hurt but any of his rats who had terrible things happen to them.

I searched deeper inside him, into the darkest part where his soul was kept. I found that spark of his life. I could either extinguish it, or I could ignite it. Was this what it felt like to play God? To have someone's life completely in my hands to do with whatever I please, the most unimaginable power trip known to man. It was up to me to either leave him be, or I could help him, and he could live. He had done so many wrongs that, by killing him, I would avenge his victims. But all the good things he had been doing were becoming more and more. He was gradually atoning for all his wrongdoing. And I could live with that. My conscious was clear.

I inhaled a deep breath and exhaled. Slowly, my white aura reached for his spark. When they touched, his spark burst into flames. Heat cascaded around me and flared within him. The heat from his flame was so hot I felt sweat drip down my forehead. I screamed in my head, but he was screaming in the bed. My eyes fluttered open in time to see his muscles grow again, where before there was only skin and bone. His grey skin changed to a glowing tan; his thinned yellow hair thickened and was sandy blond with a surfer's wave. His cheeks plumbed out and were rosy.

I returned my white aura to its metaphysical shield and secured my walls.

Lance was still screaming when the door opened, and footsteps rushed in. Everyone behind us gasped.

Lance was the man he once was before falling ill.

Just as his body became whole again, his skin flowed with thick fur. His face changed into a large jaw with sharp teeth, and his eyes glowed red. Bones snapped painfully in place, and claws grew.

I felt his hands become coarse with fur, and sharp nails dug into me. But I was human slow. I was too slow to get out of the way, to get out of his grip. He had held onto me as he changed into the large were-rat, and, before I could comprehend what had happened, I was on the floor with the rat king on top of me, and we were both covered in blood.

Chapter Six

As quickly as he shifted into his were-rat, the fur receded until he was back to human. He straddled my waist naked, and one of us was hurt. I only saw tattoos on him but no open wounds.

"Blaire, you're bleeding," Rory said, rushing to my side. When he was in my line of sight, he snarled, "Get off her, Rat King, or I'll force you off her myself."

Lance rose slowly and towered over me, all his nakedness for everyone to see. He stepped away, shouting, "Sally, we need you in here, now!"

The woman who had been tending to his wounds crouched by my side with her black medical bag. "Let me see, dear." She cut my top from the bottom up and opened it, so she could have a look. Her gaze flittered from the wound to my face and then upward. Her fingers traced the large scar that extended from my bellybutton, around my waist and to my spine. She glanced at someone standing behind me.

"She helps you, and you thank her by cutting her up!" Rory yelled. "This is reason enough to kill you, rat."

"Don't tempt me, dog. I'll rip your head off," Lance growled back.

I couldn't have Rory fight the king rat in his home city. We didn't have any other back up, and enough were-rats were in this room to kill us all.

"Rory, no."

"Blaire?"

"It's just a scratch, Rory." I said, staring into Sally's sky-blue eyes. I saw a hint of uneasiness in that blue, and I knew it wasn't just a scratch.

"Let me clean you up, and then we can take it from there. Everybody else, get out," Sally said.

"We aren't leaving you alone again, Blaire, or Sebastian will kill us."

Dammit.

The pain came in what felt like stinging shards of glass low in my pelvis. I tried to move my head, so I could see the damage, but Sally was blurry around the edges and sparkly stars flashed in my vision, and my head hit the floor again.

"Blaire, you're hurt. I shouldn't have allowed you to go," a voice sounded in my head.

"Sebastian, is that you?"

"Yes. I can feel your pain."

"It was an accident, Sebastian. It all happened so quickly."

"I'll feed enough to give us both strength."

"Will that really work?"

He laughed with a soft growl—it was pleasant—and I relaxed like I usually would in his arms. *"Yes, it'll work and help heal you quicker."*

"That was nice. Laugh again."

And he did.

Someone's phone rang, and I heard Rory answer then step away.

"I don't think your uterus is damaged, Blaire. You were very lucky," Sally said with concern. "But we do need to test your blood, dear. There is a very good chance Lance has infected you."

Not again!

Sally tended to the wound. My skin pulled and tightened every time Sally pierced my skin with the needle as she sutured the wound. The smell of antiseptic wafted in the air. I counted twenty sutures, and then she taped a large plaster low on my waist and hips.

"Can you sit up?" she asked, holding her hand to me.

I took her hand, and she slowly pulled me to my feet. The pain was manageable as my skin pulled on the sutures when I moved.

The bathroom door opened with Lance standing in the doorjamb. He was the man he was supposed to be—tall, strong, and formidable. He boasted short sandy-blond hair, high cheek bones, and cerulean eyes. He wore sweatpants low on his waist, and I could still see all those tattoos. The eight-point star and epaulettes on his shoulders reminded me of the Russian military.

He moved toward me, but Sawyer touched his chest and shook his head. "Perhaps it's best if you don't go near her again."

Lance raised his hands. "I won't hurt her." He paused. "Again." He regarded me with regret in his eyes. "I'm sorry, Blaire." He stepped forward, swiping Sawyer's hand from his chest. "I hadn't been able to shift since the fight. I think if I could, I would've healed myself, but whatever I was injected with stopped me from shifting and healing. When you brought me back to life, Blaire, everything happened so quickly, and, by the time I saw what I had done, it was too late."

"I think it's partly my fault, Lance. I did do it too fast. I'm still trying to figure out things. And I think your body was still in shock from the sudden change."

"Don't apologize for what he did to you, Blaire," Sawyer retorted.

"That's enough, Sawyer." I glared at him. "Please."

"I'm forever in your debt, Blaire. For anything, anytime, and always." He went down on one knee, took my hand in his and kissed my knuckles. His lips felt hot against my hand.

"I need to sit," I said, doubling over. My hand was still in Lance's when Sawyer came between us and held me up.

"Put your arm around me," Sawyer said.

I did, and he picked me up. I winced and bit my lip. "I think we should leave, so I can get some rest. Where is our hotel?" I asked no one in particular. I knew Lance had arranged for us to stay at a hotel, and, if he hadn't, Sawyer would sort out something for us.

"Absolutely not," Lance said. "I have more than enough room for all of you here. I don't think you're in any condition to be moved in any case. Monique!"

Monique skipped into the room. "Yeah?"

I wished her sister had half her spunk and energy. Mandy stood against the wall with malice behind those blue eyes.

"Tell Florence to ready three rooms."

"One of us will stay with Blaire. Do you have anything big enough with a cot or couch for me to sleep on?" Sawyer asked, still holding me in his arm.

"Fine. Tell Florence to arrange for the Boogaloo room and the one across from it."

"I'm on it," Monique said and skipped out the room again.

"Perhaps put me down somewhere, Sawyer. Aren't I heavy?"

"No," he said, walking toward the living room. The couch was large, and, when Sawyer set me on it, it felt soft against my aching body.

I winced, and a yelp escaped my lips as I relaxed my body into the soft cushions.

Mandy clung to Lance like he was the air she needed to breathe.

Sawyer sat beside me while Sally stood across from us, and Lance was in the far chair with Mandy draped over his lap.

"How are you with painkillers, Blaire?" Sally asked, digging inside her medical bag and removing a silver sleeve.

"Fine. I don't have allergies."

She handed me a glass of water with two capsules. "Good. And have you eaten anything today?"

"Just a snack on the plane."

"Should be fine."

I swallowed the capsules, set the glass on the table beside me and glanced up. "You know, Mandy. I don't know what the fuck your problem is, but don't take it out on me. I cut up bitches like you for breakfast."

Her mouth made a surprised *O*. She gasped, her hands covering her mouth. "How dare you!" She glanced from me to Lance, speaking with her eyes for him to stand up for her.

Sawyer giggled beside me then straightened his face, but his lips kept curving upward.

"You must forgive her, Blaire. That is my fault too."

I narrowed my eyes at both of them. "Your hospitality hasn't been wonderful, Lance. Please don't make it worse." I exhaled and relaxed my hands until my knuckles stopped hurting.

"After the fight and the attack with the needle, Mandy wanted to help me. But I kept chasing her away, because I thought I was dying. Then, when I heard what you did for Ivy, I said the only person who could help me was you. And unfortunately, Mandy is the jealous type. Then, when I said *'I only needed you'*, that just made things worse."

"Like I said, it's not my fucking problem. I don't want your man, Mandy. I have my own back home, and I wish I was there instead." I said, wishing Mel was here. Somehow, she was the only werewolf who could calm me down when I was this angry. Sebastian could help me sleep.

I cried out as pain ripped through the wound. I rested my head against the soft sofa as I thought of the pain and how to push it aside. Dark claws swiped at my face, and teeth bit into my side. Large claws dug into the ground, slowly at first then into an accelerated sprint. The muscles moved like liquid metal until the large furry animal was on me. It jumped into the air and hit me in the chest. I flew off the couch and crashed to the floor, the wound thumping in my pelvis. There was hammering in my ears, and then the pain of hitting the floor reverberated in my bones.

The glowing red eyes stared at me, its sharp jaws near my face, the white-grey were-rat wanted *out*. She was metaphysically inside of me, and she wanted out and to shift into her were-rat form. She lifted me off the floor until I hit the ceiling. When I opened my eyes, I was staring down at everyone. Everybody stood still with their mouths agape, shock all over their faces—or was it horror?

My feet and body were pressed firmly against the ceiling, like I was stuck there.

"Blaire? Are you all right?" Sawyer asked directly below me with his arms out, ready to catch me when I fell.

"I don't think I need that blood test, Sally. It seems I have the were-rat strain as well."

Sally gasped. "Oh my god, that quickly? This is unheard of."

My white-grey were-rat metaphysically licked my face and ran into her cave. When she disappeared, I fell forward, and Sawyer caught the top half of my body as my feet touched the floor.

"How's that room coming along, Lance?" Sawyer grunted, setting me gently on the floor and waiting until I could stand unaided before he let me go.

Monique skipped into the room at the right time. "All done. Luckily, we didn't have much to tidy up, as Florence is super anal when it comes to cleaning the rooms." She approached me, hooking her arm through mine. "Come. I'll get you settled. You're looking a little shaken, Blaire."

Rory reentered the room with a blank face, but his brown eyes panned from me to Sawyer; the look behind his eyes screamed how upset Sebastian was.

I pulled down Rory, so I could whisper in his ear. "I'll phone him when we settle in the rooms."

"He's not happy."

"Hmm, I know. I can feel him. He's worried."

Monique had to be on drugs or something; she was the human equivalent of a ball bouncing off the walls. She couldn't stand still and jabbered on about all the high-profile were-animals who had stayed in this very room. Lance only used it for the best and most powerful, and I should feel privileged.

I thought not, after what he had done. It was only the beginning of what he had to pay me.

I felt homesick, and I needed to be with Sebastian.

The king-sized bed was adorned with dark blue silk bedding. It looked inviting. I wanted to run and jump on the bed but thought better of it. In the small living space was a fold-out double-sized couch.

Monique threw white silk bedding onto it.

Rory and Sawyer agreed to stay in the room with me and share the double bed. I felt sorry for them—these two extra-large guards sharing a double bed but neither of them was about to sleep beside me; Sebastian would kill them. Would they spoon on that tiny double bed? I held back my grin while they made the bed together. At least the bathroom had a door.

We had some privacy when Monique finally left. I went into the bathroom with my cellphone and called Sebastian and told him a short version of what had happened.

"I'm coming to you."

"No, Sebastian. Please don't. I'm fine. Did you feed?"

"Yes. It seems to help. I don't feel as bad as I did earlier."

"Do you feel everything when I get hurt?"

"Yes."

"What happens?"

"I feel your pain, and I become incredibly weak. But all I have to do is feed to keep my strength."

"Blood?"

"Uh-huh. Is that an issue?"

"No. You're a were-animal and a vampire, and you need to feed."

"We need to find out what all this means, Blaire. You have were-rat lycanthropy in you now. It's like you're collecting them. Are you sure you don't need me to come through?"

I sighed, squeezing my eyes tight. One lonely tear slid down my cheek, and I wiped it away. "I know you're worried, but I really am fine. It's done, and I just need to rest. We'll stay the night and fly home first thing in the morning. So, there's no need for you to worry or come through to me."

He was silent, but I heard him breathe into the receiver.

"Sebastian, you still there?"

A moment passed. "I'm still here. How are you feeling from last night?"

"Better, thanks."

"Are you sure? I keep thinking about what I did in the shower, and all I remember was how good you felt. I didn't hear you cry out, Blaire. I could've hurt you badly."

"It's okay, Sebastian. Really."

The silence stretched.

He felt bad for hurting me last night and again for not coming with me to Chicago. I could feel his remorse; it was our metaphysical link to one another—with every day that passed, it became stronger. I didn't want him to feel bad. I wanted him to feel loved. We had known each other for six months, and every day we spent together, the closer we grew. I was falling for him, and hard.

"Love you," I blurted without thinking. Then I pursed my lips. Shit. I didn't want to say that to him for the first time over the phone. It was something we should have shared face to face, so I could hug him when I said it and do other things. Dammit. What if it was the wrong time? What if he didn't want to hear it and didn't feel the same way? I knew he had feelings for me, but did he love me?

The silence was long and thunderous, even his breathing had stopped. Had I mistakenly said something he wasn't ready for?

"Sebastian?"

The silence stretched. My pulse beat loud in my ears.

"Blaire?"

"Yeah?" I whispered and wiped away a tear.

"I didn't want to say it over the phone. I wanted to have you in my arms when I said I love you for the first time. And I do. I do love you."

I pulled toilet paper off the roll and wiped my nose then grabbed a fistful of toilet paper to wipe my face. I would not ugly-cry.

"I love you too," I said, swallowing so hard the back of my throat hurt, and my chest pained—or was it coming from my heart? It was an ache that tugged at my very core. A part of my heart chipped away as I offered a slice of it and my soul to him.

"Please come home to me, Blaire. I need to see you. I need to hold you in my arms and look into those beautiful green eyes to see for myself that you're okay."

I nodded then realized he couldn't see me. "Yes, yes. We'll leave first thing in the morning." I swallowed hard again, wiping another tear of joy. With a smile on my face, I changed the subject. "What are you doing now?"

"I'm still at Anne's. It's just a small meeting, nothing too serious."

"Okay. Get home safely. I'm tired and want to sleep. I'll talk to you in the morning."

"Sleep tight." And he ended the call first.

I blew my nose in between sobs and dried my puffy eyes. I opened the water in the shower, stripped and removed the plaster from my waist. I touched the raised ruby scar running from one hip to the other. Whatever I was becoming, my aura allowed me to heal others and myself incredibly fast. Sebastian had said he had fed; that must have helped me as well. The latest wound was already a scar and only sensitive to my touch as I traced my finger over it. It was amazing how quickly I could heal, and I smiled to myself.

After the shower, I pulled on one of Sebastian t-shirts. It was large and comfortable to sleep in, and it smelled of him. When I stepped out the bathroom, Sawyer and Rory glanced at me like I had sprouted a third head.

"What's up, guys?"

"Are you all right? We wanted to break down the door earlier when we heard you crying."

My smile faltered at the sides. "Thanks, but I'm fine. The bathroom is available, if you need to use it. I'm going to bed." I climbed under the covers. "And we're leaving first thing in the morning. I want to go home."

Both guards nodded at the same time. Sawyer went into the bathroom next while Rory sat on the sleeper couch and stared at me.

I could feel his gaze and sat upright. "I'm all right, Rory. Please stop staring at me like that."

"I can't allow you to get hurt again, Blaire. Sebastian has warned me. Again."

"We're safe. Just stop staring at me. And you couldn't have done anything in any case. It all happened so quickly. I'll handle Sebastian."

He grabbed a magazine and started reading it.

Exhaustion took over, and I fell asleep.

Chapter Seven

As we landed in Sterling Meadow, I saw Sebastian standing beside his Jeep, waiting for us. The back of my throat ached, and I swallowed hard.

The entire return flight, everyone remained silent. It felt uncomfortable and awkward. Rory sat in front with his back to me while Sawyer sat behind me. Neither of them wanted to look or talk to me.

We didn't discuss what had happened, and I wanted to ask if my crawling on the ceiling had been what disturbed them. For bodyguards, they were easily freaked out and were keeping their distance.

Before we had left, I had asked Lance who was the person he had fought and then later had attacked him with a syringe. He said it was his friend Billy; they had been best friends since childhood, and they used to do everything together. They were both bluebloods; they were born were-rats, and their families were very close. They had attended the same schools, had worked for the same boss after school to make extra money until they were old enough for more important work that turned them into made men.

Then Lance had become king of the Chicago were-rats, and their relationship had turned a bit sour. Billy had started working for their sworn enemy, which didn't sit right with their old boss.

"Then one day, he showed up again and challenged me. And I accepted," Lance said, recalling the memory.

"Didn't you find that strange? After all this time, he suddenly wanted to challenge you."

"At the time, no. But in hindsight, yes. I should have known, but I wanted us to be friends like we used to be," he said, staring off into the corner.

"Did you find out what he injected you with?"

"Sally said it was some kind of blocker. It stopped my animal from appearing. It prevented me from shifting and healing myself."

"Do you think Sally could send me her results?"

"Sure. I'll ask her to send it as soon as she can. You saved my life, Blaire. If ever you need anything else, please don't hesitate," Lance said with a smile.

The corners of my mouth curved upward but not by much; I felt my rat sniffing just below the surface, smelling Lance. She liked what she smelled.

"You even smell like rat now," Lance said, sniffing the air around me. "You say this is your fourth strain, and you haven't shifted yet? Surely that can't be."

"Yeah, apparently it is."

He grinned. "I can find some answers for you, if you like. We have a few old fuddy-duddies who might know a thing or two."

"Thanks. I'd appreciate that."

As we taxied, I turned on my cellphone, and a message

from Sally popped on my screen with the results from the tests she had run on Lance's blood. I would read it later; I was keeping an eye on Sebastian, who stood there, waiting patiently for me.

The airplane door opened, and I sprang from my seat and ran down the stairs. Sebastian waited at the bottom, and I leapt into his arms. I wrapped my legs around his waist, kissing his cheeks, forehead, lips, and chin then explored his mouth like I was about to eat him alive.

When I finally stopped kissing him, I stared into his eyes and waited for something ... for him to look away from me, to flinch. But he didn't. He gazed into my eyes and straight into my soul. Time stood still for those seconds, and it was only for us, so we could reconnect, even though we had been apart for only one day.

"I love you," I said, watching for that telltale sign I might be wrong; it's only the mark, none of it was real.

With the weight of his stare, I was in his line of sight the whole time, and he didn't falter. He didn't blink; he didn't look away. He gave me his all.

"I love you too, Blaire Oona Thorne."

I loved it when he used my full name, and my heart gushed with deep affection for the man holding me. We kissed harder this time, with every inch of our souls. We kissed with all our heart as we offered a piece of it to the other. We came back from that kiss breathless.

"Why are you crying?" he asked, wiping away my tears.

"'Cause I'm happy." I burst out laughing. "I don't get it either, but I'm very happy."

He set me on the tarmac and hugged me again, crushing me against his chest for a few more seconds. We walked to his Jeep as Rory and Sawyer trailed behind us with the luggage.

"What's up, guys?" Sebastian asked as Sawyer pulled the car onto the road. "You haven't said a word."

The two men shared a knowing look but remained silent.

"Sawyer?" Sebastian made it a command.

"It's nothing, sir. But perhaps, in the future, we may need more guards. Just in case."

"Is that all?"

They nodded.

"There could be one other thing," I said, glancing at Sawyer then Rory, but they wouldn't meet my eyes. "I crawled on the ceiling last night."

Sebastian regarded me with wide eyes. "Excuse me?"

"When my were-rat showed her white and grey furry self to me, she pushed against me so hard I landed on the ceiling. And I think I hovered there for a few seconds before Sawyer caught me."

"Jesus, Blaire. Why didn't you tell me?"

"You should see your face, Sebastian. That's why I didn't tell you. You would have freaked out, hopped on a plane and come to me."

"Exactly," he said with deep lines between his eyes. "Is Seraphine still helping you?"

I nodded.

"We need to find out what's happening to you, Blaire. And whether this has happened to anyone else before. You're a collector of lycanthropy strains."

I didn't know how to answer that, so I kept quiet, watching the road as we drove. We passed the exit for my house. I assumed we were going to the Labyrinth. Then we passed that exit too.

I faced Sebastian. "Where are we going? We've missed all the exits."

"To the hospital."

I felt my eyes widen. "Why?"

"Mel is waiting for you."

"Again, why?"

"To draw some blood and run more tests."

"I really wish you would discuss this with me first instead of just assuming it's what I want."

"I need to understand what's happening with you, Blaire. Metaphysically, you're collecting were-animals but changing into none of them. I want Mel to give you a physical, and afterward, we're going to Seraphine."

"It's something *you* want to know. Don't you think I'm the one who really needs to know, Sebastian? This affects me, not you!" He presumed this only affected him, but it was me it was happening to.

He just blinked at me, not knowing what to say.

I crossed my arms the rest of the ride to the hospital.

Sawyer found a parking spot near the front next to a handicap space.

Sebastian reached for my hand as we approached the entrance, but I ignored him. "You can't still be mad, Blaire. Besides, I know you want to do this too. You're also wondering what's happening."

"That's beside the point, Sebastian. This is exactly what happened when you introduced me to Anne and your leap. You blurted out to everyone that I had all these strains instead of discussing it with me first. Now you're carrying on like this only affects you and arranging things like this without consulting me first."

A loud sigh escaped his lips, and he stopped walking and caught me in the circle of his arms. When I struggled to get out of his grip, he squeezed me against his body, not easing up.

"I'm sorry," he whispered. "I guess I'm still used to doing everything on my own, or for Léon, and I hardly discuss anything with him before I act." He released me, inhaled deeply and gave me the full force of those serious eyes. "When it comes to you, I need to pause. I know this now. And I'll try harder."

I frowned at him. "What does that mean?" My arms still hugged my body. I refused to give into the temptation of his velvet voice and soothing touch and dug my fingers into my arms.

"I've been around for centuries, Blaire, and I've had many women." He raised his hand. "Before you complain, they were *all* before you. It was a different time back then, and they all loved that I did *everything* for them. And, I mean *everything*. And I made all the decisions, even some of the women of today."

"Are you saying I'm difficult? Or that I don't want you to do things for me?"

"No. You're twisting my words. All I'm saying is you know what you want. You're my equal, and I need to start respecting you like one."

My hands moved to my hips, but my frown remained. I did that slow blink where I was busy processing information.

"You're different, in every way possible. And I love that about you. However, I'll try to remember to ask your opinion first before I make any decision." He stepped forward.

When I didn't stop him from coming near me, he embraced me, pulling me in for a chaste kiss. "Come. Mel is expecting you."

Chapter Eight

We passed the nursery where ten babies were waiting for their parents to give them cuddles or fetch them for a feeding.

Cradled in my arms was a newborn girl with a full head of silky-soft dark hair. Her big green eyes stared up at me. She had that knowing look that told me she knew I was her mother and that I would care for her for the rest of her life. Her skin was pure, and her scent new and of mine. I nuzzled her cheek, and her breath was warm against my face. She cried softly to let me know she was hungry, so I offered her my breast—that instant connection between mother and child, the bond that was now permanently formed and never broken.

When a pregnant, soon-to-be mother who questioned herself constantly on whether she would be the best mother, it instantly dissolved the moment she held her baby in her arms—in most cases. Those familiar instincts kicked in, like a jolt of lightning.

A hand touched my shoulder, and I looked up into bright green eyes.

"Blaire? Are you all right?" I *heard* Sebastian, but I couldn't *see* him. This was someone else's face.

I blinked and glanced down at my baby, but my arms were empty, and we were still near the nursery we had walked past. I was staring at the babies through the window. After another blink and turning to my side, I saw Sebastian beside me again.

"I saw Scout after I gave birth to her," I said, my voice sounding distant, dreamy-like. "I held her in my arms, and she was so tiny." The back of my throat hurt.

Fingers curled around my shoulders, and I felt him standing behind me, and he held me tight against the front of him.

"We can stay here for as long as you need, Blaire."

"When we're done with Mel, I want to go home, please. I want to show you the room with all of Scout's things, and I would prefer to just phone Seraphine from the car."

He kissed the top of my head. "Whatever you want."

We left the nursery and went to one of the pediatric rooms Mel had readied for me. It had Winnie the Pooh splattered across the walls, with Piglet beside him. Next to the bed on a metal tray resting on a side table were vials, needles, tape, and plasters. My hands felt clammy, and a cold sweat ran down my spine.

"I know you're not fond of needles, Blaire, that's why I've asked you to meet me here. You can look at the cute walls while I take some blood."

I wanted to laugh and cry. I sounded pathetic. But I did appreciate the thought behind it.

Mel grabbed the tray with the instruments while I sat on the bed, kicking off my shoes. I laid down on the bed, and

Sebastian sat beside me, holding my hand. Mel did what she needed to do, and I did not want to know that she was squeezing my arm with that tourniquet or to feel the sharp prick of the needle digging into my skin, into my vein, drawing my blood. I squeezed my eyes tight.

"All done."

"What?" I glanced at my arm and then at the table with four vials full of blood, each labeled with my name. "Okay, that wasn't so bad." My smile reached my eyes as I eyed Sebastian, assuming he must've pushed some of his power in me to help me relax. I squeezed his hand knowingly.

He winked as one side of his mouth curved upward.

"I'll put a rush on these and call you when I get the results. Now, for the physical. Everyone, out."

When Mel was done with my physical, I dressed and sat back on the bed.

"I see you're closer to Sebastian. What about Léon?" Mel asked, busying herself with the various items on the tray.

"After you and I spoke, and after they fought, things haven't been that strained between them. And Léon hasn't tried to kiss me again. It doesn't feel as awkward when I'm alone with him anymore." I shrugged. "I suspect he and Sebastian may have spoken afterward again. Their relationship seems to be okay."

"I'm glad. The last thing you need is another complication."

I couldn't agree more. I'd had enough on my plate, overflowing with complications.

"Physically you seem okay, apart from the fact that you are collecting lycanthropy strains." She said, back to being my doctor. "And I'm still running tests on that dart you gave me. I'll let you know as soon as I do."

That reminded me of the results from Sally, Lance's doctor. I had sent Mel those results, and she said she would compare the two sets and let me know of any similarities.

We thanked Mel and left the hospital. We stopped outside my house, and Sebastian accompanied me to my neighbor's house.

Jermaine answered the door. "Blaire, are you back from your trip so soon?"

"Hi, Jermaine. This is Sebastian. Would you mind terribly if we visited the room?"

"Of course not. Please come in. I was just about to make some coffee. Would you like some?"

"Please. Can you bring it downstairs?"

"Sure."

We left Jermaine in the kitchen while we went to the basement. I unlocked the door, and the same smell of lavender and cotton tickled my nose.

"Wow," Sebastian said upon entering. "It's like time stood still inside here."

"Yeah. It's eerie, but I love it."

I inspected the picture frames hanging on one side of the bedroom wall. With the shock of the initial discovery gone, I could take my time and study the black and white photos. Scout was a baby in all of them, and I was either holding her, or a young Mason was. In some, he had his arms around me as we both held her. I glanced from one to the other and was slow to process it. My mind took its time to wrap around what I was staring at, rubbing my eyes and scrutinizing them again.

It was my face. Something seemed off about my face; I couldn't pinpoint exactly what it was, just … something. In each one, I looked the same. Exactly the same. I picked up a mirror sitting on the table beside the cot and stared at myself and then at the pictures again.

"You haven't aged since she was born," Sebastian said behind me.

He realized it before I did, before my mind could piece it together.

When I didn't say anything, he stood beside me with a sly grin. "Your parents must have great genes."

I shrugged. "I don't know. There aren't any pictures of them here."

"Have you searched the desk?"

"No. I haven't searched anything. When I first came here, I think I was in awe of the place."

I sat in the desk chair and rummaged through each drawer. The top drawer contained receipts and spare pens; the middle drawer held a few folders with insurance documents; and the bottom had a photo album. I removed the album and paged through it. The photos were similar to what was on the walls, except they were in color. There were other photos of Scout during her birth, her purple skin covered in the white vernix goo, her mouth open as she was screaming. Another of her clean and wrapped in a pink blanket while I held her. The memory of holding her flooded my vision again, and it felt like I was there—that instant love a mother feels for her newborn— and I felt her delicate skin against my cheek, and her smell filled the air around me.

Blinking, I turned the page and saw pictures of a cake with a large number two stuck in the middle with Scout blowing it out. Mason and I stood behind her for one photo, and the other was only of her. The rest of the album was blank after that. I returned it to the drawer. A sharp pain burst through my chest as the raw emotions of losing a child flooded over me. I needed to know more about that day and why they had to leave me in haste. Perhaps the desk held secrets, I just had to find them.

I felt the bottom and top part inside each drawer for anything that could be loose but found no hidden compartments. I felt under the desk by my legs, and something slid away. For a second, hope fluttered through me, but, before I lost myself to excitement, I needed to investigate further. Sitting on the floor, I searched under the desk. In the middle under the desk was a secret panel. I had to lift it and slide it toward the wall. I stuck my fingers inside the opening. I felt around until something moved, a corner of something. I pulled it out—a brown envelope containing a small key with a weird bit or blade that slid into the keyhole.

"That first time I tried the safety deposit box, one of the other people there had a small key that looked like this one. I wonder if this is it, Sebastian?" I said optimistically.

Sebastian glanced at his watch. "There's still time if you want to have a look."

"Yes," I said, nodding and standing up.

We rushed past Jermaine as he was about to come down the stairs with the coffee. I apologized and told him I might be back.

Sawyer maneuvered through the traffic at the maximum he could drive without technically speeding, as not to alert any traffic cops. We managed to arrive at the bank twenty minutes before closing time.

Sebastian and I entered at a brisk pace. We passed the offices and flagged down the manager I had spoken with the last time I was there. He recognized me and grabbed his keys. He ushered us to the safety deposit room.

I exhaled and smoothly slipped the key into the hole and

turned it. I heard a click, and it opened. Blinking back tears, I removed the box.

The bank manager escorted us toward a private room to view the contents, but Sebastian stayed outside. I placed the box on a table and reached inside. I removed a brown envelope and peered inside to see a piece of paper with a Portland, Oregon address scribbled on it. Nothing else was inside the envelope or the box. I memorized the address and placed it back inside the box and closed it.

I had kept her location a secret for a reason. I had to figure out why I had placed it here to find. Thoughts of visiting Scout and Mason brought tears to my eyes. Wiping away the tears, I started planning. If I were to leave in the next day or two, would that pose a risk to their safety? Was anyone watching me? If I left now, would that alert the people who had originally driven them away? As much as I longed to see them, did they want to see me? Were we even on good terms with one another?

Doubt and broken dreams overcame my sudden sense of longing, and something about this address on a note was a warning to me. I had to tread very carefully and not be seen. Things might not be as they seemed.

Then I remembered I was supposed to attend an upcoming dinner with Sebastian and Léon, and I was due back at work the following week. I could arrange for a long weekend away, but Sebastian would insist he came with or that I brought Sawyer or Rory—or both. I couldn't risk having them with me.

I needed to find a way to travel alone.

Chapter Nine

It was a formal black-tie dinner with evening gowns and heels. We were going to rub shoulders with the elite, the rich, and those ass-deep in politics. Sawyer fetched me early that morning, so I could get ready. I laughed and told them they were ridiculous to start so early, but apparently, I needed help getting dressed. The gown I chose was a plain black dress with thin straps; evidently, it was not suitable, and they arranged another one for me.

The hairdresser washed my hair, put in curlers and placed me under the dryer while someone gave me a manicure and a pedicure. I tried to relax and pretend I was at a spa for a pampering, but guards kept checking on me.

Almost three months had passed, and no one had tried to grab me off the street, let alone the Labyrinth. No witch had tried to curse me or add me to their broth. Seraphine would have a heart attack if I said that out loud. She said no witch—or rather, no modern witch—did spells in a pot anymore. *"What nonsense,"* I could hear her say.

A soft knock came on the door for the umpteenth time,

and the first thing I saw was a crimson silk gown with a bodice and a wide skirt in a plastic garment bag.

A wide-eyed girl popped her head through the open door, still holding up the gown. "They asked me to bring you this, Blaire."

"Where did Léon get that from at such short notice?" I asked the girl as she entered the room.

"Not sure. I'm just the runner," she said as she hung it up and straightened the plastic cover so it left no creases.

"What does a runner do?"

"I fetch this, I take it there. I take that and drop it off elsewhere. This place is huge, so they need someone quick." Her smile reached her eyes.

"Which animal are you?" I asked, my smile matching hers.

"Were-tiger."

"I wasn't aware of any tiger clans in town."

"There aren't, but I'm new in town, and I wanted to work for Léon. I wanted to be a guard, but they said I'm not ready yet, so they're training me. They gave me a job as a runner until my fighting skills improve."

"Aren't you a bit young to be a guard?"

She shrugged. "I'm out of school and everything. I just need to bulk up and practice my fighting."

"Why do you want to be a guard?"

"What else is there for me to do?"

"I don't know, but there should be other things you could do."

"Nah, I want to guard for Léon."

The door opened again, and Sawyer entered. "Natalie, you're wanted in the stock room."

"Bye, Blaire. It was nice meeting you, and enjoy your evening," she said and was gone.

"Since when does Léon hire kids to work for him?"

"She's a runaway, and she had nothing and no one to help her. Léon is helping her without putting her in harm's way."

I crossed my arms. "Why do you and Rory keep checking on me every twenty minutes, and do you know when Sebastian will be back?"

"We're making sure you're comfortable. And Sebastian is still at the leap. I can ask him to call you, if you like."

"Please, and would you mind handing me my phone?"

Sawyer grabbed my phone from the bedside table and handed it to me.

"What time is this dinner starting?"

"At seven. Léon should be getting up soon."

"Are you telling me it's almost four already?"

"Yep."

"Only three more hours to get ready." I stared into the wall behind the woman painting my toenails.

"I'll be back a bit later to bring you something to snack on."

"Thanks, Sawyer."

Even though the chair I was sitting on was comfortable, being stuck to it was a different story, and I was just about ready to get off. My toes were a crimson color that looked suspiciously like the gown Natalie had delivered. I sensed it was all planned.

Two and a half hours later, I was finally done. My hair hung in soft curls down my open back, and the crimson gown fit me perfectly. The bodice accentuated my waistline with straps running across my back; the skirt's delicate texture and the blues and greens of my Ulysses butterfly tattoo worked well. The heels were comfortable, and I didn't wobble in them.

My arm was through Sawyer's as he led me toward the garage where the limo was waiting. Rory was already in the driver's seat dressed in a neat tuxedo similar to what Sawyer wore. Their clothing tailored to fit them perfectly. Sawyer opened the door for me.

My heart stopped when the first thing I saw was Léon's smile. I caught a hint of the sharp edges of his fangs through his smile, his ocean-blue eyes glinting in the limo's dim interior lights. As I climbed in to sit, I got the full picture of his beauty, his high cheek bones and full lips framed by dark hair.

He sat still for a heartbeat as if he was too afraid to move in case the mere sight of him alone in a car with me might cause me to ruin his perfectly carved face. His eyes never faulted as he watched me climb into the seat beside him. Léon was a powerful vampire, and the master of the city. A friend had invited him to this dinner, and they needed us to attend it with him.

"You're a breath of fresh air, Blaire. Absolutely beautiful." His smooth voice caressed my naked flesh.

Heat crept up my neck and cheeks. "Thank you, Léon. You don't look too bad yourself." I tried masking the quiver in my voice with humor.

He chuckled as if he had never received any compliments before.

"I assume Sebastian has spoken with you?"

He nodded slowly. "Yes, that he might be a few minutes late." His chest rose as he inhaled to speak. "I hope you don't mind accompanying me on your own. Well, that's until Sebastian arrives, of course."

"Of course." I swallowed hard. "It's not a problem." The corners of my smile quivered. I just knew he could taste my lies on the tip of his tongue.

One side of his mouth curled upward. It's not that I didn't mind being alone with him, I just didn't want him touching me. The mere thought of his touch made me lick my lips in anticipation.

This was the first time I had been alone with him and without Sebastian being nearby. After Léon had kissed me in my dream a few months ago, it sent Sebastian into a rage—to put it lightly. Since then, and after many, many discussions, they had seemed to have finally kissed and made up and were the same brothers as they were before. But Léon and I were always awkward in one another's company.

Sawyer climbed into the passenger seat with Rory, and we were on our way.

After a few minutes of travel and having sensed a steady weight fall over me like a thin blanket, I glanced in Léon's direction, but he quickly averted his gaze out the window. Keeping an eye on him seemed to ease the tension between us, until his gaze flitted in my direction, causing me to glance in the opposite direction, and that heavy blanket was on me again. A faint smile played on my face, and I could feel him smile too. It was hard to describe how I knew this, I just did somehow. It felt like a cat-and-mouse game—and I was the mouse. He hadn't even touched me, and my cheeks were on fire, my breath short and labored. My heart was racing, and everything tightened down below.

I needed him to stop, but I didn't want him to know how much he affected me. The bodice felt tight around my waist. The limo blurred as my vision tunneled, and all I could see was the blue glow of his eyes.

"Léon."

He stared at me. "Yes, Blaire?" he whispered. The way he said my name was smooth and velvety as his words nipped delicately at my neck, causing my breath to catch.

"Please." I said, whimpering.

"Please what?" he replied, huskily.

"Stop what you're doing to me."

"I'm not doing anything. My power only works when your heart desires something." Mischief glistened in his dark gaze.

I glared at him, my fists bunching and my knuckles turning white. I pressed my fingernails into my arms, and pain shot to my shoulders. Ice washed away the heat I had felt. I could see clearer, my breathing returned to normal, and my heart steadied.

Anger was a deterrent to Léon's desire. He grinned knowingly at me.

I scooted closer to the door and farther from him for the remainder of the ride.

When we finally arrived, the crowd outside caught my attention. Our limo was behind a sea of black limos, and we moved at a turtle's pace toward the red carpet.

I flinched when my phone rang. "Hello?"

"It's me. You're going to be angry, but I'm going to be very, very late," Sebastian said, sounding apologetic.

I frowned. "How late?" I sounded angry, and I was. He was leaving me alone—with Léon.

"About another hour, I promise."

"Never promise anything if you can't keep it, Sebastian. What's happening that's so important?"

"Remember Corey? Sawyer mentioned him to us the other day?"

"Yes. What about him?" I stared at the back of Sawyer's head. I was sure he could hear our conversation from where he sat.

"Something happened, and I am hanging around to ensure there isn't a full-on war with the werewolves."

"Can't someone else handle it?"

"No. It has to be me. I'll make it up to you, I promise. I have to go." As if sensing my unease, he quickly added, "I trust Léon. He'll take great care of you. Love you."

Before I could say anything else, he ended the call. I turned to Léon.

As I opened my mouth, he raised his hand. "Say no more, Blaire. I heard every word. Come, they're waiting for us."

The door on my side opened, and Rory held out his hand for me. I took his hand and climbed out. He offered me his elbow. I slipped my arm through his, and we walked around the limo to where Léon waited with his elbow out.

"I promise I won't bite," he whispered near my ear when I stopped in front of him.

Reluctantly, I hooked my arm through his, waiting for that sudden surge of sexual electricity to zap me off my feet. But there was nothing. It was only my arm through his. He patted my hand with his free hand in an attempt at consoling me.

Ha! Funny joke. Especially with what just happened in the limo. I simply couldn't trust him.

"It's not only your bite I'm worried about," I whispered only for him to hear.

His slight touch could do things to me that men had to do with their entire bodies. I was sure his bite would be right up there with unholy secrets of the flesh.

As we traversed the red carpet, Léon pulled me in closer with Rory and Sawyer on either side of us. The valet drove the limo to the parking lot.

Lights flashed up ahead, like mini lightning strikes. The bright flashes from the cameras were blinding as a swarm of photographers descended the steps to take pictures of all the monsters walking up the red carpet. My eyes watered so, instead of looking at the crowd, I cast my eyes downward to stare at the red carpet, watching my skirt shimmer in the bright lights as they took our picture.

A hand came before my eyes, and I stared up to look at Léon. "Don't look down, Blaire. There's too much beauty that should never be hidden."

"It's the flashes. They make my eyes water."

Léon turned to Rory and returned with sunglasses. "Put these on."

I did as suggested; the sunglasses helped, and I could walk with my head held high, catching glimpses of everyone either taking pictures or asking questions. The closer we got to the entrance, the more the press yelled questions at Léon.

"Who is she?"

"You've never walked with anyone by your side before, why now?"

"Is she with you only because you are the master vampire of the city?"

"What are your ties to Shannon?"

Léon stopped us from walking, squeezing my arm when I tensed. When he spoke, that smooth silky voice stroked my skin and everyone around us. "This is Blaire Thorne. She's a family friend and keeping me company for the evening. And Shannon and I go back many, many years. And I'm here tonight to support him in his run for Sterling Meadow Governor."

"Léon, what are your views on Shannon wanting to cut funding to the police force and employ monsters?"

"Don't you think the best people to catch the bad monsters are the monsters themselves?" Léon winked darkly.

Some reporters laughed while others yelled more questions at us. Léon ignored them, smiling and continuing up the red carpet until we reached the grand entrance, where no press was allowed.

We entered with the rest of the attendees and followed the red carpet into the lavish banquet hall. Someone rang a bell, sounding for us to find our places. Sawyer and Rory followed us along the wall while we found our seats near the front at table one.

"How close are you really to these people?" I whispered near his ear.

"Too close for comfort. We only have to stay for the opening speech, shake a few hands, and then we can leave, if you like." He grinned and watched the various monsters occupy their tables.

Two empty seats were beside Léon. I sat beside him, leaving Sebastian's seat open, the last one at the table. Our table was a long rectangle right in front, with a white cloth draped over it. The rest of the tables were round and spread across the hall. The seats filled quickly as everyone entered.

Table two was the nearest to us and featured a man with a red coat draped around him with a silver strand adorning the front of the material on both sides of the opening. A thin red veil covered the lower part of his face, which only highlighted his pointy nose. Since only his eyes were visible, I noted they were the shade of lavender flowers—very pretty for a man. His ears were the shape of Darwin's tubercle, and twigs protruded from his head instead of hair. A tall and gangly woman sat beside him. Her face was shaped like a heart, and her ears were elongated at the top. Her eyes were mauve and her lips delicately thin. Her crystal wings glinted in the lights and stood out behind her. She had to lift her emerald dress to sit down beside him. Her hair was ash-blond, and the finest of twigs and leaves decorated her head with yellow flowers that had already bloomed.

I'd only read about the faeries—fay or flower guardians, as they were known—in my history books. And we would hear about their plight on radio or television when a corporate CEO monster wanted to flatten the land and build concrete apartments in parts of the forest that lies on the outskirts of Sterling Meadow. It was the same forest all the were-animals shared with them, but a large section was designated for the faeries.

This man in the red coat had to be their fay king. More fay joined table two, until they occupied all eight seats.

Glancing to my right at Sawyer and Rory, I saw them speaking with a man in armor; his olive skin was barely visible. I caught a glimpse of his face—smooth and the color of hazel fay flowers, a gentle brown. Only his piercing green eyes were visible through his visor. I wasn't sure what they were discussing, but all three men wore serious faces.

Scanning the room and two tables across, Shawn sat with seven of his werewolves, including Mel. The table next to theirs sat Troy drinking and laughing with his were-lions. The table designated for the were-leopards remained empty. When Sebastian had said he was busy with leap business, I didn't understand it was with Anne and the rest too.

Seraphine sat near the back with people I didn't recognize. Another table over was Désiré and her coven. I had never met Arturo before—the were-rat king—but he was there with seven of his best.

Other tables featured jars filled with thick maroon liquid as the vampires sat at their various seats. One table in the far back corner sat large creatures built like the mountains where they stayed. They lived far away from humans and the rest of the creatures, much like the fay and faeries. The trolls were solitude creatures, so it was strange they were here. Were they offered something they could not refuse to attend?

Then again, who wouldn't side with a vampire if he had every single creature behind him? It made him incredibly powerful, and I was amazed the humans weren't trying to stop him from gaining so much support.

Two bells tolled, and everybody stood.

As I pushed the chair backward, my skirt caught under one of the feet. With the momentum of me pushing my chair, trying to stand up and my skirt getting stuck, I started to fall to one side. I was about to put out my hand so I didn't crash to the floor face first, when Léon caught me midair. My pulse thundered in my ears from the near fall, and the hall's silence was deafening on its own. Luckily, no one saw us. My face was near Léon's, and a hint of the ocean hid beneath his cologne—a faint yet fresh musk—and then there was the smell of him. I grabbed his shoulders as he helped me to my feet, our lips only inches apart. Heat rose up my neck and face, and I had to resist the urge to press my lips against his for another slice of passion Léon had previously shared with me.

"You okay?" he asked, his hand still at the small of my back and our bodies close.

"Yes, thanks." I righted myself and fidgeted inside my small purse to avoid any more eye contact. I glanced at my face in the small compact mirror and saw I was as red as I felt, groaning inwardly.

"Let the games begin," he said, letting go of my back and turning his attention to the crowd walking down the middle aisle toward our table.

My eyes panned from the approaching crowd to Léon's profile to the lines running along his jaw and neck. A pulse still beat in that vein in his neck; for a dead man, his heart seemed to beat every now and then, but I suspected it was only when he fed well enough beforehand.

He turned and stared at me, his blue eyes glistening in the lambency. The darkness in his eyes hinted at the forbidden pleasures he could offer me. I wanted to run my fingers across his jaw, caress his lips with mine then taste his lips. I wanted to lick down his neck and kiss his bare chest, and things tightened down below. Glancing at his chest and back to his face, all I wanted to do was drown in his ocean-blue eyes.

Léon blinked as he turned from me.

A cold wash trailed down my body, and my skin pebbled, like someone had poured a bucket of ice-cold water over me, except I was still dry. Swallowing hard and with a shaky hand, I poured water from the jug on the table into a glass and drank all of it. The liquid cooled me from the inside.

I knew better than to look a vampire in the eyes, especially a vampire like Léon, who didn't need to touch to elicit undisclosed desires. But he did touch me, and he did look at me. And that small caress against the naked skin on my back gave me urges I did not want to explore. Not with him anyway. I was shocked he had that kind of power over me, but he was a vampire—and powerful and very, very talented.

The crowd reached our table and stopped. A woman covered head to toe with a metallic-colored cloak moved in front of the crowd. Her face was visible except for a grey mask covering her eyes. She lifted the cloak from her head and pushed the mask from her eyes. Her eyes were white— no iris, no pupil ... only white. She faced me as if she were looking directly at me. Her piercing gaze brought tension into my shoulders.

I couldn't understand why, but I didn't want her to stare at me. I needed to block her view of me. I closed the gap between Léon and me. He was perceptive, realizing my discomfort, and grabbed my hand. He stood slightly in front of me, blocking the woman's view of me. He wrapped my hand around his waist, pulling my cheek against his shoulder blade. I instantly felt at ease, and all my tension dissipated. Just by standing near me, he had managed to block whatever that woman was trying to do to me. I didn't want to admit it, but I was glad he was here.

The no-eyed woman faced the rest of the hall and raised her arms as if to pray. "Thank you for joining us this evening. You all are so important to us. If we did not have your support, we would not be where we are today." The woman bowed then went to her seat at our table. She glanced in our direction before sitting down.

Her entourage followed and sat down, which made everyone else also sit, including us. The last person from her crowd didn't sit; he marched across the floor and stood against the wall, like the other guards. He was close to eight feet tall and broad. He wore black leather patched with silver thread. Straps held his mask together, and clips covered his right eye, while the left eye surveyed his surroundings. Markings lined his leather mask where his mouth should be, a mix of hieroglyphics and something else I couldn't decipher.

Sweat beaded down my back, and my hands were clammy. I grabbed a material napkin and pretended to put it over my lap; instead, I gripped it as I dried my hands. I kept spying the masked giant who stood against the far wall, trying to see if that one eye was watching me.

He was.

I sensed Léon next to me, like he was seeing what I was

seeing, and he took my hand again. I hadn't noticed before, but his hand felt warm and comforting. I forgot what his touch could do; the thought of these monsters hurting me seemed to matter more.

Léon's action must have been enough for the masked giant, because he looked away. I exhaled and wished the evening would end. These monsters were crawling under my skin, and I wanted to go home.

A man rose, his long blond hair flowing like a waterfall around his shoulders, and he thanked everyone for joining him at his fundraiser dinner. Each table had cost a fortune, which he would use to bolster his race to be governor. He would be the first vampire in history to climb the political ranks and wouldn't stop at just being the governor; his next step would be the presidency. He rambled about the changes he would make once he was governor; the first would be to the police force, taxes, healthcare, and finally, jobs—that nobody would be discriminated against because of who they were, just because they were a monster.

As Shannon started to sit, one of the trolls in the back stood from the floor. His skin was a dark mixture between brown and green. Tusks extended from his mouth, two on each side near his bottom lip. His large muscular arms and chest was covered in a variety of tusks on strings, while a fur loincloth covered his front. I couldn't see any further due to the tables and the other monsters in front of him. His voice was deep and raspy. "Now that you have all of us in one room, Shannon. What will you give us in return for all the support we're showing you?" He flopped on the floor with a thump.

Shannon coughed politely then replied with confidence. "Apart from what I've already shared, whatever support you need, my friend. We're here together, standing up for our rights for once. It's time one of us rises from the dark ashes and brings all of us to the surface as one. We need to remain united if we are to make any kind of dent in this human world."

The trolls grunted as if that was their way of approving. I didn't know much about them, so I could only hope they were pleased. I'd only heard of angry trolls and the destruction they left in their path.

The fay king rose from his chair. "Do you swear you'll consider everyone, even the little people who stay deep in the forest and never come to town?"

"Yes, King. You have my word." Shannon clutched both his hands and pressed them to his heart and bowed.

The fay king grunted and sat.

Rumblings emanated from all the tables as each monster conversed among themselves.

Shawn, the wolf king, stood. "One of our wolves was murdered yesterday with a poisonous dart. What will you do to ensure our safety?"

Gasps and audible mumblings swept through the hall.

"This is the first I'm hearing this, Wolf King. Meet with me afterward, so we can review the details, and I'll ensure you and everyone else is kept safe from harm. Then whoever is causing this will be brought to *our* kind of justice."

I understood that meaning, that the monster responsible would be put to instant death.

There were cheers, then Shannon lifted his hands to quieten the monsters. "Please, when I say I'm standing here before you tonight, it's because I'm here on your behalf. If you experience any kind of problem, monster or not, or are afraid of anything, you need to speak up. It is our time now. It is our time to be heard. And we can only do this if we all stand together and rise like never before. We'll be the first non-human to reach this status within the government. Let us find joy and peace in that and celebrate. Will you all join me and celebrate tonight?"

Every monster either grunted or shouted affirmations, with a few fists hitting the table and toppling glasses.

It would be the first time a monster would have the monster's best interests at heart.

Chapter Ten

After all the speeches were made and dinner was served, Léon called me to where he was standing and took my hand. "I just want to greet Shannon, and then we can leave. I've already spoken with Sebastian. He'll meet us at home when he's done."

I nodded and bit on my lip. I had already greeted the witches and was ready to leave when he was. My hands were still damp, and I hoped Léon didn't mind. He squeezed my hand as if he had eavesdropped on my concern. That was one of the powers he held; he could hear thoughts if he stood close enough to a person.

The sound of glass shattering near us was followed by giggles. The lavish dinner had turned into a party for those monsters who were still around and enjoying their various drinks.

As we walked through the crowds, music started playing and some of those on the floor started dancing. Soon we were caught between couples. When one man threatened to separate us, Léon pulled me in closer to him. I felt the heat come off his body as he held my right hand with his left and his right hand held the small of my back, pulling me in closer still.

He wanted to dance.

My chest rose and fell, heat blossoming up my neck, and I felt my cheeks warm. Léon grinned sinisterly, and we glided toward the dance floor. Narrowing my eyes at him, this was all a ploy for him to get closer to me and dance.

"I know what you're thinking, Blaire, and I promise you it was entirely coincidental," he said, winking.

Even though I knew I had to stay away from him, I couldn't. We had no bond, yet we shared a deep connection, one similar to what I shared with Sebastian. Was it because they were brothers and I was bonded to Sebastian, or was there some other underlining cause? Was it Léon's machinations that kept bridging that gap I kept making between us? It was undeniable though; I was having fun with him.

A smile tugged on my face, which he took as affirmation, and we swayed through the crowd. We danced circles around the other couples, while some had even stopped to watch us. I felt drunk on the very air we breathed.

I was abruptly snapped out of my daydream dance when we bumped into Shannon. Like hitting a brick wall, we were stunned into silence as the tall blond man stood before us, his eyes dancing with mischief and a predatory grin stretching his cheeks. My good mood instantly evaporated.

"Léon, my dearest friend, so good to have you beside me like old times." Shannon put his arms around Léon and pulled him into a hug.

Léon had to let go of me to hug the other man. That

action alone made me feel vulnerable, not having Léon to shield me anymore.

Shannon stared at me while they embraced then pulled away. "Who's this creature, Léon? Surely she can't be *yours*." His eyebrows furrowed, and his blue eyes scrutinized me as he contemplated something. "She's marked though, but not by you, old friend." He slapped Léon's shoulder.

Léon faced me with a flash of panic in his face. He grabbed my hand, wrapping it around his waist, and held onto my shoulder, pulling me closer to his body to protect me. He shifted back to his stoic demeanor.

My eyes flitted from Léon to Shannon.

"She is Sebastian's."

"Of course, the handsome brother. I should have realized." Shannon nudged Léon. "But there's something else, isn't there."

They were talking about me like I wasn't there.

"No, there's nothing else."

Shannon kept his gaze on me for what felt like an eternity. He stared from my feet to my head like I was a prized possession he was admiring. I felt like squirmy away. My free hand clutched the front of my body, the soft dress creasing in my damp grasp.

"Oh, wow, I see it now. I see *her*. She is gorgeous, Léon. She certainly is one of a kind. I would guard this one with more than two guards, if I were you ... or Sebastian."

"Is that a threat, Shannon?" Léon arched an eyebrow.

"Oh, heavens no, old friend. But it is a warning. I see what she *truly* is, and, as you know, others would kill for her. How on earth did you come about finding her? She isn't quite like those already dead and buried, but she is most certainly a unique specimen."

He seemed to know something I didn't. "What is it you see, Shannon?" I asked.

"I like that she has spunk." Again, he spoke about me like I wasn't there, and he didn't bother answering my question.

The skin around my neck tingled, like insects were crawling up my neck and onto my head. I felt eyes boring into the back of me. I turned around slowly. That eight-foot giant towered over me, his one dark eye piercing through my soul. The smell of soot trailed behind him.

"Is it time to go, Raphael?" Shannon asked the giant.

"Yes," Raphael said, that one eye focusing on Shannon and then back on me.

"Give me a second." Shannon turned back to Léon.

Léon and Shannon discussed land prospects as I kept watch on Raphael. He was so large that he casted dark shadows around me. That one deep-set eye glared down at me. Not wanting to show how afraid he made me feel, I frowned up at him. "What are you looking at?" I asked with a hint of anger.

Without muttering a word, he stared down at me, as if waiting for me to say something else.

Léon was still speaking with Shannon when a man stood from his seat. He had made enough space for me to walk past him. I released Léon's hand and walked until I reached the far wall. Following the wall until I entered the large foyer, I scanned the various signs for the one indicating the bathroom.

When I exited the bathroom, Sawyer and Rory were waiting for me. I exhaled and approached them.

"Can we go now?" I asked, eyeing the exit doors.

"Léon is almost done, then we can go."

"Can I wait in the car please?" I asked, approaching the exit then halted.

The blind woman in the metallic coat and the man who had sat beside Shannon during dinner approached me. They stopped in front of me and, in effect, blocked my exit. She smelled faintly like vinegar, gripping my elbows in her rough hands. The whites of her eyes stared into mine. While the man towered above me, the light was behind him, so I couldn't see his features clearly; his hair and eyes seemed brown in the dim light, while his facial features were nondescript.

As I stared at him, my reality abruptly shifted, my vision rippling for a moment. Then when she spoke, it broke whatever power the man had blasted over me, and I could see clearly again.

"Where are you rushing off to, dear?" She stepped closer, her grip on my elbows burning.

Sawyer came between us and removed her hands from me. "Ma'am, please do not touch her."

"Yes, yes, I'm sorry, dear. But I see you for what you *truly* are. No amount of shielding can hide you from *me*." She pulled a bone that had been filed into a sharp point from her sleeve. She raised her hand high, and, for an old woman, she was fast, stabbing me in the chest in one swift movement—so quick that neither Sawyer nor Rory had seen her do it, but I felt it.

The sharp bone wedged between two breast bones and only inches from my heart. When she removed it, the tip of the bone pulled my skin. She licked my blood from the bone. Her eyes bled to maroon, and her pale cheeks turned rosy.

I cried out, clutching my chest and waiting for blood to

pour out, but nothing spilled apart from one drop near the wound.

"Ooh, yes." She nodded quickly, eyeing the man beside her. "Yes, indeed. The vampire who marked you won't be for long, my dear. Not long now, he won't be for long now." Her beady red eyes assessed me hungrily.

"What? What do you mean? Is someone going to hurt him?" I asked, feeling the sting of panic.

The man beside her threw back his head with laughter, sending shivers down my spine. And again, as I stared at him, my vision rippled and shook as reality turned in on itself.

Léon pushed past, almost knocking the blind lady out of the way. "What did the witch do to you?"

"She stabbed me with that." I pointed a shaking finger at the bone in the witch's hand.

"Kasdeya, what did you do to her?"

"I only wanted to know how pure she was, Léon. She shields her body so tightly, but I saw her white aura peeking at me through those tiny holes she forgot to close. I had to know what she *was*. You know an old lady like me couldn't resist temptation." She smiled with teeth stained black, and her eyes reverted to its ghostly white.

"What happened?" Shannon asked as he approached us. He leered at the witch Kasdeya, to the man beside her then at me. "Kasdeya, Simon, we don't *ever* touch. Am I making myself clear?"

"I remember, Shannon, but I had to know if I was right," the old woman said, walking away, her coat billowing behind her.

The man who was beside her, Simon, grunted and walked with her.

"Please forgive them, Blaire. You come here to support me, and this is the welcome you get."

"I want to leave, Léon. Please take me home," I said, whimpering, as my body trembled.

"Keep your witch and Simon away from her, Shannon." Léon's command was icy and filled with so much more.

Shannon nodded in agreement. "Yes, of course, Léon. Please accept my sincerest apologies, Blaire." Shannon took my hand in his and kissed my knuckles.

I retracted my hand.

Léon leered at Shannon as he took me by the elbow, guiding me toward the exit.

Chapter Eleven

I was still shaking when we arrived at my house. That little altercation with the witch had affected me more than I wanted to admit. And that other man, Simon, freaked me the fuck out. Every time I stared in his direction, my world tilted on its axis.

A car was parked in the shadows of my driveway. Under the light of the porch swing sat Sebastian, beautifully draped over it like he was in an advertising campaign. I glanced at Léon who raised an eyebrow in response.

"He wanted it to be a surprise, and I think to make up for leaving you alone in my company all evening," Léon said, with a hint of sarcasm.

"It's not that …" I said, my voice trailing off into the silent night.

We hadn't spoken after he invaded my dream and shared that passionate kiss. He had proclaimed how much he was drawn to me, and I felt the attraction too. But I was with his brother. No matter how strong the pull was I felt for Léon, I couldn't betray Sebastian. They already had a few disagreements, which I assumed were because of me. I didn't want to put a permanent wedge between them; they were brothers. So, Léon and I had left many things unsaid.

"Thanks for—"

He raised his hand to stop me. "You don't have to say anything. Just know I'll always be there to protect you, no matter what. Go now. He waits for you."

Léon took my hand and brought it to his mouth, letting it linger near his lips, as if teasing me. I felt his warm breath against my fingers before he kissed my knuckles. My chest tightened by his slight touch. I took back my hand, with the heat of his kiss still lingering. I said goodnight, and, before I climbed out the limo, Léon was beside me, capturing me in his gaze.

One hand was behind my head, the other around my waist. His face near mine, our lips barely touching. He closed his eyes and breathed me in then kissed my cheek.

"Goodnight, Blaire. Know I'll always cherish our time together. No matter how short." His whisper was a velvet caress against my cheek and down my neck, contracting my loins in fearful pleasure. I gasped, and he let go. I would've stumbled from the limo if I didn't grab hold of the door to steady myself. I heard Léon chuckle behind me, and I cursed him silently under my breath. Everything was a game to him. I focused on Sebastian, and my steps quickened as I traversed the path.

"You look beautiful in that dress," Sebastian said as I climbed the steps. "I heard you had a rough time."

"Something like that. Wait ... How did you know? I didn't see Léon use the phone. Or was it Sawyer or Rory?" I glanced over my shoulder. The limo pulled away and then was gone. The knot in my stomach dropped as I watched him leave. I returned my attention to Sebastian, to the man I loved.

"We're brothers. We have our own shared connection." He stood and closed the gap between us.

I wrapped my arms around his waist and squeezed, feeling the muscles underneath his clothing move as he pulled me in tighter, and it was comforting. I felt safe, especially after the evening I'd just had.

Once we were inside the house, I made us coffee and explained what the old, blind woman did and how Simon messed with my vision. I even mentioned the eight-foot giant with one eye.

"I wouldn't worry too much about Raphael. He's Shannon's bodyguard. And Simon is a vampire, but Shannon controls him."

"It didn't seem like it," I answered, not comforted by his words. My fingers wrapped around the warm mug of coffee, the dark liquid making ripples against the inside of the mug.

Sebastian put his hand over mine and the mug. "You're going to mess."

A tingle ran up my arm as light as a feather, and the shaking receded. With my free hand, I touched the small scab on my chest where the old woman had pierced me with the sharp bone, wincing.

"Does it hurt?"

"Only when I touch it."

He smirked. "Don't touch it then."

"Do you know who she was?"

"Kasdeya? She's an old witch. She still practices the *old way*." He eyed the scab on my chest. "She wanted to know what you were."

"So, she knows what I can do?"

"Most probably." He sipped from his cup, his hand still over mine, keeping the shaking at bay.

"She also said something about you, about the mark you left on me. That you won't be for long," I said, raising my voice. "I don't know what she means or if you are in danger, Sebastian."

A hot breeze caressed my face, and warmth travelled up my hand. I removed his hand and brought the mug to my lips, the absence of steam letting me know the coffee wasn't hot anymore. My shoulders relaxed, and the tension between my blades eased. "I love that your touch can relax me so quickly."

He reached over the kitchen island and cupped the side of my face while he kissed the other side near my temple. "I'll be fine, and the mark I have on you will stay there. You don't have to worry about it."

I wanted to ask, *'Do you promise?'* but I wasn't a child. I knew he couldn't make promises like that and keep it. I would trust that he would be okay, and the mark we shared would be all right. I wouldn't worry about it unless I had to.

"But if you did the second mark, it would be stronger?"

He nodded.

I cringed. My stomach dropped, and I was worried all over again. I didn't want to know what would happen if the mark was broken, our link snapped in two. Would I survive it? I needed to change the subject to avoid a full-on war of the mind, volleying with things that might not even happen.

"What happened at the leap that you couldn't make it tonight?"

"Corey and some younger werewolves broke the treaty. They were in our territory and hunting our game. They had to jump over some fences. They had to have known where they were going and what they were doing was wrong. It's like they wanted to piss us off and pit the two groups against each other."

"What'll happen now?"

"Because Shawn was at the dinner, we couldn't discuss it with him, but we will tomorrow."

"What does Anne want to do?"

"We don't want to fight, but ..." He trailed off, thinking as concern etched across his face. "We can't let the werewolves think they can invade our territory without any repercussions."

"I'm sure it'll be sorted out with Shawn, and Corey will be punished."

"Hmm," Sebastian confirmed.

I set my mug on the table, stood and wrapped my arms around his neck and said near his ear, "Are you staying with me tonight?"

He lifted me up, cupping my ass. "Definitely, baby." And carried me to the bed.

The sunlight and butterfly kisses Sebastian planted across my shoulders woke me.

"I need to go," he said, climbing out of bed. "What are your plans for today?"

"I'm meeting Ralph and Devan at the lion pride."

"I hope Marcus can give you more information about your past."

"He better. His life depends on it. If he gives me nothing today, I'm letting Troy and his pride have at him. He is of no use to me if he can't offer any information," I said as Sebastian closed the shower door.

As I lay on my arm with the covers snug around me,

steam filled the bathroom. The shower's glass door was foggy but the outline of his luscious body visible. A smile crept across my face as I was in awe of the blissful sight. When he was done, I climbed out the bed as he exited the bathroom, mischief playing in his eyes. On tiptoes, I kissed him, stripped naked and went to shower.

"You know you can't parade your body in front of me like that and expect to walk away." He chuckled low and lighthearted.

"You can always join me." I pressed the front of my naked body against the glass shower door.

"God, that's torture, woman. I would love to run my hands over your naked body, my fingers touching you in places that make you scream, but I can't. Rory and Sawyer are already here."

I opened the shower door, narrowing my eyes at him. "Are both of them coming with me today?"

He arched an eyebrow at me and pulled on jeans. "I'm not going through this again, baby. Too much has happened, and, with Kasdeya last night, I want another guard with you. But because you already have an issue with two, I'm leaving it at two."

"Fine," I said, sounding angry to myself. I couldn't decide why I was angry—because he just assumed I always needed bodyguards now or because he didn't speak with me before he made these decisions? Again.

I was under the hot water for a while, and, when I touched my hair, I couldn't remember if I had used shampoo or not, so I washed my hair again, just in case.

The shower door opened, and Sebastian's gaze moved slowly up from my feet until our eyes met. He had that look of pure lust a man would get when he wanted a woman. "As much as I want to bend you over and lick all that water off your body, one inch at a time. I need to go, but I'll see you tonight." He groaned with frustration.

I nodded and kissed him, leaving damp marks all over his shirt and a grin splashed on my face. "There. I can also leave my mark on you."

His laugh was deep with an edge of a growl. As he closed the shower door, he playfully smacked my ass, and then he was gone.

Once my hair was dried and I was dressed in my favorite pair of jeans and a black vest, I grabbed my shoulder holster from the bedside table and fastened it in place then added my Glock. I stood in front of the full-length mirror, moving the holster a bit to the left then to the right until it was comfortable. I carried my gun out of habit now, instead of Ralph forcing or reminding me. Lately, I felt naked without it. The small wound on my chest was still pink and raised with a light green bruise blossoming around it. I should have had my gun on me last night. I would've killed that old vinegar-smelling witch in an instant. I pulled on a navy-blue blouse and buttoned it up halfway, allowing me enough of a gap to grab the Glock in a hurry.

Something caught my eye outside. Pulling back the curtain, I glanced out the window. The sun was shining, but the wind looked icy as it cut through the bare trees. Was it the bend of the branches that made me look out? A shiver ran along my spine. I touched my gun through the blouse, and the tension eased. It felt like someone was watching me. I shivered, remembering the new winter coat I had bought, grabbed it off the hanger and went into the living room.

Sawyer and Rory stood at attention when I entered.

"At ease, men," I said, grinning. "Are you ready to drive with me today?" I grabbed a mug that sat next to my coffee machine and filled it with my breakfast—black coffee. "Would either of you like some?"

"I'll have," Sawyer said, grabbing a cup from the cupboard without me having to say which cupboard and held it near the pot for me to pour. "How's your"—he touched his chest with his index finger—"wound?"

"Oh, fine. It's almost gone, like it never happened." I narrowed my eyes at him. "How did you know which cupboard the mugs were in? You've never had coffee here before."

Sawyer glanced at Rory then to me. "We've searched your house."

"Protocol?"

"Yes." He glanced back at Rory, waiting for his partner to add to it. When Rory kept quiet, he said, "We needed to ensure your home was safe for Sebastian ... And for you." He said the last part quickly, almost as an afterthought.

"Just don't go digging in my underwear drawer, boys. Otherwise, we're good." I grinned then sipped the hot liquid.

"Sebastian said you wanted to visit Marcus today at the lion's den. With the werewolves and were-leopards having an issue with one another, I'm not sure Troy would allow us to go in with you," Rory said and came to stand near us.

"Ralph and Devan will be there. Besides, I doubt Marcus or Troy would try anything with me."

The two guards shared a knowing look.

"What now? Come, spit it out."

"Danny might be there."

"Yeah, so?" I said, swallowing hard. Danny and his brother Miles had attacked me six months ago, leaving me for dead and with a parting gift—amnesia. I'd seen him once after the attack and then never again. It wasn't as if his presence affected me.

"You sure you still want to go?"

"Of course," I said and downed the rest of my coffee. "Let's go." I wasn't about to let Danny or anyone else mess with my good mood. And I wasn't about to hide from anyone.

With the insurance money I had received from my old Honda, I had bought a secondhand silver Ford truck without a scratch on it. The previous owner had four cars and hardly drove this one, so he sold it. It was as good as new.

Sawyer flipped a coin and won the toss, so he was riding shotgun.

Sitting behind the wheel of my own car after other people had chauffeured me for almost six months felt wonderful. I could drive the way I wanted, at the speed I wanted, and down the road I wanted to take. I didn't have to ask anyone for a lift or wait for someone to fetch me. I could get into my truck and drive where I wanted with the freedom to do so.

Sawyer slid into the seat beside me. The only thing that bothered me was this part—having two shadows who followed me everywhere I went. I understood why and was grateful, but knowing they were here—All. The. Time—bothered me.

I turned up the radio, listening to my music all the way to the lion's pride. When we arrived, I found a parking spot near the far end, one closest to the edge of the clubhouse fence and the forest. We piled out and followed the sidewalk to the clubhouse entrance.

As we entered, I heard Ralph and Devan laughing. No one greeted us at the entrance, so we followed their voices until we came upon a room. Ralph and Devan sat across from each other while Troy sat on a desk, a cigar between his lips. His wavy sandy-brown hair framed his face. His warm chocolate-colored eyes creased at the outer corners as he smiled and puffed on the cigar, exhaling two perfect smoke rings.

The three men faced us as we entered.

Ralph was his usual casual self—jeans and t-shirt with a jacket to hide his gun. His curly brown hair was long enough that he tied it up into a small tight man-bun. With his hair off his face, his broad shoulders were defined. His dark blue eyes matched the grin on his face; he made a slight gesture toward Troy, like he needed to tell me something about him.

I held my gaze for a second longer to let him know I understood, and we could discuss it later.

Devan was a clairvoyant, a witch, or a warlock—whatever he was, he was fucking powerful. He had strawberry-blond hair and pale skin dotted with freckles. But it wasn't just his hair color or his pale skin that made him stand out. I realized when I first met him, it was those eyes. One eye was blue, like a husky in Alaska with a cerulean-blue ring around the iris. And the other was lime green with no ring. Instead, the green bled into the white—if glanced at quick enough, one would think he was blind in that eye. He too smiled, and it reached his heterochromatic eyes.

I narrowed my eyes at them. Something was up. Or knowing Ralph, the joke was on me. "Hi," I said, and my two shadows entered the room with me.

Troy surveyed the men behind me, pursing his lips then puffed on the cigar again. "No dogs allowed," he said with another smoke ring floating in the air above his head.

A low growl wafted from both my bodyguards' lips,

mimicking one another. Heat beat against my back, and my breath caught in the back of my throat.

"Enough, guys. Perhaps you should wait outside. We won't be long, I promise. I just have a few questions for Marcus, and then we can leave," I said, irritated, as I turned to face them. "Do you want my keys?" I handed the keychain to Rory; he was the better driver of the two.

"Bye, dogs." Troy waved at them.

I glared at him. "If they can behave, Troy, so can you."

"My apologies, Blaire. I guess everyone is rather on edge this morning."

Maybe that's what Ralph had alluded to, that Troy was in a bad mood because of the trouble the werewolves had caused between themselves and the were-leopards.

"It's not them you need to be pissed at, it's the new werewolf."

"They're part of the same pack, Blaire."

"Never paint them all with the same brush, Troy. Or do you want to be known as a backstabbing, cure-crunching monster like Marcus and Melinda?"

Troy flew off the desk so quickly I didn't see him move. I only felt him when he pushed me into the far wall, my back and head hitting the hard surface with a loud thump. Sparkly stars clouded my vision, and, after a second or two, it cleared, and Troy's half-man, half-were-lion face stared back at me. His power seared me like sharp needles, one painful prick at a time.

Through a guttural growl and sharp teeth, he said, "Don't ever compare me to Marcus, or that whore."

"Then don't compare Sawyer or Rory to that asshole Corey, who started all the shit," I retorted through gritted teeth and a click as I took the safety off my gun and pressed it firmly under his chin, ready to blow off his face with one happy trigger.

Something registered behind the glow of his green/brown lion eyes. He hadn't expected me to be quick enough to pull my gun on him.

My lioness was out, pacing in front of her metaphysical cave. She roared, growled and then snarled. She didn't like this were-lion hurting me, hurting us. She didn't like that little power display he had flaunted. My lioness's stride slowed until she stopped and stared at me with her yellow-green eyes. I tensed but managed to steady my breathing. I didn't want her smashing into me like my were-rat did. I shielded her in as hard as I could.

"I smell your lion," Troy said through a husky purr, squeezing his eyes shut, like he was trying to block something. He licked his lips, stepping backward to give me some space but not enough for me to move completely out of his way.

I didn't trust that he wouldn't do anything else, so I kept my gun on him. "Yeah, you pissed her off by smashing into me." I rubbed the back of my head, standing straighter and holding my head high. I wasn't as tall as him, but, in that moment, I felt bigger.

"Touché, Blaire," he said and shifting into his human form, the green of his lion eyes receding until they were chestnut-brown again.

"Are you done with the pissing contest? Can I see Marcus now?"

Troy chuckled, shook his head in disbelief and headed for the door.

Ralph secured his gun into his shoulder holster, and Devan stared at me with wide eyes, mouthing, *Are you okay?* I nodded, and they both followed close behind me. We descended a flight of stairs until we reached the basement where they kept their cages for the new were-lions. It kept everyone safe during their first few full moons.

Marcus and Melinda were in separate cages. Melinda cowered in the far corner of her cage, her eyes following me as I entered the room.

I stood near Marcus's cage. The man staring back at me through the bars seemed older; dirt peppered his face, with sweat beading down the sides. He only wore his white vest —now sweat-marked and brown—and his boxers. He snarled, fell on all fours and charged the bars. He hit the cage with a loud crack and fell backward, landing on his ass. His skin receded as fur flowed over him like running water. Bones broke; bones splintered and reset; and he shifted. His small blue eyes stayed small and shone like watery gemstones. His brown hair grew until his mane fanned out. Marcus, the were-lion, was large, bigger than a small pony.

He strode toward me with large muscles that moved like flowing silver. He pushed his face against the cage, snarling again and baring sharp teeth. "Blaire, nice of you to come see me." The words were his but were muffled slightly through his lion jaw; some letters couldn't be pronounced properly due to the size and shape of his mouth. But I understood him.

"This is your last chance, Marcus. Give me something, or I'll let Troy and the rest of the pride eat your girlfriend first, so you can watch them do it, and then you." I shot him an unfriendly look devoid of any emotion.

His lips curled upward, baring sharp teeth—teeth that could rip my limbs from my body. His small blue eyes flitted from me to someone behind me. I assumed it would be Troy. I didn't want to take my eyes off the monster in front of me, even though he was caged. For all I knew, he could have found weak spots in the cage and could crash through it at any moment.

"If I give you something, would you allow us to live?" Marcus asked.

"Maybe."

"Yes," Troy said behind me. "If you give something concrete, Marcus, only then can we negotiate what that would mean for the both of you."

"What?" I yelled, not understand what had just happened. Troy had said it was my decision what the outcome would be for these two, yet he seemed to have changed his mind.

Troy leered down at me.

"When did you decide to change the rules, Troy?"

"We might need them, Blaire. Our lion pride isn't as big as the werewolves' or the were-leopards'. We need every lion available to help our pride."

I opened my mouth to say something but didn't trust my voice. I was livid.

"But"—Troy lifted his chin in Marcus's direction—"if he doesn't help you today, I'll kill him myself."

"Fine," Marcus said, sitting down, like a large tan kitty-cat. His small blue eyes stared at me. "You were fifteen years old when I found you on the streets. I, uhm, I thought you were selling a certain product." He cleared his throat—a mixture between a growl and coughing up a furball.

"What? Was I a prostitute?" I asked, my frown deepening. This was not happening.

"No, no. I thought you were, but you weren't. I'd just started my business and was on my fourth job. By the time I realized you had seen what I had done, that I had killed someone, I was afraid you would run to the police. I was about to kill you when you asked me what I did. You were genuinely interested. You wanted to know more about what it was that I did, and you wanted me to teach you. I bought you some clothes, fed you. I'd never seen anyone so hungry before in my life." He closed his eyes, as if remembering the fond memory. "And then you stayed with me. The entire time, you kept asking me to teach you, that you had to do what I did. You never did tell me what happened to you or to your parents. I guess it was easier to teach you what I did than play psychologist. I started you off with some hand-to-hand fighting then how to handle knives and throw them. Then I showed you how to handle a gun and shoot. You were a fast learner, Blaire, and you were good. Really fucking good." He paused, as if collecting his thoughts. "You had your first kill at sixteen." He cleared his throat, making that same mixture between a growl and coughing sound. "I was sick to my stomach knowing I had created a little killing machine. But you thrived in it. I'd never seen you so happy since meeting you. And you kept saying it was the best day of your life. I hired Ralph soon thereafter, and the two of you took over most of the contracts while I managed everything else. You made enough money to buy back your old family home, then you met Mason and had Scout."

The back of my throat ached when I swallowed. "Do you know what happened with Mason and Scout? Why did I make them leave in such a hurry?"

Marcus shook his head, and his large mane swayed. "No. You were very private when it came to them. When they left, you said you wanted a basement in all our houses, that you wanted us all to be safe, that if anything happened, we would be armed and ready for anything."

"Shit. What the fuck was I afraid of?" My voice faltered as I said the last few words.

"Dunno," Ralph said, like a hollow echo behind me. "I can't remember much, except that you were spooked though, like you'd seen a ghost. We were hunting a vampire, and you left me there. You took my car, left me there and drove home. I had to catch a cab back." He laughed, but there was a nervous edge to it.

I exhaled. "Anything else?"

Marcus shook his head again. "No. That's it, I swear." He turned those small blue eyes to Troy. "Can we be let out now?"

Footsteps descended the stairs. I turned to see who it was and saw a large bald man—Keegan. His mustache had grown and curled slightly down and inward and looked smooth in the dim lights. An index finger twirled one side of the mustache then the other side. Keegan said something to Troy that I couldn't hear, then they stared at us.

"I have to go. Something urgent has come up. Keegan will take care of you," Troy said and left the basement.

Keegan came to stand beside me. "You might want to step back, Blaire." It was the first time I'd heard him speak; his voice was gruff and husky.

"Why?" I asked but stepped backward anyway.

"Come forward, Marcus." Keegan lifted a large black weapon that looked like a gun but not quite. He held up a dart the size of his thumbnail. "It's a transmitter so we can track where you are. If you try to remove it, the little ball inside will explode in your body and kill you instantly." He showed Marcus the dark ball in the middle of the dart.

Keegan's bald head shone with the light glow of sweat. He inserted the transmitter dart into the gun, lifted it between the bars, aimed at Marcus and fired. The transmitter lodged itself into Marcus' skin. As if it was intelligent, it wiggled itself into his muscle, and then it disappeared.

Keegan reloaded and went to Melinda's cage. "I need you to shift, Melinda."

She shook her head, mumbling, "No, no, no, Keegan. You aren't putting that thing inside me."

Keegan pulled his pistole with his other hand and aimed at her face. "What will it be, Melinda? Option A"—he held up the transmitter gun—"or option B?" He lifted his pistol.

"Not while everyone is staring at me."

"Nobody cares what you look like naked, Melinda. You know I hate repeating myself."

I wanted to look away, to give her some privacy, but I couldn't. She removed her blouse, folded it neatly and placed it beside her on the floor then did the same with her skirt—folding it and placing it on top of her blouse. The raised scar tissue zigzagged across her body. She tried to cover the largest scar across her chest and collar bone, but her hands were too small and the scars too big and long. Her brown eyes were wide with embarrassment from the scars, not from being naked. I wondered if that was the cause of her turning into a were-lion or from before.

"Shift," Keegan demanded.

Just that one word sent a shiver down my arms, and I held myself, digging my nails into my forearms.

It was gentle at first, like butterflies fluttering against my face. Melinda's curly black hair receded as tan fur flowed over her skin. Bones popped; kneecaps snapped; and she cried out. Like an explosion of skin, muscle, and bone, she went from a woman into a lioness larger than a small pony. She was bigger than Marcus. During those seconds when she changed, the power that hit me felt like it could peel the skin off my body, and I screamed as she cried out from her violent change. I had seen were-animals shift, but none were as brutal as Melinda's. A low throaty roar escaped her huge jaws as she paced inside the cage. It was similar to the manic pace captive animals did when they were restless with nowhere to go.

"Sit, Melinda," Keegan instructed.

She growled again, snapped her jaws and sat in the middle of the cage.

Keegan inserted a new transmitter dart into the gun and fired into her large body. Melinda jerked when the transmitter dart entered her flesh and ran for the cage door. She crashed into it with such speed and strength the bars bent outward, and the door snapped open. From the impact, Melinda fell backward. She rose again, seeing the cage door ajar. Her gaze jumped from the opening to me then to Keegan. She slowly placed one foot in front of the other, edging forward, creeping closer to her freedom.

"Out! Everybody get out. *Now!*" Keegan yelled.

Ralph and Devan were already running up the stairs.

Keegan grabbed my arm and pulled me with him, his fingernails tearing into my flesh. We reached the stairs, and he leaped two steps at a time. My foot caught on the first step, and I crashed, knees first. Keegan let go of me and ran. I glanced over my shoulder and saw Melinda staring up at me, her brown eyes shining black in lion form.

With the tip of her nose, she gently nudged open the cage door, the metal grinding hard against the broken bolts, and the creaking noise was like ice in my head. Blood whooshed through my ears, and my vision tunneled as adrenaline pumped through me. I pushed through the pain in my legs, stood from the step and ran, two steps at once.

But I was too slow. Something crashed into my back, launching me into the wall at the top of the first set of stairs, and I fell to the floor, face down. Teeth pierced the back of my neck, puncturing my skin and edging closer to important bones, veins, and nerves.

"Now you know what it feels like when someone else has your life in their hands, bitch," Melinda said with her mouth full of my neck. The words weren't clear, but I understood every one of them. She pressed her large paw onto my back, her nails digging in, and something wet ran down my back.

Squeezing my eyes shut and needing to acquire some form of control. I sucked in slow shallow breaths and tried to avoid any sudden movements.

Screaming and shouting came from atop the stairs, followed by growling and a few guns being cocked and loaded.

"Get off her, Melinda. Now!" That sounded like Troy, but I couldn't be sure, as it was said through a throaty growl.

She lifted her paw off my back, a quick jerk as my skin stuck to her nails, and more liquid flowed over my back. Her warm breath was still against my neck and head though. And, for a second, she bit down, as if changing her mind, that it would be better for her to kill me, and then she relaxed her jaw. She finally released my neck, licked the puncture wounds and left me alone. She sauntered up the stairs as if nothing had happened and nothing bothered her.

A loud exhale escaped my lips as I tried to get up, first on all fours, but then I fell against the wall and back down to the floor again.

I lay there for a second, waiting for the cluster of stars to dissipate, but they didn't.

Chapter Twelve

The floor tiles were dirty, and all I felt was the stinging that burned into my back. I focused on the ants walking in a line around the parts of the floor that were dirty and into a hole. I felt another sharp sting move up my spine.

"Okay, now for your neck," Mel said behind me, her warm gloved hand was on my head, and the stinging continued in my neck.

Through gritted teeth, I said, "Please, can you work faster? Working so slowly is fucking killing me."

"Do you want this done quickly or the right way? Infection or no infection, you might collect lycanthropy like some collect stamps, but that doesn't mean you can't get infections. Now keep still, so I can suture this properly."

"I fucking hate you."

"Tough. I'm still doing it my way."

Hot and cold sensations made the hair on my body stand on end. Mel pushed some of her warm power onto my head as she cleaned the puncture wounds on my neck. It was confusing; I didn't know what to feel—warm and fuzzy or cold and stingy. At least I was calm.

All the ants were down their hole, just in time for lunch.

"I'm amazed Troy even allowed you in."

"Yeah, well, I might be a werewolf, but I'm a doctor first, and I help all the were-animals. If they kept me out, they would die."

"Thanks for coming. Again."

"You bet."

The warmth of her hand and the gentle buzz of her power made me close my eyes for a second, and I drifted off. A car approached me with their high beams on. I raised my arms to shield my eyes from the blinding light. The car stopped, and the headlights went dead. Darkness surrounded me. Grey mist circled me, swirling and thickening, until a shape materialized, and an old woman appeared. She stood before me with eyes clouded over, her skin grey and leathery. Behind her stood a tall pale figure with long blond hair and cold blue eyes. Long fingers branched toward me, touching me. I jerked away from the hands and pain tore through my neck.

I yelled.

"Hold still," Mel said, removing her hand from my head. "What was that?"

"I don't know, but I don't want to lie down anymore. I don't want to dream about that woman again." I sat upright.

"I wasn't done."

"I don't care. You can finish with me sitting up. I can't fall asleep again."

A soft knock came on the door. Mel answered. "You can come in."

Rory stuck in his head. "Heard you scream. You doing all right, Blaire?"

I pulled up the sheet to cover the front of me. "Yeah, I'll be fine. How does it look from the back?" Mel had to cut away my shirt but saved my bra.

"Not as bad as I thought it would be. Is she healing already?"

"Looks like it."

"I don't suppose anyone has a shirt I could borrow?"

"That's also why I'm here. Troy asked me to give you this." He placed a black t-shirt and jacket beside me. "It's a man's shirt, but it's small, so it should fit you. The jacket was left in the closet, women's size."

"Thanks. Did you tell Sebastian?"

"Yeah, I had to tell him," he said unhappily. "He's on his way."

Someone yelled, followed by people running past our room.

"What's happening?" I asked, jumping off the bed and clutching the sheet taut against my body.

"Stay here, Blaire. I mean it. Let me go check it out. Sawyer is out here if you need him," Rory said and closed the door behind him.

"I'm still busy, Blaire," Mel chastised.

"You said it yourself, I'm already healing." I pulled on the t-shirt and opened the door.

Sawyer stood across the hallway with his arms crossed over his broad chest, his eyes gloomy and sinister from the dim light. He looked like a dark mountain, large and unnerving. He shook his head slowly as he approached me. "Don't you ever listen?"

"No," I said and went back into the room. I strapped my holster and gun under the jacket Rory had left me. The stitches in my back were taut, and the wound in my neck ached. But I would live. "What's going on? I heard screaming." I said, returning to the door.

"Apparently, someone got hurt."

I headed toward the front doors with Sawyer so close behind me I could feel heat coming off his body.

"You aren't making this easy, Blaire. Just don't run off without me."

I stared up at the man with my friendliest smile. "Who, me?"

Outside near the entrance was a crowd gathering around someone lying in the car park. Mel ran past us with her medical bag.

I ran after her.

Mel clawed her way through the crowd until she reached a woman lying on her side, clutching her stomach in the fetal position.

I stood behind Mel, peering over her shoulder. The woman had brown hair, and, for a second, I couldn't understand what was happening, until her hair changed to white. I pegged her to be in her early twenties, considering her youthful look, until her skin greyed and tightened against her emaciated form, and her cheeks caved in. Her body shriveled until her clothing resembled bedding. The crowd gasped in horror.

"Everybody get back. Who saw what happened?" Mel asked, raising her voice.

The crowd moved out of her way.

A young man raised his hand.

Mel stared at him. "Well, go on. What happened?"

"We were shopping, when someone drove passed and shot at us, hitting her."

"Did you get a look at them?"

"I couldn't see who it was, but they smelled sour and like the dead."

"Was it zombies?" I asked, standing beside Mel now. "It's daytime, so vampires aren't even awake yet."

"I don't know, but they smelled like the dead. It was a sour, rotting stench, and blood—lots and lots of blood." He stared at the corpse at his feet. "They shot her and disappeared. She fell, and that's when I picked her up and drove back here. But I was too late. She's already dead."

"Do you know if she had any connections to any vampires or witches?" I asked.

The man shook his head, tears welling in his eyes.

"Do you know anything about her?"

"She was new. She'd only been with us about six months. She was born a were-lion and moved here from Washington. I was showing her the best places to buy laptops in town today."

I went down on my haunches. If I could find a flicker of her light left, maybe I could still help her. I touched her hand; it was cold and hard. Her fingers were already mummified, reminding me of the missing wolf Shawn had found at the outlet mall. But maybe I wasn't too late. I closed my eyes and opened my steel wall just a tiny bit, enough for my white light to search through her. My white light moved from my fingers into her hard hand and ... nothing. There was an emptiness, a nothingness. Her light was gone, stamped out in an instant.

When I opened my eyes, most of the crowd had gone. I flinched when someone touched my shoulder.

"Sorry, didn't mean to frighten you," Mel said.

I rose. "She's dead. I couldn't help her. There's nothing left of her. It's like what happened to the werewolf. It was the dart we found on her that we gave you to test."

Mel gasped. "Is this what happens to them? My team is still busy investigating, but I'll put a rush on it." She fished her cellphone out her pocket and walked inside the building to make a call.

A man lifted the woman's body and carried her through the building and out to the other side. We all followed, watching him place her body on the firepit, while others fetched wood from the shed that stood next to the clubhouse.

"What are they doing?" I asked Sawyer beside me.

"She was poisoned. They need to burn her body."

"What poison can do that to a body and so quickly? And to a were-lion? Were-animals are much tougher than humans, yet she shriveled and died within minutes."

"Wait!" Mel ran toward the firepit. "Wait! I want a tissue sample." Mel cut tissue from the thigh, arm, and abdomen of the corpse and placed them inside glass containers and into her bag. "I'm going to the hospital to have this analyzed and compare it to the results you gave me from Chicago and the dart. We need to find out what it was, and if it's the same stuff," Mel said with worry in her voice and a grave expression.

I watched Mel leave and saw someone approach us. He stopped and spoke to Mel and then continued in my direction. I recognized that walk—loose-limbed, like flowing muscles.

Sebastian approached with a smile, but it didn't match the concern in his eyes. "Baby, are you okay?" He pulled me into the circle of his arms, kissing the top of my head. "You scared me. When Rory called, telling me you were attacked, I got here as fast as I could."

"I'm fine. But someone killed a were-lion." I pointed to

the firepit where a man lit the wood and her body with a torch.

"Where's Rory?"

Sawyer came closer. "With Troy. They had to restrain Marcus and Melinda after the attack on Blaire and question those who brought the body here."

"Blaire was his number one priority. He should never have left her alone, under no circumstances." Anger flared from Sebastian like a heatwave and hit me head on, almost knocking me off my feet. Then it was gone in an instance.

"I'm fine, Sebastian. And Sawyer was with me."

"They're back," Sebastian said, letting me go.

Four men emerged from the building, two in their half-beast, half-human form. As they neared us, I could see them better. Rory's huge head was that of his wolf, his eyes glowing yellow with hints of brown and green. Grey fur covered his face, and his large jaw bared sharp teeth. His hands were big claws. Troy's mane fanned around his massive lion-head, towering over Rory in his half-beast form.

After I blinked, their half-beast shrunk, their skin shifting to normal. By the time they reached us, they had morphed into their human form. They made it look so easy and effortless.

"Where is Marcus and Melinda?" I asked.

"After Melinda attacked you, we had to restrain her, and then Marcus went all ape-shit on us. That's why we were half-beasts," Rory answered nervously upon seeing Sebastian's stern glance.

"We need to inform everyone at the WAA about what's been happening the last couple of days, in case it happens again," Troy said, panning from the fire behind me then back at us, his expression grave.

"Agreed," Sebastian said. "I need to get back to the wolves. I'll tell Shawn and Anne when I get there."

"You aren't finished?" I asked, my frown matching his.

"No. We were just about to close off, when I heard you were attacked."

"I'm coming with you."

He nodded reluctantly. "Fine."

"I'll call Arturo. He can let the rest of the were-rats know," Troy said and returned to the clubhouse.

As we headed to our cars, Sebastian took Rory aside. I could only assume it was to chastise him for leaving me alone. Rory paled, glancing at me with regret, nodding in agreement to whatever Sebastian was saying to him.

When they were done talking, Sebastian wrapped an arm around me, pulling me in close to his body, as if he was afraid of something else but too afraid to tell me about it.

Chapter Thirteen

Rory drove my car while I sat in the passenger seat, my back and neck still ached from Melinda's bite and claw marks. I was amazed that I already had that tight itchy feeling that indicated I was busy healing even though it still hurt. Glancing out the window as we drove in the late afternoon traffic, I watched the orange and yellow from the sun splashing across the sky like a water painting. Why couldn't my days be normal?

Sawyer sat behind me; he and Rory were discussing what had happened at the lion pride. They thought it was Corey who had killed the were-lion. Ever since he had arrived in town, trouble had seemed to follow him, and the shit had hit the fan in every possible way.

"What would his motive be?" I asked, interrupting their conversation.

"That's what we need to find out, Blaire. I'd love to get my hands on him though," Sawyer said.

I glanced at him through the little mirror on the sun visor.

His eyes glowed yellow as heat rolled off him.

I rubbed my arms.

"Sorry. Sometimes I forget you can feel when one of us allows our beast to surface," he said, his voice husky with an edge of anger.

"Just don't attack me. I don't think I'm ready for another were-animal to join the rest of my animal family."

"Sorry." He chuckled, his voice was back to normal, and his human brown eyes stared back at me.

"We're here," Rory said, parking next to Sebastian's Jeep while Ralph and Devan parked beside us.

I climbed out the car and approached Devan. "Are you sure you want to be here?"

Devan was sensitive to certain environments, and a room full of werewolves might not be the best place for him. His multi-colored eyes smiled at me, and his lips curled upward.

"You're sweet, but I've been practicing, and I think I can handle the pack tonight. Ever since I started working with you and Ralph, I've started blocking certain things, which has helped. A lot."

"Are you sure?"

Devan nodded.

"Alright, but if you become uncomfortable, let us know," I said then thought of questions about what had just happened. "You were there with the lions. Did you notice anything with the woman who died?"

"Death was surrounding her and the man. I'm going to sound strange, but a black mist trailed behind them. Whatever was in those darts that killed her was a warning."

"A warning?" I frowned at him. "What do you mean?"

"That's just it, I don't know. It's difficult to discern, but someone is sending warnings to the were-animals. And they need to start listening."

My blood ran cold. I wasn't sure what Devan meant, but I was glad Sebastian had heard him. He too had stilled, and we all stared at Devan until the shock had worn off.

"Thanks, Devan, I will bring it under advisement." Sebastian said, grabbing my hand and continued walking. "Let's go see some werewolves."

Not only could Devan perceive certain things, like whether one had certain witchy abilities or was bad, just by looking at them, but he could know intimate and private things just by touching someone. He was a good clairvoyant, and, so far, he hadn't held anything for ransom against me. He has offered to help me unlock whatever was locked inside my mind, but I didn't want him looking that deep inside me. Perhaps if I ever became desperate, I might take him up on his offer.

Now that Sebastian and I had a few minutes to ourselves as we walked along the sidewalk, I could find out about the situation with Shawn and Corey. "What was the outcome of your discussion with Shawn?"

Without looking at me, he said, "Shawn agreed that Corey needed to be punished. And that one of us could fight him."

"Something tells me that someone is *you*."

"Uh-huh."

"Have you seen him fight before?"

"No."

I squeezed his arm. "I know you're a great fighter, but do you think it's wise that it's *you*?"

"We'll see."

We entered the wolves' building and walked through the hallway until we were outside again. On one side about fifty werewolves sat while Shawn chatted to two females. On the other side was Anne with about twenty were-leopards, including her two children, Ivy and Greg.

Rory and Sawyer growled when they saw Corey, who stood in the middle with two others.

"Who are the other two with Corey?"

"Werewolves," Sebastian said coldly as if he were somewhere else and not with me.

"They're the pack's troublemakers. It's either bar fights or pissing against the women at pack meetings," Rory said before heading in Shawn's direction.

"What'll happen to them?"

"They'll be punished," Rory replied over his shoulder.

Shawn said something to the two women, and they got up and left. He rose, greeting Rory and Sawyer. Rory said something in his ear. "No harm will come to them," Shawn said, staring at Ralph and Devan—at least we knew it's safe for them to attend. "Blaire"—Shawn's smile was broad—"so glad you're all right. When I heard you were attacked, we couldn't continue until we knew you were safe."

"Thanks, Shawn. I appreciate that you could accommodate Sebastian."

"Even though Sebastian and I are old friends, we do have to settle this issue tonight." His expression was taut.

"Agreed," Sebastian said. "I will fight him."

"Are you sure? None of us has seen him fight. We don't know if he fights clean or not."

"Just understand I won't be taking it easy on him," Sebastian replied, still sounding distant in thought. In that moment, I became aware and wanted to panic. I wasn't sure what was going on with him or if he was just focused on the fight. Without causing alarm, I would wait it out and only say something if I thought his life may be in danger. I knew Rory and Sawyer would help him in any way shape or form.

Nodding, Shawn whispered only for Sebastian and me to hear. "I won't mind if you kill him, Sebastian." Then to the crowd, he said, "Sebastian has agreed to fight Corey. No dirty punches, no weapons, only a true test of your physical strength and speed."

"What about the other two?" someone from the crowd asked.

"Don't worry. They'll be whipped until sunrise. Then whipped again."

Others in the crowd laughed.

Ralph, Devan, and I stood beside Anne with the leap. The spectators formed a large circle around the two fighters, each of them sitting on opposite sides until the referee started the fight. Sebastian stayed in his jeans but threw his t-shirt at me to hold. I clung to his clothing like a lifeline, his smell caressing my senses and easing my tension. He had to beat Corey; I didn't know what would happen if he ever got hurt.

Corey wiped his face with his shirt then threw it on the floor next to him.

Sebastian was taller and bulkier. I'd seen him fight before, and the power behind his punch was enough to snap a man's neck. He had knocked another were-leopard unconscious with that one hit. But nobody knew how Corey fought or how powerful he was, if at all.

Corey was taut, and, when he started warming up, I noticed just how much quicker he was on his feet than what I'd seen with any other were-animal. He seemed young, his skin soft. He hardly had any facial hair, and even the look in his eyes as he leered at Sebastian reminded me of young boys who didn't like being told what to do. It was his whole boyish attitude that had me unnerved.

Sebastian stretched his defined legs and upper body, and his muscles moved with suppleness. He stretched his upper body one side then the other and then did splits.

The werewolf referee stood between them, calling them over. "This is a clean fight. Anyone playing dirty loses. If you tap-out, you lose. If your neck gets broken, you lose. The first one to shift also loses. Are you ready?" Sebastian and Corey nodded, and the referee blew his whistle.

Corey hit Sebastian first, but Sebastian blocked the punch and hit Corey hard enough that he stumbled backward and fell to his knees. Corey wiped his bloody nose, curling his lips into a sneer. A low throaty growl floated from his mouth, then he jumped and collided into Sebastian.

My eyes were too human-slow to follow who hit whom. I saw punches, kicks, then Sebastian falling to the ground. As he rose, I saw his split lip with blood running down his chin, but that didn't stop him. That's when he crashed into Corey as hard and as fast as he could, then the real fighting started.

I heard teeth snapping and cries but wasn't sure from whom. A jaw crunched, and two teeth flew onto the grass near my feet. The fighting eased when Corey cowered on his side with two fingers in his mouth. It had been his teeth. I covered my mouth to hide the giggling.

Sebastian stood back, watching Corey with a predatory gaze. His form towered over the werewolf boy. My body pebbled at the sight of Sebastian; he was scary and delicious.

The referee blew his whistle, giving them two minutes to rest before the fight would continue. He went to Corey and asked whether he still wanted to fight.

Corey yelled, "Yes!"

After two minutes, the referee blew his whistle, and the fighting commenced. I heard another loud blow with a crunch, and Corey flew across the lawn. His jaw was slack, his eyes rolling into the back of his head.

"Is he dead?" I asked, leaning into Ralph.

"Sure looks like it."

Corey's eyes fluttered open and focused. He reset his jaw into place with a crunching sound. Corey moved it sideways unaided, yet it still seemed like a painful movement. The cut above his eye was knitting together while his swollen eye was smoothing out. He was a very fast healer.

But so was Sebastian. His split lip was perfect again, and he only had blood marks on his face without any visible wounds.

"Have you had enough?" Sebastian called out, taunting him.

Corey ignored Sebastian as he charged him, screaming as he smashed into Sebastian. This time they both flew above the crowd and across the field.

The crowd were a nosy bunch, and we followed them with the referee running faster toward them, so he could continue judging the fight. The fighting speed increased and intensified.

Light pinpricks fell on my skin. Wintery snow fell gently on the outskirts of the field. As if united, the were-animals radiated as their beasts' power pounded heat so hot into the air that it melted the snow before it landed on the ground. The jacket I wore was damp. Everybody's hair was wet from the droplets.

The fighting was harsh, the blows from each of their fists harder than the last. I couldn't see it, but I heard it.

Then the last thing I heard was a loud snap, and the fighting ceased. A body lay crumpled on the ground.

Sebastian approached me, his body healing itself without having to shift.

The two werewolves who were in trouble because of Corey went to his body. The familiar sound of bones snapping, skin stretching, and muscles moving as Corey shifted into his werewolf form wafted across the hushed crowd. Sebastian had broken Corey's neck, and if Corey wanted to live, he had to shift. And quickly. But that also meant he had lost the fight. It was over. Sebastian had won.

I put my arms around Sebastian, kissing him chastely on the lips. "You were wonderful out there. Are you okay?"

"I'm fine. It was a good fight, and he was strong."

"But not strong enough," I said teasing, my lips curling upward in a mischievous grin.

Sebastian knocked me to the ground, pinning me in place. I struggled for air as he lay on top of me, crushing my lungs. I didn't remember his weight being so heavy. People were screaming. Others were running. Movement surrounded us. The click of guns sounded near us. Then that heavy weight was gone, and it was only Sebastian on top of me. I was still seeing stars when I heard fighting, teeth snapping, and flesh tearing.

Sebastian rolled off me, then his hands cupped my face. "Blaire? Blaire, can you hear me? Talk to me, Blaire!"

My body froze in place. Everything ached as I tried to relearn how to breathe. A *gah* sound escaped my lips as I exhaled. When I could swallow, clearing my throat, my eyes fluttered open. I managed to say, "Uh-huh."

"Shawn is fighting Corey. They're both in their animal form. Stay out of their way," Sebastian said, glancing at someone beside me. "Keep her safe. If anything happens to her, I'll kill you myself." His command sent shivers down my entire body. He stood and went toward the fight.

Sawyer sat beside me, asking if I was okay.

I muttered that I was and tried to sit up. "Help me up, Sawyer. What was that just now?"

"Corey and Shawn were both in their animal form. They started fighting and crashed into Sebastian and you," Sawyer said then sat behind me, propping me up and protecting me with his body.

The two wolves fought violently; blood splattered across the grass, and the mixture of red, black, and grey blurs moved against one another.

"Can't we just shoot him?"

"No." Sawyer chuckled. "Not when they're fighting. Maybe if it was in self-defense ..." Sawyer's words trailed off as if contemplating what he could do.

I knew *I* wanted to shoot him.

The crowd fell silent when bones snapped, flesh tore, and one of them fell. A shape covered in black fur crept toward the grey figure on the ground, snarling at the limp body, and gripped his neck between his strong jaws and ripped out his throat.

"Please tell me that was Shawn doing the ripping."

"Yes," Sawyer said, nodding.

I saw Shawn's black form crouched over Corey's lifeless grey body. Shawn bit into the side of Corey's face and removed a sizable chunk of his cheek. He chewed it then swallowed it. He moved down to his abdomen and started eating the tender belly flesh.

"Is he *eating* him?" I asked, my eyes widening. I turned to Sawyer as a sickness burned in my stomach from the sounds of Shawn eating flesh.

"Yes," Sawyer said, staring out at the forest.

The sound of bones crunching echoed through the grassy bowl that lay between the wolf pack building and the forest. The lights that surrounded the field blinked on as the sun disappeared behind the trees. Shawn had eaten much of Corey when he invited some of the other wolves to join in.

I swallowed hard. "Is this what you do? Eat the loser?"

"When it's to the death, yes, but I don't stay. But I'm glad I did for this one." Sawyer's brown eyes glistening in the dim lights.

I shuddered at the thought.

A light breeze swept through the trees with the sound of dry leaves crushing under foot. I glanced over my shoulder and saw Sawyer already staring in that direction. "What is that?"

"You heard it too?"

"Yes, like someone standing on dry leaves."

"Your hearing has improved."

I grinned. "I think it's all the strains of lycanthropy I have."

We saw a coat float over dry hedges and stood at the same time.

"What is it?" Sebastian asked behind me.

I leaned my head against his chest. "Someone's out there."

"Vampires," he said and kissed the top of my head and held me in the circle of his arms.

I tensed.

Sebastian rubbed my arms as he moved us toward the sounds. He pulled me around his body so I was walking behind him—protecting me.

A gust of wind blew in from the far left-hand side of the field, and, for a second, the light near the feasting werewolves darkened, as if a shadow flew underneath it, blocking the light.

I touched Sebastian's back. "What's happening?"

He offered me his hand, and I took it. The three of us edged closer to the forest. Dark shadows played along the trees, the swaying branches casting spine-chilling silhouettes against the other. The wind dissipated, and the chirps of stridulating crickets filled the silence.

Four shots rang out. Multiple cries sounded behind us. We turned together as four bodies fell to the ground. We ran toward them. Sebastian led the way as he parted the crowd for us with Sawyer closely behind me. Rory came from the other side, eyes wide and mouth parted. He panned from the injured bodies to the fence, but no one was there.

"Shouldn't we go after who did this? They were right here a second ago!"

"No, Blaire. They've already flown away. It was vampires. I could smell them when they were here, but they were quick and are long gone," Sebastian said.

I only saw blood and Corey's half-eaten corpse. I realized what had happened when everybody stood back to clear the area, and I saw the other bodies now—another female and three males. The female and one male were were-leopards, while two males were werewolves. Their fur flowed back, and their faces changed to reveal their human face. All four lay naked and unmoving with a dart protruding somewhere from their bodies.

"Don't touch them!" I yelled as I approached the bodies.

"Blaire, what are you doing?" Sebastian asked, trying to pull me away from the first body.

"It's the same thing that happened to the others, except

this time they did it in front of us, and the darts are still in them. We need to retrieve them for Mel, so we know exactly what this stuff is that's killing the were-animals."

I used the tissue I found in the jacket pocket to pull the first dart out the female's back. I was careful not to touch the sharp end of the dart as I wrapped it in the tissue. Once I had removed the dart, the woman's skin shrank. The soft tissue of her cheeks caved in, and she was instantly gaunt. Her muscles and fat dissolved, leaving behind wrinkled and leathery skin. A husk of a human.

Shit.

"She looks like a mummy," someone said from the side.

"Mel is running tests on the other victim's tissue. We need to give her all these darts." I rose and held the dart carefully in my hand. Some of the liquid was still inside the glass casing; it was a yellow-brown-green sludge.

Shawn approached me, his massive black form towering over me.

I touched the butt of my gun, just in case.

"I won't hurt you, Blaire," Shawn said through his large muzzle. "It's the same thing that killed one of our wolves." His blue eyes held a yellow hue while in his wolf form. His fur disappeared, like the wind had blown it off him, leaving him in his human form. The shape of his human face pushed through his wolf's as his sharp teeth and muzzle inverted inside him. Shawn's shift was silent and calm.

"How can you shift so easily?"

"Some can do it." He shrugged. "If you're strong and powerful enough, it doesn't hurt as much." He smirked.

"You aren't tired?"

"A little, but it passes quickly."

I stared at his naked body and felt heat creep up my neck. He was shorter than Sebastian but more defined and toned. His short black hair was ruffled from the change, and his crystal blue eyes hinted at mischief. One side of his lips curled upward.

"Let me get you something to put the darts in." Shawn summoned one of his wolves, who handed him a large plastic bag, then asked him to retrieve the other three darts and put them all in the bag.

"Is Mel still at the hospital?" Sebastian asked.

"I hope so. Let's get these to her." I turned to Shawn. "We need to find out if this was random or if the victims knew each other or knew the attacker."

"I'm not sure. The wolves had been in the pack for some time and were low in the ranks."

Sebastian added, "The leopards were also low in rank."

"The were-lion who was shot earlier had joined the pride about six months ago. The were-lion who was there had said he smelled the dead or a zombie, and it was a sour smell."

Shawn considered this. "It could have been either, not sure, but what I can guarantee you is that I smelled a vampire earlier." He glanced at Sebastian. "Will you find out from your brother whether there are any rogue vampires or any new ones in town?"

"He's already inquiring. He doesn't like this more than anyone else. If vampires are doing this to were-animals, they need to be managed now. Plus, Shannon is in the run for governor. If the humans hear about this, they could put a stop to him running."

"We should ask Shannon if he knows of a vampire with a grudge against him. Maybe this was all a ploy to get revenge for something," Shawn said.

It hit me—my trip to Chicago. "This was similar to what Lance went through, only it happened at a much slower rate. But I could heal him. What happened to these were-animals was quick. They were dead within minutes. Lance said that when he was injected, it stopped him from shifting into his were-rat form, and it stopped him from healing. This seems to work in either form, whether it was animal or human, but it still kills them instantly."

"Isn't this what Melinda was working on?" Sebastian asked.

"She wanted to get rid of her animal, to stop her animal from emerging. But she and Marcus had been locked up all this time. She could never have done this. Unless ..."

I pulled my cell from my pocket and dialed Troy's number. When I reached him, I gave him a short version of what had transpired and what we think may be happening.

He said he would call me back when he had Melinda's and Marcus's location, now that they each had a tracker.

Chapter Fourteen

We phoned Mel ahead of time, and, as I drove in the ambulance lane, she was waiting for us at the casualty entrance of the hospital. I held the bag with the darts to her through the window.

"I can't believe there have been more deaths," she said, placing the darts into a plastic medical bag and sealing it. "I've already started to analyze that other dart along with the tissue samples and will compare those to this. Once all that is complete, I'll compare it to Lance's results to see whether we are working with the same monster or if we have two devils running around."

"Thanks, Mel. Let us know the moment you have anything."

"Yeah, sure," she said, staring at the darts. Her eyes narrowed at the liquid left inside it.

"Do you recognize it or know of anyone who was developing something that could do that much damage in such a short amount of time?"

"Uh, no, but it is curious. I mean, were-animals that mummify shortly after death …"

My cellphone vibrated in my pocket. I pulled it out and saw a message from Troy. To Mel I said. "We have to go. We found Melinda."

"Melinda? Why do you need to—" She stared at me with wide-eyes. "Oh, no! Do you think it's her?"

"Don't know. That's why we need to speak with her."

We arrived at Marcus' house, and I walked ahead with Sawyer and Rory while Ralph, Devan, and Sebastian followed.

Marcus opened the door without us having to knock. "What the fuck, Blaire?"

"Is Melinda here?"

"What do you want with her?"

"We just want to talk to her."

"With so much backup?" He eyed each of the men behind me.

"After you left the lion pride, people have been murdered. I just need to chat to Melinda to find out whether she knows anything."

"Fine, but not all of you. Pick two others and follow me." He narrowed his eyes at me.

I turned to look at the man at my back. Without saying anything, Sebastian pushed to the front. "Ralph, you can come with us."

Marcus closed the door behind us, leaving the others outside.

Melinda entered the living room, tightening her robe around her body. "What do you want now?"

"Only to ask you a question, then we'll leave," I said, raising my hands in surrender. She'd almost killed me when she was in her lion form; there was no way I would poke a stick at the angry animal unless it was urgent.

Melinda glanced at Marcus behind me. I moved to the side, so I could see them both.

"Do you want to sit?"

"No thanks. We won't stay long," I said to Marcus then glanced at Melinda. "That cure you were busy working on, how far are you in your progress, and where is it now?"

She stiffened at the question and tugged on the cord of her gown. "I threw it away."

I leered at her. "You're lying." I needed to change tactic. She seemed like the type of person to close up when pushed. "Please, Melinda. Six were-animals are already dead, and I need to see if there's a connection with what you were working on and how they were killed."

"How did they die?"

I gave her the short version of what had happened and the speed with which the victims died.

Melinda sat down, biting nervously on her thumbnail. She glanced at Marcus. "I have to tell her."

Marcus nodded. "Do what's right, Melinda." He sat beside her and pulled her into an embrace.

Melinda sucked in a deep breath and shook her head. "Those scars you saw are from when I was attacked. I almost died. Unfortunately I didn't heal as well as I should've. Then, when I first turned into a were-lion, I was distraught, as you can imagine. I was left for dead, had just lost my job and was told I could never work in a lab again. I thought my life was over. A friend recommended I see this witch. She was old, and everything about her made my skin crawl. But I saw her, and she gave me something that would remove my animal. It would basically allow my lion to lie dormant. But being the skeptical scientist I was, I was curious with the ingredients, so I tested the stuff she gave me. What I found is it would've killed me and not make my animal sleep forever. So, I tweaked it, adding other ingredients I thought would work better, and then I met Marcus. That's when I almost killed him. I refined it some more, but, before I could use it on myself, you had us locked up." The stare she gave me was full of rage and hate. I wouldn't want to be left alone in a room with her again, not after having to dig her claws out my back once already.

"Did anyone come to you and ask you for it?"

She was quiet, her gaze jumped to Marcus.

Marcus raised his eyebrows. "Tell her."

"Someone did come. A vampire, one I'd never seen before. Somehow, he had heard of my work and wanted access to it. When I thought I was going to die, I didn't want my work to die with me. I'd hoped someone would use it for good, but not to do this." She choked on her last words. "I didn't think they'd use it on innocent people."

"Thanks for telling the truth, Melinda. I don't suppose this vampire gave you his name?"

"Jones. He said his name was Jones."

I turned to Sebastian. "Do you know him?"

He shook his head. "No. I have a stronger connection to the were-leopards than to the vampires. We can ask Léon if he knows a vampire by that name."

"Thanks," I said, heading for the front door.

"They had to have someone helping them, Blaire. My serum wouldn't have killed anyone. Perhaps they had another scientist or someone who at least knows a little bit about chemistry. To kill someone within minutes, they had to have added something incredibly potent. If not a chemist, perhaps a witch helped them?"

"Do you remember the witch's name who gave you the original serum?"

She bit her other thumbnail and blood dripped down the side of her hand. "I can't remember. It started with an S or something. Sorry, I can't think now. Marcus will call you if I remember anything more."

"Thanks, Melinda."

We left Marcus and Melinda on the couch as she started biting on her index finger. I'd only seen Melinda a few times, and this was the first time she looked genuinely worried. I guess guilt would do that to anyone, especially when it was possibly your fault for releasing a potential killer into the open and that killer was targeting were-animals.

"It's already evening, so Léon is awake," Sebastian said, turning to me. "But first we should go by your house and drop off your car. It's on our way to the Labyrinth. Then you can drive with me."

"It's fine, thanks. I can follow you," I said when we reached my car.

"Guys, give Blaire and me a second."

Sawyer and Rory went and stood near Ralph and Devan at Ralph's car.

"What's wrong now?" He cocked his head to one side, his expression deadpan.

"Nothing's wrong, Sebastian. It'd just be easier if I was in my own car. If something urgent arises, I can leave if I need to."

"I don't mind taking you home, Blaire. I don't mind looking after you." He crossed his arms. "Besides, it's safer if I took you home."

I touched his forearm. "I know."

"You aren't going to drop off your car?"

"No." I rocked onto my tiptoes and kissed him. His full lips felt cool and unwelcoming. I pulled his arms open, so the line of my body touched as much of his. I cupped his face with my hands and kissed him again. His lips were warm, soft, and intense. "I know you care for me, Sebastian. We've even said we loved each other. But please don't smother me."

He tensed in my arms. "Do you feel like I'm smothering you?"

"Not all the time, only some of the time, like now."

"Fine," he said, sounding hurt.

"Don't say it like that. If I want to drive myself, let me. That's all I'm asking." I pressed my chin against his chest and stared up at him.

"Then either I or one of them will stay over," he said and leaned in for a chaste kiss.

"Fine. We'll compromise," I said with a smile.

"And you should leave more clothing at the Labyrinth."

"Next time, but right now we need to see if Léon knows a vampire named Jones."

Chapter Fifteen

We parted ways with Ralph and Devan while we were still at Marcus' house. They had Ulysses work they needed to do at a cemetery. Apparently, ghouls were eating the recently buried, and they needed to get rid of them.

The four of us headed to the Labyrinth to speak with Léon about a vampire named Jones. Sebastian and I walked the maze of the Labyrinth with Sawyer and Rory close behind us.

When we entered the office, Léon and Salvador were whispering in what sounded like French, busy leafing through aged documents. Both vampires looked up at us at the same time. Léon's startlingly vivid ocean-blue eyes followed me as I sat on a sofa, Sebastian sitting beside me.

"What brings you here, Sebastian?" Léon asked as he moved to sit across from us.

Salvador sat on Léon's chair behind the large wrought iron desk with a knowing look in his eye I couldn't place, like he wanted to say something to me but couldn't. I found it unnerving, but I ignored it as best I could.

Sebastian explained to Léon what had happened with the were-lions and werewolves and our conversation with Melinda. While Sebastian was speaking, movement caught my eye. Salvador's demeanor changed, and what looked like fury flickered in his wild eyes.

Salvador shifted in the chair, interrupting Sebastian. "I know who you seek. He's a madman. We should have killed him when we had the chance."

"Yes, we should have." Léon's eyes glowed a shade darker.

"Who is he, and why didn't you kill him?" I asked.

"With a witch's help, we had him banished to the mountains a very, very long time ago. The spell was supposed to keep him there. He should be killed for having the spell broken and coming into town." Salvador rose to stand closer. "I know where he sleeps. I can take you there. You get the information you need, then we must kill him." He placed his hand on Léon's shoulder. "The council need not know about this. And you two must not utter what I am about to do. Understood?"

"Are you sure you should be going, Father?" Léon asked. "I can handle this on your behalf."

"I'll be all right, my son. This is my doing, I will correct it."

"Why don't you want Salvador to go with?" I asked, panning from a set of dark blues eyes to Salvador's lighter shade.

Sebastian squeezed my hand. "Father had a habit of doing things the council never approved of and has been warned not to do anything similar again. If they found out, well, let's just say they would all fight him to the death."

"Oh," I said with wide eyes.

"What did Jones do that you had to banish him with a spell?" Sebastian asked.

"He had a nasty habit, son." Salvador cleared his throat. He pulled a chair closer, that was usually reserved for Léon's guests, and sat. "He enjoys turning little boys and girls into little vampires for his personal enjoyment. Before Alex was on the Vampire Council, he, Léon, and I discovered Jones's playroom. It was disgusting. Use your imagination. It's not something I wish to revisit visually. But we should have just killed him then and there. We destroyed his little toys, as they had already started going mad. They were so young and bloodthirsty. They were badly used, and it wouldn't have worked in their favor to remain alive. After we cleaned up his mess, a powerful witch placed a spell and banished him to the mountains with warning. If he somehow managed to break the spell and entered any town at any time, we would destroy him."

I felt the blood drain from my face. My nails dug into my arms until crescent shapes formed into my skin.

"We need to tell Alex, Father. He can help," Léon said.

"No!" Salvador abruptly said, standing by the door with one hand on the handle; it was such a quick and limber movement. "He's on the council now. We need to do this on our own. It is better that he does not know. Come. I want to do this tonight."

Sebastian told Sawyer and Rory to drive behind us in his car. Léon, Salvador, and Sebastian drove with me. When Salvador first mentioned mountains, I imagined the one near town, near the leap. We drove for two hours on roads I didn't know Sterling Meadow even had. Eventually, we reached a mountain cast in shadows that sent shivers down my spine. One side of the mountain was a high cliff, while the rest had the usual terrain from what I could tell. It was dark with only half a moon to light our way.

When the road forked, I stopped the car and glanced in the rearview mirror. "Which way, Salvador?"

"Left ..." He paused as if wanting to say something else but thought against it.

When I pulled away and went left, I could feel his stare. I glanced at him in the mirror again, but he wasn't looking at me.

"What did you ever do with those jewels, Blaire?" Salvador eventually asked, but something told me that wasn't what he really wanted to say.

"They're in a safe place."

"Just don't think it, or Léon will hear your thoughts and know where you have hidden them."

I glanced in the mirror again, this time at Léon, but his face was hidden in shadows. I caught a glimpse of his eyes though; for a split second they glowed a soft blue.

"Stop!" Sebastian yelled, grabbing my arm.

I refocused my attention onto the road, and both of my feet flattened the brake pedal. My car skidded to the side and collided with a tree. My head hit the window from the impact, cracking the glass.

"Are you okay?" Sebastian asked when the vehicle stopped. He unbuckled his safety belt as well as mine and touched the side of my head that had hit the window. His hand came back dripping with my blood. "You're bleeding," he said hungrily.

"Grab the first-aid kit in the glove compartment," I said quickly.

"Aah!" Salvador hissed, swore under his breath in French and pulled on my seat. "Your blood smells delicious, Blaire."

"No, Father!" Sebastian pushed Salvador back with one hand.

"Please tell me you've tasted that sweet-smelling ichor, Sebastian," Salvador purred behind my seat.

Sebastian scowled. "Don't go there, Father."

"I don't know how you could not, son. Surely you can smell that honey essence. The gods have blessed her in more ways than one. Aah, I need to get out of here before I devour her." Salvador hit the door so hard it flew off the car and landed somewhere far. I couldn't even hear it land. And then Salvador was a dark blur, disappearing into the trees.

"Now that her blood isn't cursed with that black poison, she smells different from that first night, Sebastian. Oh my god, it's too tempting," Léon uttered through clenched teeth. "When she has cleaned up, meet us at the mouth of the mountain up ahead." Léon flew out his open window.

My eyes widened; I hadn't known my blood could make vampires react like *that*.

"What about you, Sebastian? Is my blood that tempting?" I asked with a quiver in my voice.

I heard Sebastian swallow, and it sounded like it hurt.

"Sebastian?" I whispered, switching on the car's interior light. One half of Sebastian's face was hidden in shadows while the other illuminated. Hair rose on my neck, and, for the first time since I'd known him, I trembled. "Sebastian? Can you hear me?"

Sebastian stared at his hand still covered in my blood. He raised his hand to his mouth and licked his blood-soaked palm. He sucked on his fingers until nothing remained. His eyes rolled back into his head, and he made a low guttural sound that vibrated in my bones. A moment passed where I thought everything would be okay. Sebastian's eyes were still closed, and he seemed calm. I told myself it had just been a weak moment when Sebastian forgot I was his girlfriend and he had never really *tasted* me before, that he wouldn't *hurt* me.

Then he opened his eyes; they both glowed yellow, and his mouth parted, revealing fangs. He stared at me, but it didn't look like he was really *seeing* me. He hissed and edged on closer. One of his hands was on the dashboard while the other on my seat, and his body hovered above mine. His face was close to me, then he sniffed the air. Closing his eyes, he savored whatever he was smelling as if it was the best thing ever. A purr escaped his lips, and I felt it in my bones.

The thick liquid dripped down the side of my head, through my hair and along my neck. I wanted to look where it was dripping or wipe it away, but I didn't want to break eye contact with Sebastian.

His pupils dilated. He knew. He could smell it or hear my blood running down my neck. The blood trickled over my collar bone, and I wanted to zipper my jacket to hide it, but I wasn't sure if Sebastian would do something if I moved suddenly.

Sebastian's stare was filled with an intensity I had never seen before—*hunger, lust*. He was both a were-leopard *and* a vampire. He was a hybrid. He had the best of both worlds. He was hungry for flesh *and* blood. And I was food.

He broke eye contact first, staring lower on my chest, and I knew he was eyeing the blood soaking my collar bone. I still felt blood dripping down my neck. He hovered so close to me that I could feel heat radiate off him.

"Sebastian?" I whimpered. "Please talk to me. You're scaring me." I raised my hand to touch his face, and he snarled, growling at my hand. I froze without having touched him.

He moved closer, nuzzling my neck with his nose, and then he licked my collarbone and up my neck. He moaned in pleasure against my skin. Then something sharp trailed my neck. With one of his hands, he pushed my head to the side, so he had a better angle of my neck.

"No, Sebastian. *No!*" I pushed against him.

He was much stronger than me, and, even though I was pushing against him, he still managed to sink his fangs into my neck. He gripped my head with one hand and held me in place with the other. And he drank from me. I froze. My pulse thundered in my ears as I squeezed my eyes shut. Heat coursed through my veins. I heard and felt my heartbeat, and there was another—Sebastian's. Our beating hearts were in sync. My breathing steadied and complimented his. Opening my eyes, I saw a butterfly inside the car. It slowly flapped its wings, and the wind beat off it against my face.

The movement was slow. I was slow. The wind from its wings was hot and heavy. The sucking on my neck was slow. The blood leaving my body was slow *and* sensual. It all happened at a deliberate and steady pace, as if time had stood still for us.

The heat radiating from Sebastian was intense, scorching, yet comforting against my neck. I had felt other vampire's bites, but nothing quite like *this*. Sebastian's bite was meticulous, precise, and I felt every sense of mine tingle in that nanosecond when time stood still. I wished we were at my house naked and doing this; I was sure the experience would've been different. But not now, now I only felt pain and terror. I'd seen other women blush when asked about Sebastian's bite. The way he was biting me wasn't arousing in the least, almost as if it wasn't really Sebastian doing this at all.

The butterfly continued flapping its wings at a slow leisurely pace; the wind casting off its wings had hit me, as if waking me from a slumber. I blinked again and felt more pain.

"Get off me, Sebastian," I managed to say through clenched teeth. My hands still pushed against his chest.

He bit harder. His hand on my neck squeezed, and I feared he would snap my neck. He wasn't hearing me or *couldn't* hear me.

All I knew was I had to stop him, and, if he wasn't responding verbally, I had to try reach him metaphysically. I spoke to him through our connection, through the mark he made on me. I thought my fear would help him understand what he was doing to me.

"Sebastian, please stop. You're hurting me."

Time moved a little quicker. The butterfly was out the window and gone. My heartbeat was no longer in sync with Sebastian's, and the heat from his mouth was replaced by a chill that swept through my body. Slowly, he stopped sucking and unlatched his jaw from my neck, and I felt his fangs hook on my skin as he pulled them out of me. Pain teared through my flesh and into my chest and ribs.

Our eyes met with what looked like sorrow in his grass-green eyes. "Oh god, Blaire. I'm so sorry. What have I done?" He kissed me, and I tasted my own blood on his lips. He cupped my face between his hands. "Are you all right?" he asked between kisses. "God! I don't know what came over me." He released my face and sat back in his seat. He was quiet for a moment, staring at me wide eyed. After a few unpleasant seconds of us staring at each other—both unsure of what exactly just happened, he eventually said, "The smell of your blood is intoxicating. I couldn't stop myself. I should've left when Salvador did." He grabbed my hand for comfort, but I flinched. He didn't let go. "Please forgive me."

I didn't trust my voice. There were things I thought to say, and none of them would've been pleasant. Instead, I opted to say, "Don't touch me, Sebastian."

He let go of me as if I had burned him. He was in shock. I was in shock. I needed fresh air. I needed space. I needed to get away from him.

I opened my broken window as far down as it could go, and the breeze was cool against my skin. I then opened the glove compartment and removed the first-aid kit, grabbed some gauze and started cleaning the wound on the side of my head as well as I could, but my hair had already dried in clumps. Blood still dripped from the two bite mark wounds on my neck where Sebastian had ripped his fangs out of me.

I turned to Sebastian, and he was staring at me, waiting for the bomb to drop. "Get out of the car." My side of the car was against the tree we had hit, so I climbed out his side.

"Please talk to me, Blaire," he said once we were out and walked close behind me.

A rock had been in the road, and we had almost crashed into it. If Sebastian hadn't yelled at me when he did, we would've driven into it. That impact could have been much worse than the cut on the side of my head. In that scenario, my airbag could have deployed, and I might have been unconscious. Or worse. I shuddered; I didn't want to know what that would've looked like.

I raised my arm to stop him. "Don't come near me. I just need to be left alone for a bit, okay? You think you could do that for me?" I tried not to sound as angry as I felt, but I knew my anger came through in the way I said the words.

He nodded but watched me carefully, still waiting for some kind of explosion, like I would rip off his face or dig my fingernails into his chest and tear out his beating heart. I wanted to do that; I wanted to hurt him as much as he had hurt me. I wanted him to bleed and to be afraid of me, the person he was supposed to *love*.

I exhaled a shaky breath and shook away the feeling. I just needed some space. I felt violated and hurt. He had attacked me, had done something I thought was intimate, that I wanted to share with him in the privacy of our bedrooms. It was something I was considering, to be in his arms, our naked bodies pressed together. I wanted to feel his bite as it was meant to be—alluring, seductive, and desirable. Not what had just happened.

But what made it worse was he couldn't hear me. He wasn't all *there*. I loved him, but I hated him at the same time.

"Walk in front of me," I barked.

Sebastian did as I asked and walked ahead.

For the first time since I'd known Sebastian, I was afraid of him. It reminded me of when we had been in the shower a couple of days ago, when he hadn't heard me then either.

Flashes of the predatory gleam in his eyes when he saw the blood on my neck was imprinted in my vision. And then his reaction, and that he didn't hear me—or was it that he didn't want to? He didn't back away when I asked him to stop. He didn't stop on his own. I had to reach him metaphysically to stop him from draining me.

In the last three days, I had gone from saying *I love you* to being frightened. I was afraid we were losing one another, that I was losing *him*. We had just found one another.

This. Can't. Be. It.

Something sharp tugged on my heart, and it felt like it

was crushing my chest. My breath caught, and I blinked back tears. I would wait until I was home alone before I allowed my emotions to crash over me.

I stopped when Sebastian did.

Something moved to our left. I went for my gun and pointed it in the direction of the noise.

Sawyer and Rory walked out into the clear, thick in conversation and oblivious to what had happened earlier. They halted when they saw us. "Everything okay?" Sawyer asked, his brows furrowed as he panned from Sebastian to me. Then he noticed my neck. "What happened to you?"

"A misunderstanding," I said and started walking. Perhaps if I carried on as if nothing had happened, maybe we could go back to how we were before. "We need to meet Salvador and Léon at the mouth of the mountain. I think this path will lead us there."

Sebastian walked ahead of me while Sawyer and Rory trailed behind.

I heard one of them jog toward me and grab my elbow. Rory asked near my ear, "Did he do this?" He lifted his chin in Sebastian's direction.

"I hit my head when I had to brake, and the car smashed into a tree. There was blood and ... they couldn't handle it."

He sniffed the air around me. "One of us must always stay with you, all right? It's enticing, but we aren't as tempted by your blood as they are."

I nodded. "Thanks, Rory."

Chapter Sixteen

We followed the winding path through the trees until we reached large rocks that sat at the foot of the mountain. The walk up was therapeutic, and the rage I had felt minutes ago had somehow seeped out my pores. Or I was just too exhausted; either way, I was glad for it. That meant I wouldn't shoot Sebastian in the back.

Salvador and Léon were already there, sitting at the top of one of the rocks and looking down on us. As we arrived, Salvador and Léon flew off the rock to join us on the ground. Salvador grabbed Sebastian's neck and whispered for his ears only. Sebastian struggled in Salvador's grip, but the older vampire was stronger.

When Salvador was done whispering, he glanced at me and said, "Jones is here and knows we seek him." Then he turned to Sawyer and Rory. "Keep her between the two of you. Always. The smell of her blood is still fresh in the air, and Jones will want her. Do you understand? Either she stays here, or you guard her with your lives."

"Oh, I'm coming with, all right," I said, squeezing my

gun in my hand. My anger was back, and I relished in it as a surge of energy flooded my veins; the excitement of killing a monster overrode the memory of Sebastian's bite. Pulling a blade from my wrist sheath and holding it in my left hand, I was ready to go hunting.

Rory and Sawyer stood closer to me but back enough not to get in my way. "Thanks guys," I said, approaching Sebastian and Salvador.

"Maybe you shouldn't come, Blaire," Sebastian said with pain etched on his face. He tried to hide his fangs, but they were still out, with hunger in his eyes.

"Don't tell me what I can and can't do, Sebastian. You've never done that before. Don't start now."

"Leave her be, Sebastian. I'll walk with her if she's too tempting for you." Léon said, maneuvering around Sebastian and Salvador to stand near me.

"Always the opportunist, aren't you, brother?" Sebastian pointed a finger at Léon.

"I'll be the first to admit that the smell of her blood drove me crazy, the temptation to sink my teeth into her soft, delicate skin ..." The tips of Léon's fangs peaked out. "But I have it under control now. And so should you, if you're to continue seeing her, *brother*."

The muscles in Sebastian's jaw flexed, and he bunched his hands into tight fists until his knuckles whitened.

"That's enough! You two are acting like children," Salvador said, walking farther up the path and deeper into the mountain. "We have much ground to cover still. Come."

Sebastian growled then realized his outburst was childish and stopped, turning to follow Salvador.

Léon was between Sebastian and me. Sawyer walked beside me while Rory brought up the rear. It was silly to have so many men protect me, but Salvador knew what kind of vampire Jones was. And I suspected it could get ugly once Jones got a whiff of my blood. I touched the bite marks on my neck, flinching at the pain, and then my fingers came back with blood on them. It was still bleeding. I was about to wipe my fingers on my jeans when a white handkerchief came into view.

Léon offered the soft fabric adorned with beautifully embroidered patters. "Don't make it worse by wiping your blood on your clothing, my darling. It'll only drive a vampire mad. Rather, use this."

I took it from his hands and wiped my fingers then pressed it against the wound in my neck and on the side of my head. I touched the head wound; luckily, it had stopped bleeding, but the bite hadn't.

"It doesn't want to stop bleeding," I said with a tinge of panic.

"In Sebastian's rush, he didn't apply enough pressure or saliva onto the wound. Can I help?"

I narrowed my eyes at him. "What does that mean?"

"Vampire's saliva can stop the bleeding, but, if they don't apply the pressure after the bite, it may continue bleeding. I think he panicked and didn't do it. He probably hurt you when he pulled out his fangs."

I nodded.

"I promise not to do anything else. I only want to stop the bleeding."

"How will you do that?"

He grinned. "With a kiss, of course." I knew Léon's touch alone could send pleasure throughout my body, so for him to offer a kiss, made me wonder what that would do to me. But I didn't want to know, and the shock on my face must have revealed enough, because Léon added, "I promise not to do anything else. I swear. You can trust me."

"Fine." I stopped walking, and Léon closed the gap.

My heart rate ticked up a few beats, and I knew he could hear it. He cupped my face in his warm hands and gently moved my face to one side, so he had access to the bite wound. His touch was soft, delicate. His breath was hot against my neck, and his lips were warm. The kiss was wet, but he didn't linger. He did what he had promised and only kissed the wound with his lips full of his saliva and applied the smallest amount of pressure.

A slight moan came from my throat, and even I was surprised.

"There, I'm all done. And it's stopped bleeding." Léon chuckled, licking blood from his lips, savoring it in his mouth. His hands still cupped me, and I felt comfort when I leaned into one of them. He stared at me with eyes I could drown in. They hinted at a seduction I could not indulge in, no matter how tempting. He lingered for a heartbeat then slowly let go of my face.

My cheeks flushed when he smiled and winked darkly. Then I knew he had heard my thoughts about the possibilities of him. Quickly, I dabbed his handkerchief on the bite, and it came back clean. "Thank you." That small gesture of helping me and not doing anything else showed a different side to him—a gentler, tender side of him, instead of the flirt, the joker, or the tease.

"My pleasure, Blaire. Come, let's catch up."

We walked for what felt like hours, but it was only one. I'm sure they would've gotten there quicker by flying, but I was with, so everyone had to walk. We finally reached the mouth of the cave, and it was darker than the rest of the mountain. The only sound I heard was from an owl a few trees back. I squeezed the handle of my gun until pain shot up my forearm. Sawyer gave me a flashlight which I turned on and could illuminate a few steps in front of me.

We entered the cave, and the inside was filled with thick blackness; it enveloped us and was so dense I could only see a step ahead. I pointed the flashlight beam up, but the only thing visible was fog and more darkness. I pointed the flashlight down, casting the beam on the ground; at least I'd be able to see if anything was directly in front of me. I had lost the others. I couldn't see them, nor could I hear them. There was nothing.

The air moved around me, but I couldn't see anything. Lifting my flashlight and gun, I turned around, but all I saw was the thick dark fog. Air lifted my hair then caressed my neck as heat neared the wound on my head and bite mark on my neck.

"Sawyer? Rory?" I whispered.

The silence was so thick I could cut through it with a blade. The hairs on my body stood on end. The black fog swirled around me, wrapping itself around my legs, then it climbed around my hips and chest and lifted me. Glancing down, I was levitating about a foot above the ground.

"Okay, someone help me down," I cried out, trying to keep the panic at bay.

Ominous laughter echoed around me, and I dropped, crashing to the ground feet first. The air was quick, and whatever was out there pushed passed me. It was too late to turn around and go home. Jones already knew we were here and was fucking with us.

"Guys!" I yelled.

"Right here, Blaire." Sawyer touched my shoulder. "Just need to swap hands so I can hold my gun." His hand moved away then returned to my shoulder.

"This is me," Rory said, touching my other shoulder.

I slowed so I could feel them on either side of me; the heat they emitted was comforting. I could see the faint light from their flashlights as we walked deeper inside the vampire's cave.

"Léon? Sebastian? Salvador?" I asked under my breath. The cave ricocheted my voice in a sinister tone. An ear-piercing scream echoed deep within the cave. My pulse thumped in my ears after that.

Something whooshed passed us, the air in front moving in circles with it, then I heard a body fall with a painful grunt. It sounded like Sebastian.

I shone the flashlight beam on the ground. "Sebastian! Where are you?"

"I'm here," he croaked nearby, like it hurt for him to talk.

"Call out again, so we can come to you."

He did, and we followed his voice until the small beam of light caught the yellow tint of his blond hair. I kneeled near him, the beam of light illuminating the deep marks across his chest.

"Did Jones do this?" I asked, caressing his wounds.

"Yes, and he barely touched me."

"Shit. Can you heal?" As I said it, I watched in awe as his skin knitted together.

"Don't go farther inside, Blaire. Please. Jones will hurt you."

"Okay, fine. We'll stay here with you."

We heard shouting up ahead, followed by scuffling then a single clap so loud and powerful I felt it in my entire body. Goosebumps covered my body, and shivers shot up my spine. The prickling sensation ran up my neck and head and then down my spine again. The fog receded into the dark cave until it was gone, and the air became thin and breathable. The torches on the sides of the cave flared to life with its heat and brightness, and we could see the inside of the cave.

The other men were deeper inside the cave. The part we were in seemed to be Jones's bedroom; a coffin sat to one side, with a table and chair. I would've said it was only a room, but the items displayed on the table and on the wall near his coffin suggested nefarious deeds. Little carved bones were bound by some type of rope into items that resembled little boys and girls the size of my hand. I shuddered when I caught sight of a ribcage in the far corner with something dry and brown suspended from the top rib on the left-hand side. I suspected it to be a heart—possibly that of a child's.

Sebastian stayed on the ground and was almost healed. His skin knotted together until only a thin raised scar remained, and then it was smooth again, like nothing had happened. Sebastian sat upright, ran his fingers through his hair and stood. His eyes bled to seaweed green and glowed. He started running, and I followed with my two guards trailing behind me.

Sebastian yelled, "Stay there, Blaire! Don't come in with me!"

"Stop telling me what to do, Sebastian."

"Stubborn woman!"

Yes, I was stubborn as hell, but I had to see what was happening, and, besides, I needed to ask Jones questions. We ran deeper into the bowels of the cave until we reached Salvador and Léon. The two men were hunched over a figure on the ground. We stopped near them.

"So this is Jones." I said, moving around them to stand near his head. His auburn hair was stained black from the blood pouring out the cut across his head. He was tall and lean, his features chiseled. But it was the yellow glow of his eyes that caught my attention for a moment, and then I stared at his forehead. I didn't know what his powers were and wasn't sure what he would make me do with his vampiric wiles if I stared into his eyes for too long.

"This is him," Salvador said through gritted teeth. "Ask him your questions now, Blaire. He doesn't have long to live."

Salvador's right knee leaned onto Jones's chest; it seemed that action alone was keeping Jones bound and on the stone floor.

"You can't kill me, Salvador. Or it'll finally be a good enough excuse for the council to have your head."

Salvador ignored his comment and tapped Jones's head. "Ask quickly, Blaire. I can't keep him like this for long."

I hesitantly moved closer. Jones couldn't move at all with Salvador's knee on him. When I was positive no harm would come to me, I crouched beside him. "Why did you ask Melinda for her research on the serum she was working on?"

"That's not the right question, little one," Jones hissed, turning that villainous glare to me with a vile smirk.

I had been around enough vampires to understand what they were like, but none were quite like *him*. Evil surrounded his very core. His essence was a tapestry of dark and loathsome things.

"Who asked you to get it?"

"Ah, this one is bright, Salvador. Is she your little slave or one of your son's?"

Salvador didn't answer; instead, he applied pressure onto Jones's chest until the vampire cried out, answering my question. "I don't know his name, but I know he was a were-rat." Jones brought his hands under Salvador's knee, as if wanting to keep him from crushing his chest. A letter 'V' was engraved on the top of his hand.

"Why would you even help a were-rat?" I asked.

"Because he offered me something I simply couldn't refuse." He spied something behind me. I turned to see what it was and gagged. In the dark corner, I could decipher the outline of a child—a boy—bound and in a sleeping position, but he was not asleep. His skin reminded me of dark brown leather, his life essence sucked right out of him.

As upsetting as that was, I needed more answers from Jones before Salvador took his life, like Jones had that boy's. "Why did the were-rat want the serum?"

A rumble shook beneath our feet, and rocks fell from the cave's high ceiling. A strong wind blew in from the outside, and something that sounded like wings flapped inside the cave, edging closer to us.

"I'm here!" Jones called out to whatever creature was flying inside the cave.

"You aren't going anywhere," Salvador said, closing his eyes. He opened his arms, as if to hug the air, then screaming pierced the air. The shrill cries neared until a black figure flew in with its outspread wings.

"Master, I am here to serve you," the dark figure said, its large black wings flapping. The daemon's body was dark like charcoal and cracked like lava that had cooled over many years. As it hovered in the air, ash fell from his chapped body.

Salvador opened his eyes, and they burned bright blue, and he clapped. Again, it was just that one clap. The daemon flew against the side of the cave, hitting the stone with a loud crunch. The daemon ended up lying in a heap of broken wings.

At my feet, a dark murky liquid spilled from Jones's

mouth, ears, nose, and eyes. His eyes bugged then rolled into his head.

"No!" I screamed.

"Stand back, Blaire and everyone else. This will get messy." Salvador rose to his feet.

"Wait, Salvador! He didn't answer me."

"His daemon will know, Blaire. I need to do this now before he regains his strength."

"I hope you're right," I said angrily, backing up until I stood behind the curve of a large rock.

Salvador raised his hands, and Jones levitated. Sebastian, Léon, Sawyer, and Rory all took cover behind or under something. Salvador clapped again, and blood splattered everywhere. Jones was liquidized in that one clap. I did one of those slow blinks—my mind's way of processing all this information. It all happened so suddenly I was still trying to comprehend what had just happened. It was all very similar to what Alex had done to Roland. Alex, who was on the Vampire Council, had visited to sentence Roland. He had levitated Roland's body, had pulled his limbs from his body and had pulverize what was left until his blood rained on us. That was about all I could handle and had ran for an exit, but I had slipped in Roland's blood; it was awful how sticky and thick his blood had felt as it dripped down my body, and my clothing had clung to me. Shuddering, I pushed the memory aside. I didn't want to relive the feeling of his warm blood over me. And now I understood how powerful Salvador was too. That could be why the council didn't want Salvador doing anything without their permission. I was sure he could cause all sorts of trouble.

"That's one powerful clap you have, Salvador," I eventually said, still hiding behind the rock.

He faced me, his body and clothing still pristine; amazingly, not a drop of blood was anywhere on him. He cocked half a smile. "That's not all I can do with my hands."

Someone moaned.

I moved from my hiding spot and tried not to step in any of the deep maroon puddles due to the uneven floor. Everyone else emerged from their hiding area, and we cautiously approached the daemon still lying on the floor.

He sat up wincing and leaned against the wall when we circled him. "You broke my wing."

Salvador scowled. "I can always clap again, daemon."

"No! That won't be necessary."

"Do you know what your master was up to?"

"Do you mean the children or that vile concoction?"

"The concoction," Salvador said, towering over the dark and broken figure on the ground.

"The lions would have smelled the were-rat a mile away, so he approached Jones to enter the lion's den for him."

"Who was this were-rat?"

"Dunno, but he had tattoos over his chest—one large cross on his chest, with epaulettes on his shoulders." The daemon pointed to his own chest and made the sign of the cross then pointed to his shoulders where he saw the epaulettes.

I bit my lip. This were-rat sounded familiar. It reminded me of all the tattoos Lance had on his chest when I healed him. He had mentioned his friend Billy and how close they once were. I had to speak with Lance; if it was indeed someone he knew, possibly his friend, who had this concoction and managed to improve on it since attacking him, that meant a lot of were-animals were in danger.

"Do you know what he wants to do with it?" I asked.

"No, but I suspected he got it for someone else." The daemon shuddered, causing some of his feathers to loosen and float around him. What sounded like bones snapping back into place as his body knitted together again, like nothing had happened, reverberated through the cave. The daemon stood, towering over all of us with his dark form and large wings. It was true, daemons could not be killed. They had to be sent back from where they had originally come from, either by a necromancer or a witch, I wasn't sure. Neither of those were available, and I wasn't sure what Salvador was about to do.

"Why do you say that?" I asked, stepping backward so I could see his ash-covered face.

"This rat takes orders; he doesn't give them. He's a soldier. I could tell in the way he asked Jones to get that concoction and how Jones played him for what he wanted." The daemon glanced at the dead boy in the corner.

"Do you know where this rat is?"

"No, but he couldn't have gone far. He mentioned he still had work to do here."

"He is still in Sterling Meadow," I said to no one in particular.

"What should we do with him?" Sebastian asked, pointing to the daemon.

The daemon glanced at each of us in turn then stopped at Salvador. "You've freed me from my cruel master. I am yours now." In front of Salvador, the daemon got down on one knee and bowed with his head hung low. He waited for his new master to either claim him or set him free.

"You could be useful, daemon. Where do you usually stay?"

"Here."

"Continue to stay here. I'll call upon you when needed."

"Yes, Master." The daemon rose again, opened his

wings and shook his body, causing little feathers to float all around us.

Salvador hissed, lifting his arm as the letter '*V*' formed on his hand, marking him. "What is your name, daemon?"

"Verin, Master."

"Well then, Verin, I command you to stay here until I summon you. You're not allowed to leave, and you certainly may not harm anyone. Do you understand?"

"Yes, Master." Verin swept one hand to the side while he brought the other to his chest and bowed in front of his new master again. It was elegant and strange all at once, to see a large, dark, and dangerous daemon behave himself for a master vampire.

Chapter Seventeen

The moment we were outside in the fresh air and back on the path, we descended the mountain toward the cars. I used my cellphone to call Lance in Chicago. He thanked me again for saving his life, and I jumped right in to question him about his friend Billy.

Before he answered me, he said he had some news. He had consulted an oracle, and I needed to see her immediately. She knew me and said she could help me understand more about who I was. I asked him to text me her details, and I would contact her when I had time. I could only manage one problem at a time.

Lance said Billy hadn't been seen since the attack, which was almost two months ago. As I listened to Lance give me information and dates, I realized the attack on Lance happened after Billy had arranged for Jones to ask Melinda for her recipe. Perhaps Billy had used Melinda's serum as is when he had injected it into Lance, hence the reason why he had survived the initial attack even though he was dying slowly.

Lance described Billy, and, apart from his tattoos, he would resemble half the men in Sterling Meadow. He wore his brown hair long and boasted brown eyes and an athletic build. But that was over two months ago. Billy could've cut his hair, dyed it, or shaved it. I had to keep an eye out for those tattoos though. Lance did mention Billy had a tattoo of the Virgin Mary. Unfortunately, for me to know whether it was Billy or not, I had to see him half naked, which would not happen.

Lance said he would send one of his were-rats to help me track him down, adding that Billy was extremely dangerous and had been trained by the best. I thanked him and ended the call.

I walked ahead of Sebastian with Rory and Sawyer trailing close by. Even though they blocked Sebastian from my view, I could still feel his eyes on me. Maybe it was the mark we shared, because I felt him the entire time. It only made me walk faster.

Once we reached the cars, Sawyer and Rory pushed my car away from the tree I had crashed into. They turned it around, as there was no way I had enough space to turn around or reverse without hitting another tree. Having super-strong were-animals as friends or bodyguards certainly had its advantages.

Salvador and Léon glanced between Sebastian and me, but it was Léon who finally spoke. "We'll fly ahead and meet you at the Labyrinth."

Sebastian grunted.

I said, "Sure."

"Perhaps one of us should ride with?" Sawyer suggested, stepping closer to me.

"No," Sebastian grumbled. "Ride with Rory."

"Let me know if you need anything, Blaire," Sawyer said, walking with Rory to Sebastian's vehicle.

When it was just the two of us in my car and we were driving on the open road, I gave Sebastian a concise version of my conversation with Lance. He nodded as he listened, still grumpy.

After a moment's silence, Sebastian finally spoke. "We should probably meet with Arturo. He might know who Billy is and his whereabouts."

"Do you know where their colony is?"

Arturo was the King Rat of Sterling Meadow. I had never spoken with him personally, but I knew of him and had seen him at the dinner.

"It might go quicker if I drive instead of giving you directions," Sebastian said, motioning for me to pull to the side.

I sighed reluctantly, veering into the emergency lane. When Sebastian got out to walk around the vehicle, I climbed into the passenger seat.

"How's your neck?" he asked, steering the car onto the roadway. When I didn't answer him, he glanced at me, his lips in a tight line and his eyes pleading. Even though in some instances I couldn't read his expression, right then I could tell he was sorry. He hadn't meant to hurt me.

"It's okay," I said, touching the bite wound on my neck. "It doesn't hurt as much as it did before. Luckily, Léon stopped it from bleeding."

"What?" The car swerved left then right, and a look full of fury crossed his face.

"The bite wound was still bleeding. Léon said you didn't apply enough pressure or saliva when you stopped biting me."

He hit the steering wheel so hard it dented. The car

swerved from the impact, and we almost struck an oncoming car.

"Sebastian! What's wrong with you? Why are you so angry lately?" I gripped the handle above my door for safety.

"He had no right to touch you, Blaire. You are mine." He glowered.

"I'm not your possession, Sebastian." My own anger bubbled to the surface. "You don't own me. And besides, I didn't want you near me again so soon after biting me like that. You hurt me. And ... you scared me." I whispered the last part.

Sebastian braked so hard the tires screeched on the tarmac, and my body jerked forward, hurting my neck and the seatbelt cutting into my chest, burning my skin. "Fuck!"

He swerved into the emergency lane and stopped. He leered at me with an expression I'd never seen before, but I knew that look. I had one just like it. *Hate*.

I swallowed hard enough to hurt the back of my throat but kept quiet as I assessed my injuries. I rubbed my aching neck, but luckily, it was only whiplash. My concern was for my chest; it was still burning from the seatbelt pulling taut against me.

This wasn't the Sebastian I had come to know, to love. This was not like him at all. Glancing at him, I saw he was momentarily frozen where he sat; white-knuckled fingers squeezed the steering wheel, and he stared far out onto the road. His chest rose and fell as he sucked in deep breaths to calm down.

Someone opened the door and pulled Sebastian from the seat. "How about you drive with me, Sebastian?" Rory said, dragging Sebastian to his car.

"Let go of me, Rory," Sebastian yelled, flailing from

Rory's grip and rewarding him with a right hook to the jaw. Rory yelled, hitting Sebastian back.

I climbed out the car, but Sawyer blocked me from going closer. Sebastian bounced on the balls of his feet, Rory mimicking him.

"Stop it, Sebastian."

Sebastian glanced at me, his eyes dark, not an inch of green in them.

"What's going on with you?"

Sebastian stopped bouncing but staring at me as his eyes bled back to green, his shoulders sagging. He shook his head, rolling his shoulders then stretching them out. "I'm okay." Sebastian raised his hands. "I'm fine." He glanced at Rory. "You all right?"

"Yeah."

"Ride with Rory, and Sawyer will drive my car," I said.

Sebastian pursed his lips; he was unhappy with the arrangement but obliged with a nod, climbing into the passenger side of his car.

Sawyer slid into the driver's seat when I sat down and eyed me. "Are you all right?"

"No!" Tears streaked my face. "I don't know what the fuck is wrong with him." I pulled down my shirt and looked in the little mirror on the visor; the burn marks cut across my chest from the seatbelt.

"Let me take you to Mel."

"No, I'll be fine. Do you know your way to the were-rat colony?"

"Yes."

"Then go there. And tell Rory to take Sebastian home."

Sawyer pulled his cellphone out his pocket and dialed Rory's number. I could hear Sebastian yelling in the background and warning Rory. Sawyer ended the call. He didn't have to say anything; I had heard how Sebastian refused to go home and leave me to deal with Arturo on my own.

"Sawyer, ever since you've worked for Sebastian and Léon, has Sebastian ever behaved like this? Fine one moment, extremely angry and violent the next?"

He shook his head. "Never. He's usually the calmest out of the two brothers."

"Something happened to him," I said, afraid of the possibilities something had happened to Sebastian to make him like this. And it all had started from the shower we shared. Before then, he had been attending a lot of leap business and, more recently, some vampire business. So somewhere in between, something had happened.

I would speak to Sebastian about what's been going on with him once he had calmed down. But before I could figure all that out, we needed to see Arturo and then find Billy.

I said as much to Sawyer, who nodded and drove us to the were-rat colony.

Chapter Eighteen

As we drove through the city, I was exhausted and hungry. We stopped at a twenty-four-hour drive-thru for dinner. The guy behind the little window gave my car one glance, shaking his head slowly. Yeah, my new car was already a mess with one side full of dents and missing a passenger door.

Sawyer greeted him with a smile and ordered classic burgers with fries. Sawyer ate while he drove, one hand on the steering wheel, the other holding the burger. I had to hold my burger with both hands it was so big, but it was divine. Rory and Sebastian also grabbed dinner, but I wasn't sure what they had.

We arrived at the were-rat colony after midnight—a large ominous building on the outskirts of town. A large red neon sign that read, *Dirty Chains*, hung above the entrance. It was the only building for at least a mile in either direction. I so would not stop here if I was on my own.

People gathered near the entrance, and they turned to stare at us as we parked. Some wore vinyl hot pants or skirts with tight shirts, some only wore vinyl pants and were naked above the waist, while the others wore black dresses and stilettos.

"Are you sure this is the place?" I asked, swallowing hard.

"Yep."

"Is this where all the were-rats come to play? Or is it a nightclub?"

"It's a bit of everything, I think. Although, I wouldn't leave you alone in this place. And definitely wouldn't let you go in one of the rooms with anyone, even Arturo. I don't care if he is king."

"Okay, you aren't making me feel any better about this. But let's get this over and done with," I said, climbing out the car. "Don't bother locking it. With the door missing, I actually hope someone steals it." I giggled. My insurance company was going to flip out.

Sawyer smiled, pocketing the car keys.

"Feeling better?" I asked Sebastian when he neared.

"Yes, sorry about earlier. I don't know what's happening to me." He wrapped his arms around me. I squeezed him tightly, pressing one side of my face against his chest, and listened to that strong rhythm of his heart. He kissed the top of my head. "We've been together a few months, Blaire, so you know I'm not like this. It's not in my nature to behave that way. You believe me, don't you?"

I stared into his kitty-cat eyes, smiling. "When we're done here, we need to see Mel. Have *you* tested, for a change. And then we must find Billy."

"What are you thinking?" The lines between his eyes deepened.

"It's not only from today, Sebastian, but from our shower. Do you remember?" I whispered.

"How could I forget?" He kissed the top of my head again. "I would never hurt you like that, Blaire. Ever."

"I know, yet you are. That's why we need to figure this out. Before our date, where were you?"

"Leap business."

"Did anything out of the ordinary happen while you were there?"

"No." He shrugged those large shoulders. "It was the usual meeting. I did drink a weird-tasting tea though, but it was only a few sips, and I threw it out."

I stepped back from him, so I could see his face. "Who made it?"

"She was new. I think she said her name was Claire. She made everyone's tea that day, but I threw mine out after I tasted it."

"Did you feel different afterward? Or ill?"

He shrugged again. "Maybe. I can't remember."

"Okay, when we're done here, either we locate Billy first or this Claire and find out what she gave you."

"Yeah, let me tell Anne."

"No, don't tell anyone. Not yet in any case. I don't want her getting spooked and running away."

"Okay. Fine. Let's get this over and done with." He glanced at Dirty Chains. "This is not one of my favorite places, but it should be fine with all of us near you. Just don't go off with anyone."

We approached the building. Apparently, we were safer in numbers. The were-rats parted, allowing us access through the front door. We traversed a dark narrow hallway until we reached a woman sitting behind thick glass with a tiny window only big enough to hand her money or a credit card.

"How many?" she asked, tucking purple hair behind her pointy ears.

"Four."

She leered at the men behind me. "You're in luck, sweetheart. All is welcome tonight. Even dogs."

I faced the men, then I turned back at her. "Yeah, why is that?"

"At open night, all animals are allowed to enter. But, you my dear, you can come every night if you want." She purred, winking at me. "That will be forty."

I gave her the cash, and she handed us the tickets.

Up ahead was a black curtain where a large olive-skinned bouncer in the standard black security uniform leered down at us. I wasn't sure if it was because of the type of animals with me or if the guard was just miserable. He confirmed my suspicions by grunting as he took the tickets from me and parted the curtains. He was just a miserable guy.

I walked through the black sea of material first, halting when a hand grabbed my elbow. "Let me go first, Blaire," Sebastian said, passing me.

I allowed him to walk in front as we entered another short hallway; this one was dark and painted with photoluminescent scenes of various stages of carnal pleasures. An odor assaulted my nose, a mixture between latex, bodily fluids, and smoke. I shuddered when I stepped on something squishy and was grateful I wore my knee-high boots.

We walked through double doors into a vast room with a bar on either side and a stage in the middle. The music had been muffled in the dark hallways, but now that we were in the club, it was ear-shattering loud. The woman on stage had just thrown her red top into the crowd and danced provocatively in her white negligée; both men and women showered her with notes.

Against the far wall was a flight of stairs that spiraled to the high ceiling, seeming to be the only access to each of the four floors. On each of these floors were at least ten doors. I frowned. What type of place was this?

We continued to follow Sebastian as he approached the bar on our right-hand side. A man three times as tall as Sebastian passed us wearing a vinyl suit that covered him from head to toe, leaving his face visible and his long rat tail sticking out the back. He was juggling with what looked like three black candles, but I couldn't be sure; he was too quick with his hands. One look at his feet and I saw the circular rubber bottoms from the stilts he was standing on. Another man, also dressed head to toe in vinyl with his face and tail visible, passed us and threw something up at the man on stilts, and they juggled items to one another, reminding me of a circus.

Once we reached the bar, I didn't dare lean against it. The damp bar held the smell of stained wood with years of vomit and alcohol etched between the wooden cracks. Over the loud music, I heard Sebastian ask the bartender where he could find Arturo. The barman pointed to the spiral staircase and said to go to room 119.

Before we reached the staircase, a woman taller than Sebastian walked in front of us. She had flowing blond hair and wore a tight red vinyl dress. When she turned around to hug a friend, I noted the large ears, furry face, flat hairy chest, and bulge between his/her legs.

Maneuvering around the encounter, we finally reached the stairs where a couple was kissing on the first step. Both were feminine and infatuated with one another. We had to step over them to climb the stairs.

When the lady with the purple hair behind the thick glass had said, *'All was welcome,'* she really did mean it. People from all were-animal territories crowded downstairs, and they were into very different things—and each other. No one was discriminated against.

As we reached room 119, the door opened before we could knock. A woman stood in the doorjamb, trailing her eyes up and down Sebastian's body, licking her lips seductively and smiling. "What do you want, honey?" She purred. "We didn't order a kitty-cat or a couple of dogs." She leered behind Sebastian at Rory and Sawyer. When her eyes met mine, her face softened. But that softness didn't last long. "Arturo! I think they're here for you."

"Let them through, Darlene!" a man yelled from inside the room. Darlene opened the door wider and stood to one side.

We entered the murky room, smoke filling my lungs which caused me to cough. The walls were maroon with a white floor and ceiling. The contrast was startling as my eyes adjusted to the colors. A black curtain was draped on one side, and chains were rustling beyond it. I had no idea who or what was behind that black curtain, but I had a sense they were bound and gagged.

Arturo sat behind his white desk, watching us as we entered his office. His earthy tones complimented his honey-colored eyes, as his black hair reached his shoulders, framing his face. The way he tucked wild strands of hair behind his ears seemed a little too bashful for the were-rat king. And I wondered whether that gesture worked with the ladies.

"Sebastian and friends ..." Arturo rose from his chair and approached us. "My old friend, so glad you've come to visit me again. Is this business, or are you looking for some pleasure?" He spoke to Sebastian but stared at me and winked.

I noticed then that he was naked from the waist up and wore tight black vinyl pants that looked painted on his body.

"Did Troy notify you about the were-animal deaths?"

His face sobered. "Yes. I was shocked to hear what had happened. Just awful!"

"We need some information, friend." Sebastian hugged Arturo; it was that sideways manly hug that didn't involve too much touching. They slapped one another's back, then Arturo motioned for us to sit when he sat on the edge of his desk. None of us did; we all remained standing.

"Yeah? Not sure how I could help though. I don't know much about the murders."

"We may have a lead on the person who was tinkering with the serum Melinda started. From what we hear, he's a were-rat."

Arturo's eyes widened, and he white knuckled his desk. "From my colony?"

"No. We suspect he's from Chicago. He has a tattoo of a cross on his chest, epaulettes on his shoulders, and the Virgin Mary on his back."

Wood splintered, and shavings fell to the floor. Arturo broke the edge of his desk like it was a match. The muscles in his chest and forearms flexed, and I could hear him grind his teeth. "Billy?"

"Yes," I said, stepping closer to him. "Do you know where he is?"

"No. He left this morning, said he was going back to Chicago."

"How long did he stay here?"

"A little over two months. He said he was offered

employment and needed a place to crash for a while. I provided him one of the suites, which he paid for in cash."

"What do you want to do about him, King?" Darlene asked behind me.

I felt Darlene's presence then; it was like she was touching my shoulders and neck with her eyes and breath. A shiver ran along my spine. I turned my back to the wall, so I could see everyone in the room and not have my back exposed. She bore those beady brown eyes at me, like I insulted her by moving.

"I heard what you did for Lance, Blaire, and I knew about his and Billy's falling out." Arturo moved around his desk to sit again and dusted the wood shavings from his hands.

"Why did you help him then, if you knew who he was and what he did?" I bit my tongue to not say anything more. We were in rat territory and had to play nice.

Arturo glared at me. "I only knew of their feud. And I would rather he stayed here, where I could keep an eye on him than somewhere he could cause more trouble."

A pang of guilt sunk to the pit of my stomach.

"Do you know if he was associated with the new werewolf named Corey?" Sebastian asked, sitting in the visitor's chair across from Arturo's desk.

I scanned the gloomy room. Sawyer and Rory were still standing near the door. They both glanced in my direction then turned back to stare at Sebastian and Arturo.

"The wolf from Vegas? Yeah. He'd been here a couple of times, causing trouble with a pair of his friends. We kicked them all out for pissing on the ladies. I warned Billy not to bring them back, and I haven't seen them since."

"And you're certain they were with Billy?" I asked.

Arturo nodded.

"They've been working together all this time. We need to find out what happened in Vegas that prompted Corey to come here. And we need to find Billy," I said to no one in particular and didn't expect anyone to answer.

"My rats will find Billy. But let me know if you need any manpower, Blaire. If it was these two were-animals killing our kind, we need to stop Billy before he hurts anyone else. The more of us out looking for him, the better."

"Thank you, Arturo. We'll let you know when we need your help."

A knock on the door startled me.

"Enter!" Arturo shouted.

I saw his dark hair first then the tattoos of two teardrops by his right eye. Derick, one of Lance's were-rats, entered the room. "King Arturo, King Lance has sent me here to assist Blaire." He eyed me when he said my name, nodding in greeting.

"Good. You know what Billy looks like and can help her track him down," Arturo said then addressed me. "Derick here might be small in stature, but he is big in tracking. He can find Billy for you."

"Thank you," I said to Arturo. "How did you know I was here?" I asked Derick.

"I didn't. When an out-of-town were-rat enters another's territory, they have to greet the king before they can stay. I guess I came at the right time." He grinned.

"Thanks, Derick. And thank you, King Arturo, for speaking with us."

"A pleasure, Blaire, but please let me know the moment you need any of my men."

"I will," I said, pushing away from the wall.

Sebastian stood and put his arm around my shoulders possessively as we headed toward the door.

Something cold touched my left arm. When I turned to see what it was, Darlene's predatory gaze locked onto mine as she walked behind us, sending shivers up my spine. "I hope to see you real soon, Blaire." She purred.

I walked out the room without answering Darlene. I did not want to give her any impression of me other than what she already had. I hoped not answering her meant she would leave me alone.

Derick followed behind us as we descended the spiral staircase. The two women were still making out on the bottom step, and we had to climb over them again. As we passed the bathrooms, I realized I needed to go. I let go of Sebastian and told him I would be right back and went to the ladies restroom.

When I exited the cubicle and started washing my hands, a woman entered the bathroom. Her acorn-colored hair was twisted into curls and spiraled down her back. Her honey-colored eyes glanced at me then at the cubicles behind me. She wore a vinyl dress that looked painted on; the top part wasn't nearly enough to cover all of her. She opened the first cubicle door. It banged against the side, revealing nobody inside. She repeated the process on the second, third, and last. We were the only ones inside the restroom.

As I dried my hands on a paper towel and was just about to throw it away, the woman stood behind me, a whole head taller. She stared at me knowingly, but I didn't recognize her. The hairs on the back of my neck stood on end as she studied me. I wasn't accustomed to meeting women in the bathroom, so I wasn't familiar with the etiquette.

"Blaire?"

I tensed, staring up at her, then managed to answer her.

"Yes?" I threw away the paper towel and stood with my back to the basins. "Do I know you?"

"No, but I saw you at the dinner, the one for Shannon."

"I don't remember seeing you there," I said, frowning.

She glanced at herself in the mirror, shook her body as if something was on her, and tiny dust particles floated around her body and glowed. The particles swirled around her faster, and her vinyl dress disappeared, leaving her in a brown cloak. She had a heart-shaped face; her ears were elongated at the top; her eyes were mauve and her lips delicately thin. Crystal wings unfurled from behind her and glinted in the dim restroom lights and stood out behind her. Her acorn-colored hair turned to ash blond with the finest of twigs and leaves pushing through her head, blossoming with yellow flowers.

"You sat at table two, with the fay king."

She nodded delicately. "My name is Moonbeam, and King Shimmertree has kindly requested your presence."

"How could I possibly help you? I only know about the fay from what I learned at school, which wasn't much. What I do know, is secrecy surrounds you and your kind."

"We're afraid for our lives, Blaire," Moonbeam said, her eyes misty.

"Tell me."

"Everyone is afraid. We heard you're seeking the one causing all the deaths among the were-animals. In our quest to locate you, we were informed you were here and knew we had to seek you out." She made it sound like everyone knew who we were and what we were doing.

"Yes. We need to stop him before anyone else gets hurt." I frowned, wondering how she had heard about this so quickly when our investigation had only just begun.

"One of our own needs your help. We heard what you

did for King Lance, the were-rat in Chicago. And what you did for Ivy. We desperately need your help too."

"What happened?"

"She fell gravely ill after she drank tea."

"Who gave her the tea?" A knot formed in the pit of my stomach. The mere mention of this tea made my hands bunch into fists.

"A were-leopard."

I froze. It had to be Claire.

A knock on the door distracted me.

"Blaire? Are you okay in there?"

"I'll be right out, Sebastian." To Moonbeam, I whispered, "Take me to her. But I can't guarantee I can save her."

"We'd be grateful if you'd just try," she replied, her floral-patterned eyes glistening in the light.

"Fine, but you can't go out like that." As I said the words, the tiny dust particles glowed again, and she reverted to the woman with the acorn-colored hair and vinyl dress. "Wow," was all I could say.

When I exited the bathroom, I told Moonbeam to stay close to me.

Sebastian glanced from me to the woman behind me. "Who's this?"

"I need to help her. If you want, you can leave with Rory, and I can take Sawyer and Derick with me."

"Nah-huh. I'm not leaving you alone with her. She doesn't smell like any were-animal."

"That's because she's not." He frowned at me. "She's fay, and she needs my help. One of her own has fallen ill by drinking tea one of the were-leopards gave her." I widened my eyes, hinting at the similarities.

"Fine, but we are all going with." He turned and headed for the exit. Rory, Derick, and Sawyer brought up the rear.

From the corner of my eye, I saw something dark move in our direction. I turned to find a large man in full body armor with barely visible olive skin. Of his face I could see, I could tell it was smooth and the color of hazel fay flowers—a gentle brown. Only his piercing green eyes were visible through his visor. He greeted Rory and Sawyer as he guarded Moonbeam.

We walked through the dark and narrow hallway with the painted photoluminescent scenes of various stages of carnal pleasures that was lit like Christmas trees. The stench of latex and body fluids was more prominent than before, and I was relieved not to step on anything gooey again. As we walked out the club and into the fresh evening air, I welcomed the cool breeze against my skin.

"Will you follow us, Blaire?" Moonbeam asked as she and her giant guard started walking down the sidewalk to my right.

"Yeah, sure." To Sawyer, I said, "Will you drive and follow their car?"

Moonbeam and the giant climbed into a black limo.

Sawyer started my car's engine as Derick climbed in and sat on the other side where there was still a door. He looked like he wanted to comment but decided against it. Good rat. Sawyer pulled in behind the limo. Rory and Sebastian were behind us.

We drove behind the limo for about an hour, and it felt like we were returning to the mountains from where we had just come from on our search for Jones. Eventually, we pulled onto a sand road that wound around stumps and trees, then I knew we were heading deeper into the forest. The road stopped, and the limo parked near a building. We were deep in the forest, surrounded by lush trees and dense brushes.

When I climbed out, the forest sounds enveloped me. I glanced at the night sky, and the stars twinkled brightly. Without the lights from the city to drown out the beauty of night, I appreciated nature around me. I heard an owl, insects chirping, running water. I exhaled and felt tension ease away.

"Blaire …" A deep voice brought me out of my Zen. I opened my eyes and saw a large man heading my way. I recognized his pointy nose and lavender eyes—the fay king.

"My name is Drew Shimmertree."

"King Shimmertree," someone blurted from behind one of the cars.

He cleared his throat. "Fine. It's King Shimmertree," he said with a pleasant smile. "Thank you for agreeing to come with Moonbeam. Her sister Moonrise has fallen ill."

"Her sister?"

"Yes. Did she not say who had fallen ill?"

"No. Only that it was fay."

"I see. She's very modest, our Moonbeam. You see"—King Shimmertree delicately grabbed my elbow, forcing me to walk with him—"one of the were-leopards and Moonrise had become close friends. Moonrise drank some herbal tea this friend made her and has fallen gravely ill."

We walked through dense bushes and tall trees. I glanced over my shoulder, and Rory, Sawyer, Derick, and Sebastian were nearby.

"Who was this were-leopard?"

"I think her name was Claire."

"The woman who gave you your tea." I glanced at Sebastian.

"Yes."

"So she poisoned him too?" King Shimmertree asked.

"Yes, we think so. But he hasn't fallen as ill. Yet." Without having to look behind me, I could feel Sebastian was much closer to me now.

"I'm not just a were-leopard, King Shimmertree," Sebastian said.

"I know what you are. And please call me Drew. I know my people want me to remain formal with outsiders, but you're about to help one of mine. I'd rather treat you as a friend." Drew stopped and released my elbow. "You must do everything you can. Help our Moonrise." To Sebastian he said, "Catch that Claire. She's poisoning people, and, if they have given it to you, who is high up in the leap ranks and a vampire, then they care little for the rest of us."

"As I said to Moonbeam, I can only promise to do my best. I won't promise I can heal her."

He turned those lavender eyes on me. "That's all I can hope for, your best. But I know Sebastian will catch Claire and take care of her."

"I'll do more than just catch her. She and everyone else involved is as good as dead."

"That's my boy," Drew said, slapping Sebastian's back.

We ventured deeper into the dense forest. My feet ached in my boots; first it was the mountain climb, then the club, now the forest. I was feeling a bit fatigued, but, when Sebastian held me with one arm around my shoulders while I clung to his waist, it gave me strength to push on.

When we came to a tree with bare branches, Drew went onto his haunches and pulled on the bark. A light cascaded from the tree. He opened the door onto a large bedroom. Behind the tree was only the forest, yet the room inside the tree was vast, like an optical illusion.

Something touched my shoulder. Whipping my head

around, I found Moonbeam behind me. "We use magic to hide our rooms. Mine is up there." She pointed to a tree to our right. "Fay use white magic. We are unlike witches and warlocks who may use grey or black magic. We draw our magic from nature to live, never to harm."

"It's impressive."

"Go in." Drew opened the door for me.

Once I was inside the large dimly lit room, I noted a bed with cupboards, a chair, desk, and a bathroom. Under the covers lay what I assumed to be Moonrise, Moonbeam's twin sister. But where Moonbeam had bright sparkly mauve eyes, Moonrise had powder-blue eyes. Her skin had lost its glow and tinged grey. Her hair was thin, and, where Moonbeam had twigs and fresh flowers blossoming from her head, Moonrise had dead leaves and withered flowers. Her face was gaunt and ghostlike.

I exhaled slowly and sat on a stool beside the bed.

She raised her hand for me to hold. "I don't expect a miracle. Just you being here means so much to me and to my sister and the fay." She smiled, but it wavered. "Do what you can, whatever it may be. If you can't do anything, I'm ready to be one with nature once again and give back to the land that has given me life."

I blinked back tears. "Nice to meet you. Sorry it's under these circumstances though. And thank you for not adding pressure. But let me see if I can do *anything*." I gently took her hand in mine. The moment we touched, a jolt of lightening hit me, but I didn't flinch or retract my hand. I held onto her delicate hand as I closed my eyes.

I opened my metaphysical shields just a smidge, lowering my tall mental walls so my white light—my white aura—could come out. It moved down my arm and into Moonrise. I searched for her life essence, for that little flicker of life that was left. I found her heart first; she was good—a wholesome soul that had never hurt anyone. Her kindness surrounded me like a warm blanket. I fought not to smile.

That's when I knew I had to help her. Someone so *pure* and so *good* couldn't die like *this*.

My white light continued searching until it came to a wooden coffin wrapped in chains and a cross. I had no idea why a coffin would be trapped near a fay, but this was the metaphysical world where it was possible that the person responsible for everything was somehow connected to the tea Moonrise had drunk.

I tugged on the chains without any effort, and they fell to floor. Opening the coffin, I found it was empty. The vampire who used to sleep here was long gone, possibly had escaped. At the bottom of the coffin near the feet section lay a tiny candle. Whoever was once inside the coffin had hidden her life candle away.

I touched the wick of the candle, and it flared to life.

In the center of the room was a candle holder where I returned the candle and created a cage so no one could disturb it again. Moonrise's candle burned brightly and would now remain unharmed.

My white aura returned behind its mental walls, and I shielded tightly once again. When I regained consciousness, bright blue eyes stared back at me.

"How are you feeling?" I asked, pleased with what I had done.

Tiny flecks of glowing dust particles danced in the air around Moonrise. Her skin was rosy, her hair shone like silver, and the flowers around her head blossomed pink. She sat upright, keeping my hand in hers and rubbing the back of my hand against her cheek. She was warm to the touch.

"So much better. Thank you." Through tears, she added, "You saved me. I owe you everything."

"No, you don't. I'm just glad I could help you. Some weren't as lucky as you."

"All of fay owe you," Drew said, still standing in the doorway. His eyes glistened with unshed tears.

I stood, approached Sebastian, mis stepped, and he caught me in his arms, keeping me in an embrace.

"You okay?" He kissed my temple.

I nodded, feeling a little shaky. When I found my voice, I said, "We need to find this Claire woman. And Billy. What they're doing to everyone needs to end now. Everybody is scared."

"Don't worry. We'll stop them," he said void of any emotion.

While I was in his embrace, I lowered my shield and mental walls and searched through Sebastian. If I could help Moonrise, surely I could help Sebastian. If he drank the same tea that had almost killed her, then it was possible it was messing with his emotions. There was hope I could help him too. I could expel whatever was damaging him.

My white aura searched through Sebastian and stopped at his heart first. I gasped. This was wrong; I had to be wrong. It couldn't be. Not *my* Sebastian. I felt a darkness I didn't want to get too close to, an evil so bad that once it had secured its hooks, it wouldn't let go. And it was in him. It was in *my* Sebastian.

This evil took me to a place I remembered from when I was young, a time when I was locked in a closet for three days before someone had found me—that dark closet where I vowed I would kill the man who had murdered my ma. That same darkness was within Sebastian. It swirled around his wholesome heart as if biding its time for something important to happen. I desperately wanted to be wrong, but it was there, surrounding his good and pure heart.

None of it made sense.

Why did I have to go and do this?

I'd tainted my feelings for Sebastian by going behind his back and working my white aura within him. But all I wanted to do was heal. Instead, I found an evil deeply embedded within him.

I was so stupid to have fallen in love with the man who had killed my ma.

My white aura returned behind my mental shields before it discovered more things I did not want to know, and I released Sebastian. I pushed away from him hard and glared into his green eyes. He blinked at me like he knew what I had just done and knew I had discovered his secret.

"It was you?" I choked on my words as the tears fell.

Sebastian tried to reach for me, but I stepped backward. "What did you just do to me?" He rubbed the left-hand side of his chest near his heart. "Did you just use your power on me?" He doubled over, clutching his chest.

"You killed my mother, didn't you?"

He shook his head, still hunched over himself. "Who was your mother?"

It came to me then, with that dream, that memory of *her*. "Alice. Her name was Alice!" My yell was laced with anger. My hands bunched into fists, and my pulse thumped in my ears as I remembered the man who used to throw me down when I was only a kid, that deep-chested breathing as he walked toward me. "I don't understand!" I cried, shaking my head. "You don't sound like him nor do you have that smell. But what I just found inside you is so evil, you must be *him*!"

My body vibrated with power. A cool white heat

coursed through my veins, like lava flowing through my body, except it was also ice. My hands found my face as I felt something move just beneath my skin, like my face had doubled. Many things happened at once as my world slowed down. White heat radiated from me. Moonbeam pulled Moonrise from her bed, and they ran for the door. Drew was already outside, calling them to follow him. Sawyer, Derick, and Rory were still standing outside the door far away from us, away from everything that was about to happen.

"I've known a few Alice's in my lifetime. I don't know whether I knew your mother or not, but I didn't kill anyone with that name."

"You. Are. Lying!" My face doubled again; the shift was sudden, then it was gone. My hands were hot as I pumped them into fists and opened them again. White heat oozed from me and away from my body, and I was about to explode.

"I promise you," Sebastian pleaded, raising his hands in surrender. It was that same gesture he had first made when he picked me up off the cold ground after I had been attacked six months ago. "I don't know what you saw or why you saw it, but it wasn't me. I would never lie to you about something like this. You have to believe me."

"Why did I sense him inside of you?" I cried out, my stare boring through Sebastian as the tears flowed.

"I don't know." His eyes widened as he stared down at me. "What's happening to you? You're glowing white. You need to calm down. Once you've relaxed, we can talk about it. I promise. But you need to calm down!"

I glanced at my glowing feet. I raised my hands near my face to see they were glowing white also. Something shifted in my face again. I looked at my stomach as something moved from within me; a hand was trying to claw its way through my skin.

Heat crept up my face as I struggled for air. My chest rose and fell as I tried to suck in air, but my throat had closed. Sweat beaded on my forehead, and my clothing clung to me. I was on fire and melting from the inside. I had to find a way to climb out of my skin, or I was about to die.

My anger was laced with white hot coals, and I didn't know how to stop it.

Panic washed over me.

My blood boiled; my bones melted; and I screamed as loud as I could. "Noooo!"

The room exploded into a white light, destroying everything in its path, obliterating everything in my way.

But I wasn't dead. I was moving. And fast.

When I opened my eyes, I was running—sprinting so fast tree branches hit my face, and my surroundings blurred past me. It felt like I was flying through the trees. I was racing toward something; I just didn't know what, but I was getting there at the speed of light.

I was by myself. It felt so wonderful. I felt free.

My anger had dissipated, and my heavy heart felt lighter, whole again.

I was at peace.

When I arrived at the top of a waterfall, I stopped to behold my surroundings. I had no idea where I was or what had happened to everyone. All the sounds echoed around me—a fly a yard away, ants walking on the ground. In the distance, the city was clear.

All this was impossible, yet I could do it.

I licked dry lips, running my tongue over razor-sharp

teeth, but I desperately needed to drink some of the water that flowed before me.

I bent down and froze when I saw my reflection.

Chapter Nineteen

I stared at my reflection, trying to comprehend the furry face staring back at me. My mind was trying to protect me from myself. I could see what I was looking at, but I couldn't believe it was *me*.

My eyes glowed blue. My fur was white, with markings similar to a leopard but so much bigger and very different. I was fluffy and had large maxillary canines sticking out my mouth. I stared at the large white paws with its sharp claws for what felt like hours.

I was still thirsty from all that running, so I drank water, my tongue lapping the cool liquid and quenching my thirst.

A twig snapped behind me. I snarled.

"Blaire?" Sebastian said through his large jaw, his black beast moving toward me.

"I'm a fucking saber-tooth."

"Yeah, I can see that." He chuckled, stopping short of me, not wanting to come too close until I was ready. "This is a dumb question, but, are you okay?"

"No! I'm not fucking okay. Look at me. How the fuck does this even happen?"

"I am looking at you. And nothing's wrong with how you look. You are ... beautiful. You're unique. Don't you see that?"

I growled. The sound was foreign to me. "How do I change back?"

"You need to eat first."

"I was afraid you would say that."

"Once you've eaten, you'll feel better. I promise."

"Why now? It's not even a full moon."

"I think your anger activated the change, and possibly parts of your memory. Something snapped inside you, and you just exploded. You blew up Moonrise's house. But luckily, no one was hurt."

"Good, but I don't remember anything. I don't even remember the change. Just a white light."

"Yeah, that was you blowing up. I just saw a white blur run into the forest, and I knew it was you. So I chased after you."

I had no reply. I was still trying to process what had happened.

"Come, let's get you something to eat."

I sighed but followed Sebastian anyway. Walking beside him, I was as big as he was in his leopard form, and that meant I was huge—larger than a pony.

Because it was my first time in my saber-tooth form, Sebastian killed the moose while I sat and watched. He made it look so easy, but I knew I would have to learn to do it myself, one day. Just not right now. The idea of eating raw meat didn't sit well, until he killed it. The smell of fresh meat stirred a hunger deep inside me I had never known before. I growled at Sebastian, pushing him out of my way. Staring down at the moose, the fresh blood, the fresh meat, I ripped apart the moose and ate it one mouthful at a time.

Only when I was full did Sebastian eat. I was kind enough to leave him half the moose. While he ate, I licked the blood off my paws and cleaned the fur around my mouth. Sebastian was right; when I was sated, I felt better. Exhaustion engulfed me, and the sun was rising, cascading golden rays across the sky.

When Sebastian was done eating, he scent marked me by rubbing against my body, then he lay beside me. When he relaxed, I rested my large head on his back, closing my eyes. We fell asleep in our embrace, one large black kitty with a large white kitty.

This was something I did not expect.

I shivered as the wind caressed my naked skin. Twigs dug into my hips and side, awakening me. I looked behind me only to be greeted by Sebastian with a smile planted on his face.

"Good morning," he said, kissing my temple. "How are you feeling?"

"I dunno. Confused, I guess." I turned and closed the gap between us. His heat was keeping me warm. "Okay, how come I still get cold? You're a were-leopard and are always hot. I should be too, obviously, yet I still get cold?" The lines between my eyes deepened.

"Like I said last night, you're unique. I've never met *anyone* quite like you before in all my years on Earth. Ever."

"I don't know about that. I feel pretty ordinary."

"Just think of all the things you can do. And with last

night …" He shrugged. "You're the first saber-tooth I'd ever heard about, never mind seen."

"Why can I change into my saber, but not any of the other were-animals that now live inside of me?"

"Maybe your saber is the alpha, and is the only animal you will change into. And perhaps it has something to do with how you can syphon powers, perhaps that's just a part of it."

I nodded. I still didn't believe it, but I knew he was right. "Anyway, how are we getting back? With no clothes."

He grinned. "Are you sure you want to go back? We could stay here all day."

I rested my head against his chest. "As tempting as that is, we need to find Claire. And we need to find Billy. And Sebastian—"

"Yeah."

"Do you promise that you didn't know my mother?"

"I knew four women with the name Alice. None were from this century." He pulled my body closer to his. "Do you remember your father's name?"

I squeezed my eyes tight. "Uh, Joe, I think. No. Joseph." I sat upright, gasping as memories flashed before me. "It was a car crash. I never knew the full story though. But he was involved in a wreck."

"And your mother? You didn't finish the story about what happened to her. Do you remember now?"

"After my dad died, she started seeing this man—a shifter." I closed my eyes. "When I picture him, all I see is a tall dark figure. I can't see his features, but I know his smell and the deep breaths he used to take. That sound always made my skin crawl. But what I can't figure out is why I saw him inside you. Like, you are him or are somehow connected. I wonder if it's the leopard part of you I'm sensing from him. That maybe he was a were-leopard and linked to the leap."

Sebastian rubbed my back tenderly. "I don't know, but I want to know as well. Someone within the leap is a murderer, and we need to find out who they are and stop them. Who knows who else they've harmed?"

I whimpered, turning toward him. "At first, he was a gentleman and did everything right for Ma. But he slowly revealed his true self to her and beat her, then he turned his anger on me and would push me down whenever he was unhappy. This man wanted my mother to run away with him. When she didn't arrive at their rendezvous, he looked for her at our house. She told me to hide in her closet—my secret hideaway for when he visited. He was so angry she didn't want to leave with him. She would never choose him over me. I was her daughter. She would never leave me. He said if he couldn't have her, no one would, and then I heard him strangle her. I remember how her body fell to the floor. That thump as she hit the ground still haunts my dreams. That's when he searched for me. But, before he could look inside the cupboard, someone called for him, and they had to leave. I stayed in that cupboard for three days before someone opened it for me." I choked back tears.

"Ah, Blaire," Sebastian said, pulling me closer. "I'm so sorry this happened to you. Can you remember who found you?"

"The neighbor. We missed her dinner, and, when she came into our house and saw my mother's body, she knew my mother would've hidden me and knew where to find me. Years after, I returned and spoke to the neighbor. She told me what she thought happened."

"And ...?"

I could smell him then, that tall dark evil figure. I could

feel his large hands push me down or push me against the wall so he could walk past. Another time, he had backhanded me against my cheek, leaving half my face bruised. Then I'd hear his deep-chested breathing, like he had smoked cigars his whole life. His dark form would tower over us, screaming at Ma then at me.

A flood of memories hit me one by one, like flashcards burning brightly. I remembered watching Marcus and how suspicious he seemed skulking the streets. That's when I had decided to follow him. I watched him kill his target and pestered him to teach me. I wanted to learn what he did, so I could kill that shifter—the one who had killed Ma.

That's why I joined Ulysses Assassins.

Why I got that tattoo.

The three of us were sitting at the tattoo parlor. Marcus got his tattoo on his left shoulder; Ralph got his on the inner part of his right arm. Me, I got mine on my back. My love of Egypt and the details of the hieroglyphics had to be included into the design of the butterfly. The pain I endured for four days for them to complete the masterpiece had been well worth it.

The thought that the flap of a butterfly's wings could cause a hurricane in another part of the world intrigued me. I wanted to be that butterfly, to cause my own destruction to those who had wronged me—to those who had hurt me and my family.

"Blaire?" Sebastian asked, bringing me out of my memories.

"Yeah?" I glanced at him, feeling the color drain from my face.

"Are you okay?"

I nodded.

"You were saying, you spoke to your neighbor years later."

"Oh, yes. Sorry. I thought of something else just now. When I was older, I spoke with her about that day. She was much older, obviously, but she still remembered it like it was yesterday. She said she thought he was married, that's why he wanted to run away with Ma. But Ma was weary of him and his anger issues. He was a powerful shifter. She didn't know which animal though, but she knew he was scary. Our neighbor warned Ma to take me and run. But Ma told her he would find her, us, no matter where we went. He was obsessed." I swallowed hard, wiping my eyes dry. "That's why I hated shifters so much."

"What?"

"Ralph told me I hated shifters. I could never understand why though. I do now." I smiled at Sebastian. "But that was the old Blaire. The new Blaire loves you."

He mirrored my smile, pulling me in for an embrace, cupped my face and kissed me. "I love you too." I held onto him a little longer than necessary. It felt so good to be here with him. It felt like home.

"Plus, I can't hate shifters anymore, especially since I am one," I said, chuckling.

"Are you ready?"

"Uh-huh."

"Good. How about we find our bad guy before he hurts another were-animal? If I remembered correctly, there's a road over there." He pointed at a cluster of trees a short distance away.

"What do we do when we get to that road? We're naked!" I giggled.

"The boys will be looking for us. I told them to drive up and down until they found us."

We walked hand in hand on the edge of the forest alongside the road and headed toward town. We were bound to meet up with one of the cars sooner or later.

Two hours later, my car sped past. Sebastian flagged them down before they passed again. Sawyer gave me his jacket, which luckily reached my thighs, while Sebastian wrapped the blanket I kept in the back seat around his waist.

When we reached town, we stopped at my place where I showered and Sebastian joined me. He lathered soap all over my body and washed me tenderly. The feel of his hands caressing my skin made me weak in the knees. With one arm around me, he kept me upright and kissed me as his hand went between my legs. I welcomed him and moaned into his mouth as his fingers found that delicate spot.

"So ready for me." He grinned in the kiss.

"U-huh, only for you."

"Only for me," he whispered, lifting my leg as he entered me. He gently moved in and out of me with care, being careful not to hurt me like he had the last time we showered together.

"I won't break." I kissed him again, "Please, harder—faster."

He did as I pleaded, going harder and faster until he built that sweet pressure between my legs and I could no longer stand. I wrapped my legs around his waist as he pushed deeper inside me, maintaining that heavenly rhythm. He grunted as he thrust one more time as hard as he could, and I squeezed my orgasm around him. I whimpered as we came together and rode that wave of pleasure over and over. Still pressed against the shower tiles, he cupped my face in his hands and kissed me with soft lips, lingering to demonstrate his love. What it would mean to spend the rest of my life with him? My heart swelled as his warmth filled my body. Our hearts entwined while our beasts scent marked one another. I loved him more than anything.

Whatever the evil was I had sensed within him, we would work through it.

"Did I hurt you?" he asked breathlessly.

"No, you were perfect." I pecked his cheek. "I think it was just what we needed."

"I agree." He slowly removed himself from me, leaving me gasping at the loss of him.

"And I'm glad our leopards like each other."

He grinned. "Of course. We were made for each other." He kissed the top of my nose. "You'll still be the death of me though."

"What?" I froze, remembering what the witch had said. "Why did you say such a thing?"

He looked as shocked as I felt, with confusion splashed all over his face. "I just meant if we keep this up"—he kissed my neck, trying to calm my nerves—"I'll get tired." He kissed the nape of my neck then moved down, nibbling on the soft skin of my breast. "And I've never gotten tired before."

"Let's finish up," I said numbly, trying my best to forget what had just happened.

"Nothing will happen to me, Blaire. Or to us." He stared, placing calm hands on my shoulders. "Nothing."

I nodded, biting back tears and trying to regain some sort of control as we washed again, attempting to detach myself from those feelings of loss.

Once I was calm and we were dry, he changed into the clothes he kept at my house. While I got dressed, I repeated my mantra that I couldn't control everything. If it was within my power, then yes, but until such time, if anything happened, I would enjoy my time with Sebastian and leave it at that. If he said nothing would happen, I had to believe him.

When we were done, we walked toward the cars. I took one look at my poor car with its door missing and the dents on the side. My insurance will have a field day with my claim. I photographed the damage and sent it to them via their app. They would contact me in forty-eight hours.

"Guess you have to ride with me now." Sebastian smirked as we climbed into his vehicle.

I elbowed him. "You always get your way, don't you?"

"Not always. Okay, maybe most times."

"Sawyer and Rory, since you were up all night trying to find us, do you want to go home and sleep?"

"No, sir. Derick and I took turns driving," Sawyer said.

"Rory?"

"I'll be fine. I'll sleep in the back until we get to the leap. I only need a power nap."

"Good, because we might need all of you."

Sebastian drove us to the leap where Anne greeted us at the front door. We gave her a short version of the events, except the part where I turned into a saber-tooth. She knew where Claire stayed and gave us her address. She would contact as many were-leopards as possible to warn them of Billy but only after we found Claire. We didn't want her to warn the others. This way, we still had the element of surprise on our side.

Chapter Twenty

We parked outside Claire's apartment building. It was mid-morning, and, after a few minutes of sitting inside the car, watching, waiting, we gathered it was safe to go in. Sebastian entered the building first, with me second, and the other three men close behind. We climbed the three flights of stairs and approached her apartment.

As we neared, Sebastian halted. The door was ajar, and the lock had been tampered with. Sebastian pushed open the broken door, pointing his gun inside. I did the same, along with the three men; whatever was inside wouldn't come out alive. The dark apartment smelled of fresh cigarette smoke still wafting in the air.

"Claire? It's Sebastian."

Silence greeted us. She wasn't in her kitchen or living area.

I faced Rory, Sawyer, and Derick. "You three stay here while Sebastian and I check out her rooms."

Sebastian blocked me from passing him and, with stern eyes, said, "I heal quicker than you. Let me go first."

"Fine."

The first bedroom was vacant, and, in the main bedroom, the smell of cigarette smoke was much stronger. A thin silver light shone through the slit between the two curtains. Her bed was unmade, a broken water jug lay on the floor, and ash littered the bedside table.

Sebastian entered the bathroom and froze.

"What is it?"

"I found her. Them."

I stood beside him and saw a body lying in the bathtub, submerged under red water. A bloody trail mark on the floor connected the doorjamb to the shower where another body was dumped. Her shoulders and head rested near the shower drain, while the rest of her lay on the tiles near the bath and toilet. Both bodies were naked and carved. The words *Venenum Daemon* were etched into their backs.

"Poison daemon."

"What?" I asked.

"Poison daemon. That's what's carved into their backs. It's Latin."

"Oh! Which one is Claire?"

"I can't be sure, but I think this one." Sebastian pointed to the body near the shower. "And that must be her roommate."

"Who would do this?"

"I might know," Sebastian said and left me standing in the bathroom. "Go home, Blaire."

"What? Where are you going? Sebastian?"

"He and Rory left," Sawyer said as he peeked his head inside.

"What do you mean he left?"

"He's gone. Said to take you to the Labyrinth."

"How can he just leave me? We still need to find Billy."

"I can help you," Derick said, also sticking his head into the bathroom.

"Okay, guys. Show's over. Who do we call when things like this happen?" I motioned to the bodies.

"I'll call Anne," Sawyer answered while pulling his cell out his pocket. "They might want to feast on her. The full moon rises in a weeks' time."

The thought took me back to when everyone had eaten Grant, the were-leopard I had shot and killed because he was about to attack me. They had passed around a glass that contained his blood. After one sip, I had gone all were-leopard on Sebastian, and they had to hold me down. That's when we realized I might change into one of my were-animals, but it didn't happen. That's all before I shifted into my saber-tooth.

Sawyer ended his call with Anne. "She'll send Greg and Kai to fetch Claire's body."

"They can't feast on her if she was poisoned with that serum."

"Then they'll burn her body."

"Don't we notify the police at all?"

"We take care of our own, Blaire. The only time police do anything is when they pulled the trigger."

"Oh, what happens to her belongings or her apartment?"

"Each animal group has someone who knows someone who can manage everything once someone passes. All that is the easy stuff. It's notifying the next of kin that's the toughest. Claire was new, from what Sebastian had said, so I'm unsure whether Anne knows who her family even is to notify, but she'll try to find out. Don't worry."

"Fine. Since everything is being taken care of here, where can we find Billy, Derick?"

He smiled a toothy grin. "Let's go have some fun."

Since Sebastian and Rory had left us at the apartment and taken his Jeep, we flagged down a cab to take us to the airfield.

"Remind me why you think he would even be here?"

"He's an adrenaline junkie, and this might be his type of place. If he's still in town, he could be parachuting. If not, I know a few bars we could try."

At the ticket office, we described Billy to the attendant and asked whether she had seen him. She said no but allowed us to enter to see if maybe he was inside. We searched the hangar and their restaurant, but he wasn't here.

"Before we check the bars, are there any other places where someone who likes falling might want to go?" Derick asked.

"Ice skate rink?" I offered, but Derick shook his head. "Trapeze?" I said, remembering my date with Sebastian and seeing Corey there.

"Maybe, I don't know, but let's check it out just in case," Derick said as we exited.

We hailed another cab to take us to the edge of town. I glanced at the *'You are now leaving Sterling Meadow'* sign. In front of me was the familiar eerie building with its ten parking spaces out front. We were on the edge of the forest, again. Sebastian had brought me here for our date before I left for Chicago. The building seemed run down and in desperate need of a coat of paint. On the outside, it looked like a place where people got killed. But inside, it was only *Jenny's Trapeze & Dine*.

Butterflies and Hurricanes

We entered the building and bouts of laughter greeted us, then we heard screams. Near the trapeze, a crowd had gathered, and all heads tilted upward at the flying men. I didn't recognize these men. One man swung and reached for the other man who leapt from his bar, and then they caught each other. The two men swung for a bit, then the one who had originally leapt to the other summersaulted to his bar and caught it with one hand. Gasps emerged from the crowd then a round of applause.

"That's Billy," Derick whispered near my ear.

Billy continued to swing while the other man let go and did at least three backflips until he landed on the net below. Then Billy swung higher and faster, and eventually, he let go and squeezed in four backflips before landing on the net beside the other man. They both laughed.

Billy looked at Derick then at me with a creepy smile across his face. I recognized him; he was one of the guys who had joined Corey when Sebastian and I were here.

Billy flew off the net and landed behind us, hitting Derick in the jugular. Derrick crumpled to the floor. Blood pooled from his throat and beneath him.

"What are you doing here, Derick?"

"We just want to talk with you," I said. "You didn't have to hurt him."

Derick leered at Billy. I didn't think Derick could speak as he gripped his throat, trying in vain to stop the bleeding.

"Blaire?"

"Yes."

"He your bodyguard?" Billy jerked his chin in Sawyer's direction.

"Yes," I replied, moving closer to Sawyer. I didn't like the way Billy had said that or the way he was staring at Sawyer.

"When I heard you've been looking for me, I knew you would find me sooner or later." He smiled sinisterly. "It made my job a lot easier." He stared at me for a heartbeat, contemplating, then added. "What's the best way to catch a mouse?"

I shrugged nervously.

"By setting a trap." He laughed and glanced at something behind me.

When I turned around, a blur of something hit me in the jaw, and I fell—darkness dragging me to the depths of Hell.

The pain in my jaw woke me. I flexed my fingers one at a time then outstretched my hands. I could move them around, allowing the blood supply to climb my arm, but they were bound too tightly behind my back and to the hard chair I was strapped to.

"Blaire?"

I raised my head, my surroundings dark and blurry.

"Blaire, to your left." It was a familiar voice.

I moved my head slowly and saw Sebastian and Rory; the men were bound in silver with their hands tied above their heads. Sebastian and Rory's faces were etched in pain, and their shirts were ripped with their skin split and the wounds still oozing blood. It looked like someone had lashed them over and over again on the same spot, creating large gaping wounds.

"You aren't healing." Through my distress, I somehow managed to state the obvious.

"This type of silver is blocking us from our change."

"You left me, Sebastian! I still can't believe you just left me at the apartment!"

"I know, and I'm sorry."

"You keep saying that, but you never do anything about it." I groaned as I stared at him, my vision clearer now that I could focus again.

"I know. And I'm very sorry. God knows how sorry I am." He fell back into his restrains, dangling in the air as if the only alternative was to give up.

"Where did you go?"

"I thought I knew who had carved those letters into Claire."

"But ...?"

"It was a trap."

"That's what Billy said before I was knocked out."

"I told Sawyer to take you home," he said with a growl.

"You always want to protect me, but you're never around to do it. And we still end up in trouble."

Sebastian pursed his lips in understanding but not wanting to confirm my statement. It was safer for him to remain silent, because he knew he had messed up. Again. The wounds on his chest stopped bleeding, but Rory's didn't; he wasn't as strong as Sebastian.

"Where are we?" I asked, wanting to change the subject. It was no use going around in circles when we were in trouble. We had to get free.

I felt for the knots that bound my hands and loosened them. Tugging one knot, I managed to free one hand and got to work loosening the other. Eventually, both hands were free. I bent over and started on the knots on each ankle.

"Once you're free, where will you go?" a deep voice with a slight Russian accent echoed from the corner on my right.

Now I know why Sebastian had kept quiet. Someone had entered the room. I froze, glancing in that direction. A man emerged from the shadows and stood in front of me. The light was behind him, so I could only see an outline of his face. My vision tunneled, then rippled as my reality abruptly shifted.

"Who are you?" I blinked and then I could see again.

"It doesn't matter who I am. Well, not yet anyway." He traced the side of my face with his index finger. His nail was sharp enough that it felt like a blade on my skin. He bent in front of me, raising his hand.

I kept my eye on his hand and watched as he sliced his fingernail-blade down my legs. I flinched, waiting for the pain or my blood to spray everywhere, but nothing happened. Instead, I could move my feet. He had freed me.

I rubbed my ankles. "What do you want with us?"

"I've been tasked with bringing the two of you to my master. That one there"—he pointed to Rory—"was just a bonus. My name is Simon. And it's time."

A door opened, and a gust of wind blew in, sending shivers down my spine. The sound of feet scraping the concrete was tedious. Eventually, a figure in a grey coat emerged. Her white eyes glowed as she stared down at me.

"Kasdeya?"

"My dear, so glad of you to drop by." She snickered and approached Sebastian and Rory.

I remembered what she had said to me that night at the dinner. *'The vampire who marked me won't be for long.'* Visions of her pulling out a blade and decapitating Sebastian shook my world as my heart dropped to my feet. The loud pounding in my ears increased as panic consumed me.

"What are you doing? No! Don't you dare touch him!" I

rose from the chair, no longer bound. I could walk faster than the witch and stepped in front of Sebastian, blocking her. "No, I won't let you touch him."

"Don't do this, Blaire," Sebastian pleaded.

"Shh."

"Simon, get her out of my way before I cut her," Kasdeya said with a threatening sparkle in her blind yet all-seeing eyes.

Simon's large hands grabbed my upper arms, and he yanked me from Sebastian. He flashed his fangs and pushed power into me. My world shook, my vision blurred, followed by thick red liquid running down the side of the walls. The floor beneath me felt soft and spongey with blood and sucked at my feet. I glanced over my shoulder, but Sebastian and Rory were no longer in the room.

Kasdeya was also gone.

It was only Simon and me.

The blood seeped through the walls faster and faster, gushing through tiny holes in the door. The levels rose. The chair I had been sitting on floated on the thick liquid. The blood noisily rushed into the room and was already up to my knees.

I was going to drown in a sea of blood.

Simon was still gripping my upper arms. The suction at my feet was pulling me into the floor. I now had my knees sucked under the floor. The blood was flowing faster as it filled the room and had now reached my hips.

Simon's hands were burning my arms. Pain shot through my veins, like a wildfire spreading up a mountain. The pressure of his tightening grip and the suction at my feet was contradicting, as I didn't know which way I could get out and free myself. I screamed as loud as I could. I had to find a way out, but first, I needed to calm down. I shoved down the panic and stopped screaming, in effect snapping me from my anxiety.

I grabbed Simon's forearms, my fingernails digging into his skin, and a smile formed on my face. I had a way to free myself and rescue Sebastian and Rory from that horrible witch. I just needed to close my eyes and concentrate hard enough and block the current world around me.

I lowered my metaphysical shield, pushed my white aura into Simon and let it go searching. My white light hovered near his heart; at first, I saw a coffin he had once been locked in but had managed to escape or was let out. It reminded me of the coffin I saw when I had helped Moonrise. Then I saw an outline of someone, and they were beating a little boy in front of Simon. Simon was crying, begging the person to stop, but they didn't. I wanted to see the face of the cruel man beating Simon's younger brother. The boy fell and couldn't get back up. Simon ran to the body on the floor and cried.

I choked up.

"No! Please stop it, Blaire. I haven't seen this memory in years. Please don't show it to me again."

When I opened my eyes, we were in Simon's childhood house with his little brother. A man who wasn't his father had beaten his brother to death. His mother lay in the corner, her neck broken, and Simon was about to be next. The man grunted as he approached Simon with a belt in his hand.

I was afraid.

It felt real enough that I tried to reach out and touch his memory.

"No!" Simon yelled, pushing me away with so much force I flew into a wall.

Butterflies and Hurricanes

In a blink, the memory was gone, the blood-soaked walls were gone, and I wasn't ass-deep in the thick maroon gore anymore. I couldn't see anyone else besides a blurry Simon and thought we were the only ones again and in another dream. Dread filled me just thinking what that witch might have done to Sebastian and Rory, but I knew I had to find them. When I could focus again, I saw a pillar ahead of me. I got to my feet and ran around it, stopping in my tracks.

Rory hung limply by the silver chains binding his hands above his head. He was motionless as blood stained his body and pooled on the ground near his feet. I couldn't comprehend what was happening or what I was seeing. Blinking back tears, I stared at the hole in his chest—the spot where his heart should be beating. Tears clouded my ability to see. My heart thumped in my chest, and blood whooshed in my ears.

Rory—my bodyguard, the man who kept me safe, who had kept me out of harm's way for six months—had his heart torn out. My chest ached as I stood there, staring in disbelief. I touched his face; he was already cold. He had been left here to die on his own. What had felt like minutes in my dream with Simon had equated to hours in the real world. Even if I had escaped sooner, it wouldn't have helped. Rory would still be dead. And no matter what powers I possessed, I couldn't save him. I couldn't heal a body so badly torn apart.

"Look at me, Blaire."

I flinched when Sebastian spoke. I hadn't even seen him when I came around the pillar; all I had seen was Rory. I choked up again when I focused on Sebastian.

"It'll be okay," he whispered sweetly and, with all the energy he had left, said, "Remember my love for you."

"Don't leave me, Sebastian."

"I'll always be with you," he said as he collapsed in his restrains. His chest still rose and fell; he was still alive, just spent.

"Stay with me, Sebastian! Stay."

"Enough of this!" I flinched when Kasdeya spoke, and placed her wrinkled sun-kissed hand on Sebastian's chest. I hadn't seen her either. Sebastian cried out the moment she touched him, and I echoed his cries.

My chest burned with fire as she tried to rip out my heart by going through Sebastian's chest, by using the mark we shared. She wanted to kill us both. I collapsed to the floor, clutching at my chest. The pain ripped through me, like lightning searing a tree.

"The bond is strong, but it's only the first mark. Once it's severed, it won't kill you." Kasdeya removed her hand from Sebastian's chest.

I could breathe again. And I heard Sebastian gasp for air.

"What do you want with us?" I sobbed once I found my breath.

"My dear, you have so much to learn." She touched my head. "And you're very important to us. We'll need you."

Her touch sent me back centuries, and I saw flashes of witches hanging by their necks, witches burning at the stake, and witches being hunted. A faint voice kept repeating poison daemon over and over. Then I saw flashes of humans dying, vampires falling to their deaths, and were-animals asleep only to never awake. These visions contained Kasdeya and empty bottles left in the deceased's hands. It had been so for all centuries. She was the daemon who specialized in poisons, the poisons that had killed so many and still killed today.

When she removed her hand from my head, I wailed. "Why, Kasdeya? Why are you killing the shifters?"

"I thought you'd be happy. It was something you've wanted for years. It has always been the powerful who prey on the weak. Century after century, the shifters have been torturing and killing my kind. Then suddenly they need us, want us to help them, to be by their side. They need us to make a potion for this and that. As if all the centuries of their torture and murder of my people didn't happen. They expect us to turn a blind eye just because they need our help now."

Without her touching me again, I saw the death of her child. And a young Sebastian.

"Sebastian, what did you do?" I said, staring up at him.

"What?" was all he managed to say.

"You killed her daughter. Esmeralda."

Realization dawned on him. He blinked wide eyes at me then at Kasdeya. "Esmeralda was centuries ago." He coughed up blood. Sucking in a deep breath, he continued hoarsely. "When times were different than they are today. Esmeralda was an evil witch who killed children. It was either her or me. I did what I had to do to protect me and my own. She lured us kids to her house in the guise of a good, beautiful witch. She was anything but a good witch." He spoke breathlessly, as if just speaking caused him more pain. "She locked us in cages after she killed and ate one of my friends. I knew the only way I could survive was to kill her."

"You tell the truth, hybrid," Kasdeya said, stepping backward. "But I must do what I've already set out to do." She placed the palm of her right hand on his chest again.

Air was sucked from my lungs. The world around me

tunneled, and I felt a crushing feeling in my ribcage as my heart contracted.

The walls that protected us crumbled, and the red floor sucked me in.

Chapter Twenty-One

I was running in the woods, searching for something. I had to find it, whatever it was. Then I remembered. My white aura was here somewhere. And I had to find it. Whatever Kasdeya did to me had wiped it out, removed it from me.

My aura.

My healing powers.

Me.

The walls that surrounded me, protected me, protected us, were gone.

Mel whispered softly to me that everything would be all right, that I was healing well, and I could wake up. I could come back to them. It was time for me to wake up.

Then there was darkness. The forest was gone.

I heard Sebastian; I felt his hands over mine, his gentle kiss at my temple. He whispered something, but I couldn't recall what he said. He sounded distant and aloof.

Darkness swallowed me again, wrapping me in its murky cocoon.

Someone whispered French words near my ear. They

sounded delicate and soothing, sending vibrations throughout my body. My arms pebbled as his words tickled down my spine. It broke me from my dark spell. I recognized Léon's voice, he whispered near my ear in a language I couldn't understand but knew it was full of tenderness and love. The hairs on my body rose as his warm breath brushed against my skin, sending delicious sensations throughout my body. And my body responded to him. He chuckled darkly, kissing me on the cheek—his warm lips on my skin. "Come back to me. I need you, *ma chérie*," he said before he left.

Neither Sebastian nor Léon came to me in my dreams. They stayed far away while I slept. And I was grateful they couldn't see me like this. The darkness surrounded me, engulfing me in the gloomy silence and smothering me in somber air.

After floating for what felt like years, I eventually came across grey ... water? clouds? soil?—not sure, but everything was grey, and the darkness still lurked nearby.

In a dark corner, a tiny spark glowed.

I found myself.

My white aura.

With a flicker of my flame, my heart beat again.

The darkness receded to where it had come from.

Even the grey was gone.

It was only the bright white light again.

It was only *me*.

Chapter Twenty-Two

My eyes fluttered open to darkness. It wasn't the darkness of my dreams or my nightmares but of a room. The lights were off, and all I heard were the beeps of the monitors. I was in a real hospital, with nurses, doctors, and bad food. A tray with food lay uneaten atop a table near my bed. The heart monitors screamed louder and infrequent.

A nurse burst through the door. "You're finally awake. Everyone was so worried about you, dear." She grabbed my hand to check my blood pressure and then my temperature. "Let me call the doctor." And she was out again.

I lay quietly, turning onto my left-hand side and faced the wall. I stared at the muted movie on the television that hung against the wall. Only the erratic sounds of the heart monitor kept me company.

Someone came through the door, out of breath. "I'm Dr. Mears. We're so glad to have you back with us." He too checked my blood pressure and my temperature. He confirmed the IV drip was still pumping me full of fluids. "You've recovered remarkably well. How are you feeling?"

"I'm fine." I really was fine—a little tired and weak but fine. "How long have I been here?"

"Three days."

I sat up. "What? Three days?"

"Yes."

"What happened?"

"You were brought here unconscious where Mel admitted you. I believe you know her."

I smiled, I was at to the same hospital where Mel worked. At least I was in good hands. "Yes, I do know Mel. Do you know what happened to me?"

"I don't know what caused your conditions, but you certainly scared everyone. Mel had to jumpstart your heart three times. But other than almost dying, we managed to stabilize you and tended to the few cuts on your body. You'll feel a little lump on your head, but, other than that, you're okay. Remarkably okay. I don't think you'll have any permanent damage. And, if all goes well tonight, you can go home tomorrow if you like."

"Great," I said, glancing at the muted advert for food. "I'm starving. Can I have some food?" I gestured at the old plate of food. "Fresh food?"

"Sure. The kitchen is closed, but I'll ask one of the nurses to get you something fresh from the canteen," he said and exited.

I lay back on the pillows, closed my eyes and tried to contact Sebastian—metaphysically. But there was nothing. I couldn't feel him, couldn't hear him. Nothing. Just a large, dark emptiness where he had once been. My chest tightened, and the heart monitors went crazy again.

The nurse ran back inside my room. Even though she was out of breath, she still managed to moan at me. "What are you doing in here? You need to relax. You've endured enough."

"Can I have my phone, or any phone?" I asked frantically.

The nurse opened the drawer and handed me my cell. "I'll be back with something for you to eat."

"Thanks," I said, dialing Sebastian's number.

"Blaire? I'm so glad to hear your voice."

Relief washed over me, and the tension in my shoulders seeped away. He was still alive. "Why can't I feel you?"

"Hold that thought. I'm coming over." And he ended the call.

I dialed Ralph's number. "Hi, Ralph. What did I miss?"

"Holy cow, you're awake. You okay?"

"Uh-huh."

"We're all good. Business is great, and there are no monsters out to kill us."

"I'm glad to hear." I smiled; it was good to hear his voice.

"And please don't rush coming back to work. Take it easy, and we'll see you next week if you're up to it."

"What day is it today?"

"Wednesday evening."

"Thanks, Ralph. I'll see you next week then."

"Get well, kid." Ralph ended the call.

A sinking feeling washed over me, followed by a cold sweat. The heart monitor made erratic noises again.

The doctor entered the room and switched off the machines. "I don't know what's going on in your head, but you need to calm down. You're way too young to give yourself a heart attack. Well, another heart attack." He removed the oximeter clip from my finger. "Someone's here to see you. Are you up for visitors?"

"Who is it?"

"Sebastian."

Damn, he was fast! "Please, I need to see him."

A few moments after Dr. Means left, Sebastian entered. The back of my throat hurt when I saw him, and I blinked back tears. I sat up and wanted to climb out of the bed.

"Stay in bed. You've been through so much." He sat on the side of the bed and wrapped his arms around me. He hesitated then kissed my temple. After a brief embrace, he let go. His stare was riddled with an expression I'd never seen before.

"What is it?" I reached for his hand. "You're scaring me."

He grabbed a chair and pushed it closer to the bed while holding my hand, then he kissed my knuckles.

"Sebastian?"

"What's the last thing you remember?"

"I don't know." I scrunched my face, deep in thought. "That witch! She was hurting you. And me."

"Anything else?"

"No." I shook my head a little too quickly and felt light-headed. "What is it?"

"Kasdeya broke my link to you."

"What?" I did one of those slow blinks, trying to process his words. "Did I hear you right? I'm no longer tied to you?" As much as I tried not to cry, a lonely tear escaped and fell down my cheek. The back of my throat hurt as I swallowed.

Sebastian gently shook his head and wiped away the tear.

"Weren't you hurt?"

"I was, but not as badly as you. When Kasdeya broke our link, you collapsed and hit your head. That gave me the energy to break free from my chains. I knocked out Kasdeya and Simon to get to you. But, when you didn't wake up, I brought you here where Mel recognized you. She had to use the defibrillator on you three times to bring you back to me." It was his turn to choke up.

More tears fell. I wiped them away with the back of my free hand. "What does this mean?" My chest tightened down on my heart, and a frown formed on my forehead. "What does it mean for you and me?"

"It means you're free of me, free from being my human servant." He smiled, but it didn't reach his eyes.

"What does this mean for us?" I whispered with a quiver in my voice. "Has it changed you? Do you still want to be with me?"

He squeezed my hand. "I don't know what this means. It's whatever you want it to be. I'm still attracted to you, if that helps." He shrugged those broad shoulders, as if to expel the weight of the world. He brought my hand to his mouth and kissed my knuckles again. "How do you feel?"

"I don't know." I didn't feel anything. Nothing for him. But ...

My gaze darted to the ceiling, and I blinked back tears —I wouldn't ugly-cry. I glanced at him again, stared at his green kitty-cat eyes, his blond hair that held the beginning of a soft curl, and I still wanted to run my fingers through it. I smiled. "I still want to touch you." I giggled. "We can see how it goes." My smile reached my eyes.

He mirrored my smile, stood up and reached for me. He cupped my face in his hands and kissed me gently enough so as not to break me. His touch was just what I was craving, and I couldn't get enough of him. His hands were all over me as he climbed onto the bed to lay beside me as we kissed. My hands touched as much of him as possible.

"When are you getting out of here?" he asked in between kisses then purred.

"Hopefully tomorrow."

"Good. I can't wait to take you home." He moved me into the circle of his arms.

I wrapped my arm around his waist, clinging to him with all my energy. I hooked my one leg over his, and we lay like that in silence until the nurse arrived with a tray of food.

"Who are you?" the nurse asked, regarding him with a frown.

"Sebastian, her boyfriend," he said with a grin.

"Oh, I didn't know she had a boyfriend. Aren't you glad she has finally woken?" The nurse said playfully, batting her eyelashes at him. Glad it wasn't just me he had that effect on.

"Yeah, very." He pulled me closer to his body and kissed the top of my head.

I could just melt in his arms.

The nurse lifted the lid, and the smell of food enticed me, forcing me to sit up. "That smells wonderful. Thank you."

The nurse brought the tray closer to the bed so I could eat. "He can stay for another ten minutes, but then he needs to leave. Visiting hours ended long ago."

"He will. And thanks again."

I had the soup and half of the roast beef sandwich then stopped eating. It was too much for me to finish. Sebastian rubbed my back while I ate, planting kisses on my shoulder, my temple, then my cheek—in that order and repeatedly.

When I was done eating, he said, "I don't want to leave you alone. Either they discharge you tonight or I stay here with you."

"I'd like either way," I replied, laying against him, nestled in his shoulder.

"Let me chat to the doctor." He climbed off the bed and left the room.

I pushed the tray to one side, glancing at the muted movie then at the door.

A few minutes passed when Sebastian and Dr. Mears entered the room like they were best friends. They were all laughs and smiles, with Sebastian squeezing the doctor's shoulder.

Sebastian gave me a thumbs up. "He'll discharge you tonight, and, if anything happens, I need to bring you back immediately. I've already signed the discharge forms."

After I dressed in the bathroom, Sebastian carried my bag as we traversed the quiet hallways of the hospital toward the exit. We passed a clock on the wall, and I saw that it was almost midnight. We approached a white Land Rover, one I'd never seen him drive before.

"I didn't know you had one of these."

"I got it today. Do you like it?"

"Yeah, it's beautiful."

We drove for a short while then entered the freeway. We passed the exit to the Labyrinth. "Sebastian, you missed the exit."

"We aren't going there tonight. I'm taking you to a special place where you'll be more comfortable." He placed my hand on his thigh and covered it with his. I closed my eyes and drifted to sleep.

When I woke, Sebastian was carrying me up a flight of stairs. "Where are we?" I asked, feeling sluggish.

"With all that you have been through, I decided to buy this place. It's out of the city, away from the monsters, and I'm the only one who knows about it. And now you know about it too. It's to keep you safe. I don't want anyone to try to hurt you again now that you're mine."

He set me on my feet at the top of the stairs. We passed a window, and I saw nothing but forest. "Where exactly are we?"

"At the edge of town, near the forest."

"Do we have any neighbors?"

"The only neighbors are miles away. We're in a very secluded area. I assure you, we're very safe here."

My stomach tightened, and I wiped my clammy hands on my pants. I didn't like not knowing exactly where I was. The forest surrounding Sterling Meadow was vast, and we could be anywhere. It's not that I didn't trust Sebastian; it was just something *different*—but, then again, he had been acting a little strange this last week. It could just be the aftereffects. And if Sebastian said we were safe, I would trust him.

Sebastian opened a door at the end of the hallway to reveal a large, newly renovated bedroom.

"Wow, you thought of everything, didn't you?"

He smiled, kissed my temple and squeezed my neck but didn't let go. He was quite possessive, but he had almost lost me, so I understood his actions. He eventually let go and closed the window blinds. "It's still dark out. Perhaps you should sleep."

"Sounds good." I kicked off my shoes and climbed under the covers, exhausted.

He climbed in behind me and kissed my temple.

After a moment, I was finally asleep.

Chapter Twenty-Three

Long bony fingers stretched in front of my face, then the hand hovered near my chest. That one long sharp nail dug into my skin until it hit my breastbone. I couldn't move, couldn't scream, couldn't do anything. When I glanced down, I saw the wound—*Venenum Daemon* carved into my chest.

I woke to an empty bed with the covers and clothing sticking to my body. "Sebastian!" I yelled. "Sebastian?" His side of the bed was empty. I pulled down my shirt to see if I still had the wound, but my chest had no carvings. I sighed with relief. It had only been a horrific dream. I climbed from the bed and used the bathroom. I couldn't remember the last time I showered, and it looked so inviting. I undressed and had a long hot shower. When I was done, with a towel wrapped around my body, I opened the dresser drawers, searching for fresh clothing. I dressed and hung the wet towel, leaving my hair damp. I tugged the bedroom door handle; it clicked but didn't open.

"Sebastian?" I yelled, banging on the door so he could hear me.

Silence.

I opened the blinds near the window, but, instead of seeing the forest or the sun, all I saw was a bricked-up window. My heart thundered in my chest, and a cold sweat washed over me. I scanned the room again; everything was new, from the bed, the bedding, side tables, a fresh coat of paint, and even the bathroom was recently renovated. The forest I saw through the window last night had been real. I'm sure I saw the trees swaying as the wind blew through them. I'm sure of it. I opened the little curtain in front of the window near the shower, and that too was bricked up.

I won't panic. I won't panic. I won't panic.

I tried the bedroom door again—still locked. I continued to yell for Sebastian while knocking and kicking on the door.

Silence.

Dammit.

I opened the window in the bedroom, placed my hand on the wall and felt the mortar between the bricks—cold and still soft. I pushed with both hands against one brick, and it slowly moved outward. My arms were burning, but I pushed through until that brick dislodged. I heard a loud thud once it hit the ground. I pressed against another brick, and it too moved out as well, with another thud as it hit the ground beside the first. Peeking through the hole I had just made, I saw the dark night and the stars. Glancing at the clock on the dresser, it read 1am. It was nighttime again, but I wasn't sure if it was the same night or the next.

The lock on the door clicked.

A gasp escaped my lips. I turned in time to watch the handle move down, and the door opened.

"You're up," Sebastian said. He went back out then reentered, holding a tray with food. "You must be hungry."

"A little ..." I stayed near the window as I watched him set the tray on a side table near the bed and sat down. "Sebastian?"

He tapped a spot on the bed beside him. "Come, sit."

I stayed put.

He raised an eyebrow and tapped the spot again.

Eventually, I approached him and sat beside him. "Why did you lock the door?" I thumbed the door behind us. "And why did you brick up the window?"

"To keep you safe. When you're done eating, you'll rest again."

"I don't want to rest. I want to get out for some fresh air."

"That'll depend on you and whether you do everything I say," he commanded, detached and mechanically.

My chest tightened; Sebastian was even more controlling than he had ever been.

He handed me a plate with a sandwich. "Eat."

I took a bite as he watched me carefully.

When I was done, he wiped my mouth with a material napkin, removed the plate from my hands and handed me a glass of water. "There. How do you feel?"

"Better ..."

"Here's your medication." He held out three tablets in the palm of his hand.

"I don't want to take any meds. I feel fine. I just need some water."

"Drink. The. Pills," he said through gritted teeth. "Doctor's orders." He smiled.

"I don't want to."

Sebastian grabbed my throat with his free hand and

squeezed, cutting my air supply. "I'm not asking, Blaire. I am telling you. Now drink them." He growled then slowly eased his grip on my throat.

I froze, my eyes widening in disbelief. I inhaled a deep shaky breath and stared at him for a heartbeat. He didn't flinch. His fiery gaze threatened to end me with one twist of his wrist. I grabbed the three tablets from his hand and swallowed them one by one, finishing the water.

He watched me drink the water and took the empty glass from my hands. "Good girl. Now get back into bed."

"But—"

"*Now!*" Sebastian grabbed my throat again and pushed me onto the bed. He let go when I started to wiggle under the covers myself.

"Good girl." Dark shadows played along his face, making him seem menacing. He collected the tray and exited the room.

What. The. Hell?

I rubbed my throat as I breathed through the pain. Whatever happened to Sebastian from drinking that tea had somehow escalated while I was unconscious the last three, four days. I didn't even know if it was still Wednesday or if it was Thursday.

He had changed so much in such a short time.

As I lay in bed, and after a few minutes, I scanned the room again, trying to take in all the details of where I was. One moment, I was staring at a picture of flowers; the next, Sebastian was above me, his body riding mine. He rocked slowly in and slowly out of me until he found his rhythm. The next moment, I was alone and lying on my side, staring at the bedside lamps then the wall. I blinked, and Sebastian was above me again, telling me how much he loved me, kissing me, licking my neck. Another slow blink and I watched as the white walls moved and slithered like snakes. A slow blink and Sebastian pushed my legs farther apart with my knees to my chest as he moved above me before climaxing.

Then there was nothing.

I woke pushing and kicking the covers off me. My chest rose and fell as I gasped for air. I sat upright, nausea threatening, and I ran to the bathroom to vomit in the toilet. Everything I had eaten had come back up until I was dry heaving. I wiped beads of sweat from my forehead, stood up off the floor, rinsed my mouth and washed my face.

When I sat on the toilet, I realized I was still wearing my underwear. Flashbacks of Sebastian washed over me, and panic settled within my bones. But somehow, I knew they were only flashbacks. Sebastian would never take advantage of me like that.

I heard the door open and click shut.

A knot formed in the pit of my stomach. I hurried on the toilet, washed my hands and stood in the bathroom's doorjamb.

"Sleep better?"

"Yes," I lied, nodding quickly. I didn't care if he sensed the deceit in my voice.

One side of his mouth curved upward. "*Riiiight* ... Come, let's go for that walk I promised you." He extended his hand to me.

At first, I hesitated, but the glare in his eyes was a warning. I pulled on the shoes that were there, took the hand he offered and followed him out the room and down the stairs.

Once outside, we stepped over the two bricks I had pushed out of the wall, but he didn't say anything about them. We walked to the edge of the forest in silence then stopped near a fallen tree. He sat and pulled me down to sit on his lap, his arms possessively around my waist. We sat like that for a while, in silence and enjoying the fresh air of the night. It was quiet.

It was too quiet.

No sounds came from the forest, nothing from the sky apart from the twinkling stars.

"When we get back to the house, can I have my phone?" I asked nervously.

"You already have everything you need. Why do you need your phone?"

I swallowed hard. "I need to phone Ralph. I'm sure he's worried sick that I haven't called him back." I lied again.

"No need to. I've already spoken with him. He knows you're safe."

I opened my mouth to say something but closed it again and frowned. "Sebastian …?"

"Yes?" He gave me his full attention, that warning from earlier still gleaming in his eyes.

"What are you doing?"

He shrugged. "I don't know what you mean."

"You're forcing me to do things I don't want to do. And you're stopping me from doing what I want and when I want to do it. I'm not some princess you can keep locked up in a tower and deny me things."

"You are *mine*, Blaire, and all I want to do is keep you *safe*. And this is how you repay me?"

Something caught my attention as it scurried in the distance. A creature in the forest—how I wished it would take me away. "I'm not ungrateful. Thank you for everything. But if I want to phone someone or go somewhere, you can't stop me."

He considered this carefully, giving me the full weight of his glare.

Butterflies and Hurricanes

Whatever was moving in the darkness of the forest got closer. "Sebastian, something is out there."

"I don't hear anything."

Leaves rustled nearer. I rose to my feet to see what it was. How could he not hear that? Whatever it was, it was loud.

Darkness moved and edged toward me.

Something grabbed me from behind, and I was airborne. The tree we were sitting on grew smaller the higher we ascended. Glancing up, I saw Sebastian behind me.

"I didn't know you could fly," I said, surprised.

He didn't answer me. Instead, we went higher until all I could see were the lights of our house and the surrounding lights from other houses miles away. We stayed airborne for a heartbeat, then we descended and landed on the roof of the house.

"What's going on, Sebastian? You're frightening me."

He didn't answer. He grabbed my hand with care, and we walked across the roof and entered the house through an open window on the far side of the house. I climbed in after Sebastian and froze. We were in a nursery. White bedding covered the cot, with light yellow walls. Sebastian pulled my arm to walk beside him.

"What's going on, Sebastian?" I halted and snatched my hand free of his. "I'm not going anywhere until you start speaking to me."

The door flung open, and Léon entered.

"Léon?"

"Get away from him, Blaire."

I sidestepped away from both of them. Why were the brothers fighting? Léon growled at Sebastian.

"*What's going on?*" I yelled, backing away from them until I hit the far wall.

Léon's eyes glowed a soft blue as stars clouded over them. He hissed at Sebastian, whose eyes glowed red. Which I found strange; why red?

"This isn't Sebastian, Blaire."

"What? What do you mean it's *not him*?"

"What were you planning on doing with her during the day? You didn't think about that, did you?" Léon questioned.

Sebastian leapt in the air and hit Léon so hard I heard bones break. Their fighting was too fast for my slow human eyes. I heard cries, more bones breaking, flesh tearing, and blood splattered over the white crib. I scampered to the far corner so I was out of their way.

Léon crashed onto the crib, splintering it.

It was my only chance; I ran for the door. As I left the room, something crashed into me, and I hit the hallway wall. Pain thumped against my skull from the impact. Red eyes glowed in my face, and sharp fangs edged near my neck, and he bit down. He moaned in the bite, vibrating my bones. When I moved, his fangs tore through my flesh, and I cried out in pain. All I could do was lay still and wait for him to finish, but could he stop in time? Would he stop before killing me?

Time didn't slow down for us like it had last time. There wasn't anything special about Sebastian's bite this time. His bite was quick but painful.

"Oh, I should have done this sooner. You taste so good, Blaire." Sebastian purred once he unhooked his fangs from my skin. He licked the bite wound, climbed off me and extended a hand.

I ignored it and stood on my own, using the wall as my

aid. I kept eye contact with him though. I didn't want to take him out of my sight.

He licked the blood from his lips and smiled mischievously. "Delicious!"

I was numb as I stared at him. "You said you wouldn't do that to me again."

Still smiling, he replied, "But you don't understand, Blaire. I'm not who you think I am."

I swallowed hard. "What do you mean?"

"That's what I've been trying to tell you," Léon said when he reached the door, the wounds on his pale chest already knitting together as he healed. "That's not Sebastian. It's Simon."

I gasped. The memory was clear, and I took another step away from Simon.

Simon tilted his head backward and laughed as he slowly morphed from Sebastian to his own face to Sebastian's then back to his own face. It was fucking freaky.

Then I remembered. When I had first met Simon, I couldn't see his face properly because the light was behind him. Now I saw him clearly—his brown hair and eyes, a nondescript face, and he was just as tall as Sebastian. I remembered how he had gripped me after he had cut my legs loose then had altered my reality, the blood pouring out the walls and the soft floor sucking me under. But he had held onto my arms to change my reality that time.

"I don't understand. How could you change into Sebastian without having to touch me this time?"

He stepped closer to me. "I too am a hybrid—a skinshifter. Except it's not an animal I can change into but other humans."

I moved backward until I bumped into a table near the stairs, noting its contents.

Simon lunged forward.

I grabbed the vase from the table and smashed it against his head.

Léon yanked him off me before he could bite me again. "No! Get away from her!" Léon hit Simon with his left fist, then his right. He pounded Simon, pushing his power into his knuckles so with each hit, the force that collided with Simon's face was so great that no identifiable facial features remained. Simon's face was a bloody, gory mess; his eyes bulged, ready to fall out his sockets; his jaw was broken and hanging on his chest, with his nose and cheeks split apart.

The violence Léon exhibited startled me. I'd only known him as someone who oozed pleasure with his soft velvety voice and caressing touches. Now, he was frightening to watch and incredibly dangerous.

"Léon, stop. He's dead!" I tried to pry his hand off Simon's lifeless body.

Léon hissed at me, his blue eyes glowing. But he continued hitting Simon over and over again until his face was a pulp. He eventually stopped and stepped backward, his fists dripping red. "That was for what he did. He deserved it. We need to remove his head and heart."

"We can't. What about the Vampire Council?"

Through a low growl, he said, "This was self-defense." He pulled a blade from his pocket and handed it to me. "You need to do it."

"What?" I cried out, shaking my head side to side.

"You need to do *this*!"

"No."

"You must, *ma chérie*." His now gentle and velvety voice caressing my cheeks and neck. That's what he had called me when I had been in the hospital. He had never called me by a pet name before. Why was he starting now?

I gasped when he pushed the blade closer to my face. With a shaky hand, I grabbed the blade from him and knelt near Simon's lifeless body.

"Take his heart."

I flinched at his words and wiped tears from my face. "I can't."

"You have to! Do it now. Cut a hole in his abdomen and go under his ribcage. It's the only way. You can't break his breast bones with that blade."

I closed my eyes, exhaled and lifted his bloody shirt. I sliced the soft tissue of his abdomen near his diaphragm on the left side of his chest. Dark blood oozed out. With a shaky hand, I entered his body. Soft, warm tissue enveloped my hand, and I gagged. I swallowed hard and soldiered through his body until I was in his ribcage.

"Faster, before he starts to heal!"

I flinched when Léon spoke again and wiped away tears with the back of my free hand. "Stop yelling at me! Just give me a second." I exhaled and went to my dark place—the place that's only mine, a place I went to when I needed to do something I didn't like. I pushed my hand through the warm, soft meat under his ribs until I found that large muscle that hadn't beat in years.

As I gripped it, it spasmed in my hand, and I screamed. His heart throbbed in my grasp.

"Do it now, Blaire. He's healing and about to wake up."

Simon moved.

I watched in silence as his face started to heal. His jaw popped into place, and his muscles knitted together to form a semblance of a face.

I held onto that large pulsing muscle and pulled.

Simon's bulging eyelids fluttered open, and he screamed.

I screamed back at him and yanked his heart. I pulled so

hard I fell backward and hit the wall, his black heart still in my hands—still beating from my touch.

In between sobs, Léon crouched beside me and kissed the top of my head. "We're almost done, *ma chérie*. Let's burn the place and get out of here."

I nodded, not trusting my voice just yet. If I spoke now, I would break down.

Simon's dead brown eyes stared at me, his body lifeless as it should be. I gagged, dropped his heart and ran into an open room I thought was the bathroom, but it was another child's room. It was too late to look for a bathroom, so I grabbed the dustbin as bile and spittle came out.

Léon came in behind me and handed me a wet washcloth to wipe my face. "Are you okay?"

"No! Why did you make me do that?"

"Because that's who you are. You kill the monsters. And this one would hurt you in ways you couldn't imagine. If you didn't do something to kill him, he would've kept coming after you until he consumed you." He stood back to give me some space, to let his words sink in.

"But you could've just done it yourself! Why make *me* do it at all?"

"Because, Blaire, it would be something you would regret not doing."

Chapter Twenty-Four

I lit the match and threw it on the wooden floor doused with an accelerant. The fire spread through the open front door and consumed the house within minutes, with the vampire's body still upstairs.

I stood two feet from Léon, the heat from the blaze caressing one side of my face. "What happened, Léon? Where's Sebastian? Why isn't he here instead of you? The last thing I remembered was Rory hanging limply in those silver chains, and that witch had her hand on Sebastian's chest."

"They're dead," he said with misty eyes. His usual dark blue eyes were drowning in soulless black as his vampiric powers flared to the surface.

"What? I don't understand." I wiped my eyes dry. "You must be mistaken. Sebastian is alive."

"He's not, *ma chérie*. My bond with him has splintered. Not even Salvador can feel him."

For the first time since knowing Léon, his emotions were raw on his face. The pain inside his heart was clearly visible. As I stared at him, in that second, my world crushed into dust. The ache I had felt was real, and the hole Sebastian had left grew bigger and was not healing. The man I had just shared my heart and soul with was gone.

I shook my head in disbelief as the tears fell.

I didn't want to believe it.

I refused to accept it. "No. There must be another way."

He remained silent as crimson tears streaked his cheeks. I ran into his outstretched arms and held onto him, as the man I loved was no longer with us. It bonded Léon and me as we shared the loss and heartache, comforting each other in our time of mourning.

"Our Sebastian is gone, *ma chérie*. That witch took him from us," He said softly with malice.

"I need to see his body. I won't believe it until I've seen it. Please take me to see him," I whimpered into his chest.

He squeezed me. "There was no body left for us to find."

"But you found Rory's."

"Yes."

"Then where's Sebastian's body?"

He shrugged.

"No, his body must be there. We need to go back and find it."

"It's not there. We searched. They took his body with them after they killed him."

"How do we find his body then? If they took it, and Simon is dead, how do we find it?"

"I do not know."

I shook my head. "How …" Something didn't make sense; how did Léon even know where to find me. "How did you find me?"

"Your earrings. Sebastian installed a GPS tracker into them."

I smiled halfheartedly. Sebastian, in his possessive way, had saved my life. But it wasn't worth anything if I didn't have him in my life. I wrapped my arms around Léon's waist, burying my face against his chest and crying until nothing was left.

I felt a hiccup-like jostle of his own chest as we cried together. Standing in Léon's embrace, his heart beating against my face, and he was warm beneath my touch. I realized the vampire who had shifted into Sebastian had been cold when I had held his hand and when he had held me in the hospital. And he'd had no heartbeat. I was too hurt to notice these differences. If I had realized this sooner, none of this would've happened. We could've stopped him and questioned him about Sebastian. We could've found his body before it was too late.

A weight pulled on my chest, and bile formed in the back of my throat again. I swallowed hard as I clung to Léon. "What happened to Kasdeya?"

"Her body was there. We think Sebastian killed her before Simon killed him and took his body. I'm not sure exactly what happened."

"How did he know where I …"

"What?" Léon broke the embrace to look at me.

"I phoned Sebastian's phone. That's how Simon knew I was awake in hospital. No wonder he was there so quickly. He was waiting for me to phone Sebastian."

"He must've taken Sebastian's phone after …" I choked up again. "Tell me everything please. I feel like I'm missing something."

Léon played with my hair to try and comfort me. He spoke softly and sweetly as one would when breaking the worst kind of news. "You were unresponsive when we found you. We brought you to the hospital where Mel shocked your heart a few times and admitted you. When your bond with Sebastian was broken, your heart suffered. But I'm sure your head will be strong enough to help you move forward. I had just lost Sebastian, and I was so afraid I would lose you too. When you were stable, they allowed us to visit you often. Each of us took turns to sit with you, talk with you, whisper to you."

That last part swirled around me and caressed the side of my face not pressed against his chest.

"When the doctor called the Labyrinth's main phone to say you were awake, I rushed over. But by then, you were already gone. The nurse and doctor said Sebastian had checked you out. That's when I realized someone else was still involved."

"And you tracked me again by using the GPS in the earrings."

"Yes."

"So I wasn't gone long?"

"No. Only a few hours."

"He made it feel as though I was here for days."

"He could alter reality. He was powerful. And I did not know he was a skin-shifter though. It's not common for a vampire to be."

The heat from the blazing house comforted me to know Simon was busy burning inside and wouldn't be hurting anyone anymore. The roof finally collapsed, shooting sparks everywhere. We stepped backward to avoid our clothing from catching alight.

Sawyer arrived in Sebastian's Jeep, with a passenger.

"Who's with Sawyer?"

"Your new personal bodyguard."

I squinted to see what he looked like. "Okay, thanks."

"Don't thank me, thank Lance. He's paying for Marc's services."

"Oh, why?"

"When he heard of Rory and Sebastian's passing, he insisted on helping. It's also great for our alliances to have were-rats from Chicago on our side."

I hated politics, but, from what I gathered, Lance's rats were excellent at what they did, and they had the numbers. Nobody would want them as enemies, so to have them as allies was great for us.

"I'm sure you approve."

Léon smirked. "Yes, of course."

"What happened to Derick?"

"He was killed at *Jenny's Trapeze and Dine*. Luckily, they only knocked Sawyer unconscious when they took you."

"Why was all this done, Léon? Why so many deaths?" I asked, choking up again. But all my tears were dry; all I had left was a pain in my chest.

"That's what we need to find out. But I swear to you, we will figure it out."

When the Jeep stopped, we climbed in the back seat. I greeted Sawyer, and Léon introduced me to Marc. He seemed to be of similar height to Sawyer, his blond hair shaved into a brush cut, with blue eyes and a square jaw. He was wide in the shoulders, with tattoo sleeves covering both arms.

"Ma'am, it's a privilege to work with you, and I'll do whatever's required to keep you safe."

"Umm, thanks, Marc. Just one thing, please don't call me ma'am."

"Sure."

The corners of my mouth curved upward. "And don't get yourself killed."

The drive back was uneventful—thank heavens. I didn't think I could handle anything else. When we reached the Labyrinth, Sawyer parked the Jeep in the garage, and we all climbed out. We went through the various hallways that shifted every twelve hours until Léon stopped outside Sebastian's room.

"I don't think I can stay here, Léon," I said.

"Would you like to stay in my room?"

I nodded. "I don't want to sleep alone though. Can you stay with me?"

He reached for my hand. "Come."

After I showered, I perused the pile of clothing Léon had brought for me from Sebastian's room. I recognized one of Sebastian's sleep shirts and pulled it on. I lifted the collar to my nose to smell him and tears fell again. I didn't want to lose his scent. I wanted to bottle it and be able to take it out whenever I craved him.

I dried my eyes, brushed hair and teeth and climbed under the satin covers while Léon showered. Just as I was about to fall asleep, Léon slid behind me and pulled me into his arms. I clung to him as we lay there, the loss we shared binding us closer. I listened to his breathing and tried to relax, to expel the dreadful events from my mind.

Flashbacks of Simon shot across my vision—first of the bloody walls dragging me to Hell, then Simon morphing into Sebastian and sneering at me. I woke with a jolt and whimpered.

"Shh, *ma chérie*. I can't push power into you like Sebastian could, but I'm here for you. I'm not going anywhere."

I nodded into his chest, listening to his rhythmic breathing, and appreciated that he was doing that to comfort me.

Chapter Twenty-Five

Léon was an absolute gentleman. His arms were snug around me while I tried to sleep. When I moved, he gave me space, and, once I settled down, he held me again. That little bit of comfort knowing he was there holding me made my heart burst with love. But it wasn't Sebastian's arms around me. A constant ache burned in my chest as I kept drifting off to sleep, and all I saw was Sebastian—his touch, his soft lips on mine, his green eyes, even his possessive nature of late.

Perhaps it was the poisoned tea he drank or the next steps in our relationship, I wasn't sure. But I knew he really cared for me, enough so that he didn't want any harm to come to me. He had been so concerned that he had installed a GPS into the beautiful earrings he gifted me.

I whimpered as quietly as I could. Although I was sure Léon could hear me, but he didn't act on my cries. He just let me be.

Our last date was still fresh in my mind—how Sebastian held me while we ice skated, how I flew in the air then he grabbed onto my ankles. A smile spread across my face, and I snuggled into Léon's chest. Again, it was not Sebastian, but it was comforting.

After about two hours of moving from one side to the other, I told Léon we should just get up. I knew day was breaking, and then he would be dead for the day. I didn't want to wake up next to a corpse, cold and alone.

He asked a guard to get me some breakfast. When it arrived, he sat and watched me eat. I had one or two bites of the egg and pushed the rest around on my plate.

"You need to eat, *ma chérie*."

"I know," I whispered, avoiding his soul-piercing stare.

"At least finish one egg."

I forked some egg into my mouth and chewed it for a really long time before swallowing. I could tell Léon was struggling to ask me something, so I stared at him while I sipped my coffee, waiting for his question.

"Do you feel like talking to me about what happened at that house of horrors?" Léon finally asked, watching me carefully as if I was about to break.

I blinked back tears, taking my time before I was ready to speak. I took another sip of coffee, sucked in some air then gave him a short version of what I could remember. Adding that Simon had given me medication and that I had been so out of it I had lost time or because Simon could manipulate time—or rather, reality—he had made it feel like time was slipping through my fingers.

It all felt strange still, especially since Léon had rescued me the same evening the hospital had discharged me. I even told him about the weird dream I had of Sebastian and I making love. I wanted to cringe while discussing Sebastian and me in that way, but it didn't seem to bother him. Léon was quiet for a really long time, and that made me nervous. "What are you thinking?" I finally asked.

"I'm sorry I can't be with you today. But, when I wake this evening, we can spend more time together. If you like."

I nodded. "I'd like that."

"What will you do while I sleep?"

"I need to find Billy. I'm sorry, but I can't just hang around all day waiting for you. I know I need to mourn Sebastian, but his death cannot be in vain. I need to find out why all this happened. Once everything is over, then we could take a day to show Sebastian how much we loved and cared for him."

"I know, and I'm grateful for what you're going to do. While you were in the bathroom, I called Ralph. He's on his way here. You'll need all the help you can get. And chat with Sawyer. He and Marc have been speaking to all the monsters in town to find out about Simon and Kasdeya. They have spoken with me already but they can provide you with more information."

"Thanks, Léon. I will." I appreciated his foresight, his tenderness, and caring nature.

If the only thing I did today was to find Billy, then I'd be happy. I needed to understand why this had to happen.

I glanced at the sun as heat fell against my face. I sucked in the cool air and exhaled until my lungs were completely empty before inhaling again. Today would be a good day. It had to be. Come Hell or high water, I would make it a good day.

Sawyer reversed the Jeep out of the garage and left it idling while we waited for Ralph. I heard his car and climbed in behind Sawyer's seat while we waited. Ralph parked, cut the engine, locked his car and climbed in beside me.

"Morning."

"How are you holding up?" Ralph asked, covering my hand with his and squeezing it tightly.

"Fine."

Marc ended his phone call and turned to me. "There have been reports of Billy sightings, which means he's still in the city. All the were-animals are banding together to locate him."

Sawyer pulled the Jeep onto the road.

"Thanks, Marc," I said.

Sawyer added, "With the WAA community scared because of that serum and of Sebastian's death, everyone is pulling together and looking for that were-rat." He glanced at Marc. "No offense, dude."

"None taken. I know we'll get him. It's not a matter of *if*, but *when*," Marc answered with glowing red eyes.

Something tugged on my stomach when I saw Marc's eyes. I flinched when Ralph squeezed my hand again.

"You okay?"

"I'm fine, just a little jumpy, I guess."

"Are you sure you're okay to be doing this today?"

I nodded.

He pulled me close to his body and held me tightly. "With the vampire and Kasdeya gone, the only loose end is Billy. We'll find him."

"Do you know about everything?"

"Yes, Léon explained it all to me when he called. I'm to be your teddy bear when you need a hug, or your guns when you need to kill something."

I laughed at him. "Thanks, Ralph. I needed that." To

the other two, I said, "Léon told me either of you could give me more information about Kasdeya and Simon."

Sawyer spoke while he drove. "While you were sleeping beauty, I spoke with some of the older, more experienced witches. At first, they were very reluctant to say anything, as you can imagine, but, after I explained everything, some of them softened up and told me Kasdeya was known within all the covens as the poison daemon. For centuries, she had worked on various types of potions and had killed wereanimals and vampires alike. But, these potions took a very long time to kill them. Apparently, it was her sick and twisted way of getting retribution at everyone for the years of abuse the witches had experienced at their hands and for the death of her daughter. But what she forgot was why some witches were burned at the stake or hung by their necks to begin with. Before everyone came out of the shadows and into the human world, no laws or rules governed them. And they basically did what they wanted. It wasn't like it is today, where the covens manage their own. Back then, it was each to his own, and they did vile and ghastly things. Assassins, such as yourself—or any of the monsters, really—would usually take out witches.

"Anyway, it was Kasdeya who gave Melinda the poison. She confirmed it when we showed her a picture of Kasdeya. In Kasdeya's eyes, she hoped Melinda would drink it and die a slow and painful death, that it would be one less shifter to worry about. But Melinda was a scientist. She tweaked it so it would make her animal dormant. Kasdeya and Simon found out what Melinda was up to and asked Billy for Melinda's work. But, because Billy was afraid the lions could smell him, he got Jones to get it from Melinda while she was locked in a cage. That is what was injected into Lance when Billy fought him. This version of the poison just stopped Lance from shifting and healing himself. Melinda was close to a breakthrough, but, it was still killing Lance—until you healed him. Melinda also shared with us, that she formulated another part of the poison that could speed up the process. It was this part that Kasdeya *really* wanted, so it could be used in those darts to kill were-animals from afar and at a much quicker rate, not forgetting the tea they also had made, which Sebastian drank. It was the same tea that had hurt Moonrise, but somehow it didn't hurt Sebastian as much as it had hurt her, and he wasn't dying from it." Sawyer's voice fell to a whisper when he said, "Although, it did drive him crazy enough to almost hurt you."

"How did the witches come to know all this?"

"Even though Kasdeya was bat-shit crazy, she still asked some witches for advice. Unfortunately, none of them tried to talk her out of her madness."

"Did any of them know why she was doing this?"

"From what I gather, for Kasdeya, it was her madness for revenge. For Simon, it was pure power."

"Léon never mentioned any of this to me. Did he say anything when he heard all this?"

"We only just informed Léon. Obviously he was glad they were dead. With Simon and Kasdeya gone, we only have to find Billy, and then hopefully it's over."

"And Shannon? What did he say? Kasdeya supported him at the dinner. How close was he to her?"

"She did some work for him, but he had no idea what she was conniving with Simon. Léon and Shannon knew Simon, but they obviously didn't condone his behavior. Léon has notified the council, and they'll send word about any repercussions for us burning him."

"Do you think we'll be in trouble?"

"No, we'll be fine."

"How can you be so sure?"

Sawyer grinned. "'Cause I am."

"Fine. Where's the serum now?"

"The only place we haven't checked yet is Kasdeya's place. Perhaps we should do that now."

"Great idea. Let's go," I said, resting my head on Ralph's shoulder.

Kasdeya's cottage sat alone on a large piece of land near one of the malls, surrounded by residential houses. The land was fenced with electricity, but I doubted it was on, as the front gate stood open when we pulled up the driveway. Either someone had left in a hurry, or they were still there.

The outside walls of her cottage were painted white, with a thatched roof. A full garden thrived out front, with a small vineyard that grew near her cottage.

I was feeling slightly better when we stopped; my mind had something else to focus on.

We climbed out the Jeep and approached the front door while Marc went around back to ensure no one ambushed us. When the front door opened, Marc smiled at us. "It's just us."

I was relieved that it was just us, but, at the same time, I was saddened because I had hoped Billy was here. The first thing I saw as we entered was vines similar to the ones outside. They crisscrossed throughout the front part of the house on the high ceiling and against the walls. Little potted plants sat on shelves that stretched against the walls encircling what I could only imagine to be her kitchen. The kitchen was not a typical kitchen for houses but a fiery pit in the middle of the room with a table, pots, vials of liquids, and a variety of other items scattered about the room. To one side was a short hallway that branched to a bathroom and two rooms.

The interior reminded me of a homemade greenhouse, except it featured weird plants I had never seen before. The little potted plants were strange looking; one seemed to be a Venus fly trap, but it only contained one *trap* that opened its mouth when I moved my hand in front of it then closed again when my hand went away—as if it sensed heat, my hand, or it was just after blood. Another plant was purple and seemed to dance when we walked near it. If I had to think about it, they all seemed *alive* and *aware* that we were here.

"Um, guys, I don't think we should touch any of these plants," I said, standing near the window where at least four pots sat on the sill and turned to face the sun. Yep, they were definitely *alive*.

"I think we should torch the place," Ralph said, looking above the fire pit. A large pot sat over the fire, held by a metal rod that extended from the ceiling. "This place is where nightmares come from." He shuddered as he lifted the lid from the large pot. He dropped the lid onto the pot and pinched his nose. "Ah, I should've known the smell was coming from this pot. Just don't open it again."

"Maybe that's the potion that's been killing the were-animals." I lifted the pot lid and picked up the ladle that was hooked on the inside of the pot. I swished around the liquid and lifted the ladle with some of the goo. It was green and the smell indescribable; it was sour, rotten, bitter, with a hint of foul breath.

"Does it smell like the rot you smelled when the were-animals were attacked? When Shawn and Corey fought?" I asked as I continued stirring the green stuff.

"Yeah, that death whiff is familiar," Sawyer replied as he exited a bedroom. "Nothing's in there except her clothing and bedding. I think all her witchy stuff is out here."

Ralph nodded. "Yeah, it smells like the stuff. And a dry green substance is on the table over there."

I put the lid on the pot and had a look at the dry substance on the table. "Maybe that's how they made the tea. See?" I pointed to dry leaves that resembled tea. "Should we take some of this stuff and have Mel test it, or should we just destroy it all?"

"Well, in my opinion, I don't want anyone to be able to replicate it. I say destroy it all," Ralph said.

I nodded in agreement.

Marc came through the front door, holding a canister. "Let's torch it now."

The four of us stood outside and watched the little house burn. They wanted to leave soon thereafter, but I wanted to wait a bit longer. I wanted to ensure nobody could save anything from that witch's house of horrors.

Sirens wailed in the background. Ralph pulled my arm to get me into the Jeep. Once I climbed inside and Sawyer pulled away, I kept watching the inferno. The roof collapsed, and a cloud of smoke rose into the air. This was my second fire in two days; I liked the idea of permanently destroying something with hot flames.

Nothing would be left, except the book in my hand.

Sawyer drove me to the bank where I had a second safety deposit box. The witch's book would be kept there. With it tucked under my arm, I inserted the key into the little hole, turned and slid out the large metal box. I carried the box to a private area, locking the door behind me, and placed the box on the table. I opened the lid, moved the three jewels to one side and placed the book beside them. I closed the lid, locked it with a second lock and key then returned it to its original spot for safe keeping.

When I climbed into the Jeep, Sawyer turned to me. "Anne wants us to come over right away."

"Why?"

"She has good news."

"Great! Let's go."

My mouth gaped open. Billy was bound, beaten, bruised, and still bleeding. Jeremiah, the nineteen-year-old were-leopard I'd met a couple of months ago, stood behind Billy. He was ensuring Billy couldn't do or say anything unless he wanted him to. Greg, Anne's son, paced in the corridor while Ivy sat on a chair in the kitchen. Anne stood beside me. Some type of tension hung in the air, but I couldn't understand why. We had Billy; this was good, yet they seemed to emanate something else.

"How?" I asked through the silence.

"He crossed into our territory," Anne said. "We suspect he was running away from others when Jeremiah detected his scent while he was hunting and brought him to us."

I glanced at Jeremiah. "By yourself?"

Jeremiah eyed me with that typical boyish expression that

told me *he was the man*. One side of his mouth curled upward, his soft brown curls framing his cheeks, and baby-blue eyes gleamed with mischief. The last time I'd seen him, he was soft around the middle; now he was all muscle, standing in the living room wearing only shorts and sneakers. His face wasn't as round or as soft as before; he was becoming a young man. And, from what I could tell, a dangerous one.

Apart from Jeremiah seeming to be happy about what he had done, I was still concerned about Greg and Ivy's tension—or whatever they were grappling with. I glanced from one to the other. Greg wouldn't meet my eyes as he paced, and Ivy stared out the window.

"What's wrong with your children, Anne?"

"They're worried about Sebastian. We know his bond with you was broken, and even Léon can't sense him anymore. But we don't think he's dead."

That made me turn to meet her gaze with a frown matching hers. "How so?"

"What he went through should have killed him, but I suspect the only reason why he isn't dead is because he has the best of both worlds, and that makes it harder to kill him. But we can still feel him. He's out there, Blaire, and we need to find him."

"If Léon or Salvador can't feel him, why would you be different?" I asked. I sounded angry and defensive, even though what I felt was much more than that. I didn't want to get my hopes up based on their so-called feelings. It was impossible for Sebastian to have survived what he went through. All his bonds were broken; he was stripped bare. He was forcefully removed from everybody's lives. Even if he was alive, where was he?

"It's hard to explain to someone who hasn't shifted into

one of us, but our leopards know his leopard is still alive. Our leopards are searching for his."

"You're right, I don't understand. How can any of that happen?" Perhaps I should let my leopard out of her cave, so she could look for him.

"Our leopards roam free in the metaphysical realm. When we meet our destined mate and our leopards meet for the first time, our holy bond takes place. And we mate for life. It's also in this metaphysical world where the leap comes together once a month when the moon is at its fullest, and we hunt together. We're all our spirit animal, and, when we're together, we all form as one unit. When one of us dies, so does the leopard, and that leopard becomes one with the leap. Sebastian isn't dead, because his leopard is still out there. Still roaming. His leopard hasn't joined the leap."

Tears streamed down my cheeks without warning. I couldn't stop the flood of emotions. If what Anne had said was true, then he really was out there. My Sebastian was still alive.

Anne embraced me, and I held onto her tiny frame while I sobbed onto her shoulder. After a few minutes, my tears subsided, and I let go of her.

Both Ivy and Greg were near us, neither of them with dry eyes. Ivy offered a box of tissues. I hadn't heard them approach. When I glanced at Anne, her face was red and marked with her own tears. In our contact, we both shared a language that couldn't be taught. In our hearts, we knew he was still alive. I had to have faith. But I also didn't want to be crushed knowing we were wrong. My mind was pulling me in different directions, which made me feel helpless.

Someone cleared their throat.

We all glanced at Billy, and I wanted to remove that smirk off his face. He was healing. I glanced at Jeremiah; he too had shed a tear. But now that we were all back in the now, Jeremiah hit the back of Billy's neck so hard it snapped, and his head lulled to the side. He stared at us with wide eyes, surprised by the hit.

"Don't hit him again, Jeremiah. I need information," I chastised.

"You have ten minutes, Blaire. Afterward, he's dead."

"Don't worry. I'll kill him myself."

Jeremiah wanted to say something, but Anne shook her head. She must've known I wanted to kill him myself and would allow it. Just like I was grateful that Léon allowed me to kill Simon, even though at the time, I didn't want to.

I approached Billy. Even though his neck was broken, the bastard was strong enough to remain alive. He watched me with careful eyes as I neared. I crouched and cupped his loose-hanging head. "Speak, Billy. If you have any ounce of a heart left in that dark cavity of yours, you'll tell us everything."

Billy closed his eyes, and that condescending smirk spread across his face.

"You once had a best friend, Billy. What happened that you wanted to hurt Lance so much?"

He snorted.

"Was it because he became *your* king? Were you jealous of him?"

Billy's smirk faded, and I felt his neck knit together as he healed. His head straightened while I still cupped his face.

"He was my best friend. We used to share everything until the moment he became king. Then, when he started treating me like one of his pawns and the love of my life left me, that was the last straw."

"Mandy?" I asked, taking a chance.

He squeezed his eyes shut as if trying to expel a memory. I let go of his face when his neck had completely healed. He opened his honey-colored eyes, unshed tears glistening in the light.

I pulled up a chair and sat next to him, my left knee touching his. "Mandy seemed very much in love with Lance. You cannot blame it all on Lance."

"You're right. I drove her to him with my behavior." His expression went from sadness to stone-cold hate as he leered at me.

"Lance had said you worked for the competition. Did that not happen?"

"It did. We drifted apart before he became king, and I guess I just hung out with the wrong crowd."

"Why hurt the shifters?" I whispered. "Get it off your chest, so you may go in peace." He wouldn't live another day; today was his end. But he could at least go knowing he gave us the information we needed to move forward.

"I'd worked with Simon before, and he asked me to help him again. He was a sick bastard. I know you've had the pleasure." He stared at me for a heartbeat.

The memory of Simon impersonating Sebastian sent chills down my spine.

"When the Vegas wolf pack expelled Corey and he came here, Simon asked him to do a few odds and ends for him. When he heard Melinda had improved on Kasdeya's poison, he asked me to retrieve it. That's when we got Jones to get it for us. Simon wanted to use that potion on the were-animals as a control mechanism and rival Shannon and Léon. Then, when everyone was scared, he wanted to produce the anti-serum and come across as the hero. That's when it all snowballed." He shook his head as if he regretted his actions, which I doubted. "But Simon worked for someone. We never knew who though. He was scared enough of this person not to tell us who it was. Him killing the shifters was just a game to him, a thrill. He enjoyed the control and power of it. But whoever he worked for ..." He hesitated as he stared at Anne then glanced back at me. "She's right, you know. Sebastian isn't dead. They need him."

My frown deepened. "Why? What do they want with him?"

"He's a hybrid, a very powerful hybrid. He's old, has the best of both shifter and vampire world, and he is a day walker. Think about it. If someone had his blood, his DNA, what could they achieve?" His honey-colored eyes darkened.

"They're using him. They're running tests." My stomach sank to my feet, and I was nauseated. The memories of the voodoo priest hit my chest, and, in my heart, I knew they were busy damaging Sebastian. Whatever they had done to Ophelia and Ross, they were doing to Sebastian as well. "Are they creating their own monsters?"

"Precisely."

Someone gasped behind me, but I couldn't look away. I needed to stare into his eyes to see if he was lying, but he didn't flinch. He was telling the truth.

"How do you know all this?"

"Simon was a constant complainer. Jeez, he was worse than the bitches at *Dirty Chains*. He didn't like that he wasn't included in his boss's secrets or plans. But he discovered something about what his boss was working on and mentioned part of it to me once then never again. I got the suspicion that whoever his master was had powers we couldn't even imagine possessing. He somehow shut up Simon. Anyway, he continued poisoning the shifters and started cleaning house; got rid of Claire and anyone else who might know about the poison. Then he wanted you." His expression softened. "He secured Sebastian for his boss in exchange to keep you."

A yelping sound escaped my lips as I sat back in my chair so hard it knocked the wind from my lungs.

"Yeah, I thought you might like that piece of information."

I wanted to hit him, but I still needed information. "He wanted to keep me?" I asked, numb with disbelief and impotent rage.

"Yes, but obviously you escaped from his clutches unharmed."

"Only because I had help." I glared at Billy. "Did you know about his house at the edge of the forest?"

"Yeah. We helped set it up for him. We knew he wanted you."

As much as I wanted to rip his head from his body, he had known about it all and did nothing to stop it. But who was I kidding? He was a bad guy, who loved doing bad things. Unfortunately, I still needed answers.

"What was with the nursery and children's bedroom?"

Billy didn't have to say it; his eyes told me. Simon wanted me to be his mate.

"But he was an old vampire. He couldn't have children," I said, trying to answer the unasked question.

"He wasn't that old. He was just freakishly powerful. He only turned into a vampire when freezing sperm became a reality. He wanted his own hybrids. Blaire, you were to have his children, whether he could do it naturally or not."

"Fuck me!" someone said behind me. I think it was Ralph; he had started to sound more and more like me—potty mouths.

It reminded me of that dream I had of Sebastian; maybe it wasn't a dream after all. Nausea bubbled to the surface. I lunged from my chair and ran to the nearest bathroom. I spilled my guts into the toilet and washed my face. Tears threatened again. But it was over. He was dead. I wouldn't be having his children. I stared at my pale reflection in the mirror and needed to speak with Mel—I needed a pregnancy test.

"You okay?" Anne asked from the doorjamb.

I flinched. I hadn't heard her approach. "Yeah, I think so."

"Did Simon hurt you?"

"Honestly, I don't know. He drugged me, so—"

"Should I ask Mel to come?"

I didn't answer. I just looked at her, my eyes speaking on my behalf.

"I'll see if she can come now, with a pregnancy test."

I choked on my tears all over again. "Thanks."

Once I felt better, I returned to the living room. I didn't look anyone in the eye, but I could feel their stares, their sympathy hitting me like a lightning bolt.

"Yeah. Simon was a piece of work," Billy said once I sat across from him again.

"It's not like you were any better. You knew what he was up to, yet you did nothing to stop him. In fact, you aided in his evil work."

"I deserve this, no doubt about it. But you must remember, the real bad guy, is still out there. I'm sorry I don't know who he is, but he's worse than Simon. All these tests he's conducting and now that Sebastian is in his clutches, you can be sure he's devising something bigger than anyone can think of. Good luck with that."

"Okay, I've had enough of this guy," Marc blurted, approaching us. "Lance wants him dead, Blaire. The sooner the better."

"He might know more, Marc."

Marc grimaced at Billy. "He doesn't have anything left to say, do you, Billy?"

"He is right, Blaire. I've said enough. Nothing more will be able to keep me alive."

Marc was right; we were done with him. He needed to die, not only because of his actions but because he had known what Simon was doing and he had not tried to prevent it. He was no worse than the person who had concocted everything, no worse than Kasdeya who had created the serum, no worse than Simon who had taken Sebastian from me and everyone else. One thing was certain, it was time for him to die.

Without thinking about it, I reached for my gun and aimed it at Billy's face. His wide eyes stared at me, then he smiled as if I wouldn't do it. I pumped five bullets into his face, obliterating it. The specialized bullets we had manufactured specifically for Ulysses Assassins would ensure nobody could recognize him.

I'd caught everyone off guard, because Ralph, Marc, and Sawyer all drew their weapons and pointed it at the bloody corpse across from me.

"Jesus, Blaire. Fucking warn us next time," Ralph chastised me from behind.

I stood and went to Anne's kitchen. I opened the cabinet where I knew she kept alcohol and poured myself a shot of whiskey. I downed it then had another. I didn't care what time it was; it was late afternoon somewhere in the world.

"Anyone want one?"

"Yeah, I'll have," Anne said as she touched my back, reaching for the full glass. She downed hers.

"We need to find Sebastian. If what Billy said was true, they're testing on him, using what they can. Who knows how long he has left to live? If it's the same people who tested on Ross and his Ophelia, I don't think he has long."

Anne nodded at me, keeping her arm around my shoulders and squeezing.

I poured another shot and downed it. It burned going down my throat, but it felt good. "I don't even know where to start, Anne. Do you?"

She shook her head with pain in her eyes.

The text ringtone on my cellphone sounded, letting me know I had a message from Lance.

Thanks for getting Billy. Don't forget the Oracle wants to speak with you.

Mel entered the living area, motioning for me to follow her to the bathroom.

"I've brought a few tests for you to try. I hope your bladder is full."

"Yeah," I said and stumbled to sit on the porcelain chair. "I've been saving all of it just for you," I slurred.

She handed me two different types of pregnancy sticks, and I urinated on both at the same time. I didn't have time to waste. When I was done, I placed them on the basin and finished up. I sat beside her on the edge of the bath, trying to balance so I didn't fall into the tub. We waited the two minutes in silence.

My headache, I blamed on the whiskey. But my twisted-feeling chest? I blamed that on my shattered heart.

But I couldn't sit still. I fidgeted with my shirt then my pants. Eventually, I gripped the bath until my knuckles ached. I hoped and prayed I wasn't pregnant, that it was only a dream and that Simon hadn't had his way with me. I was on oral contraceptive and it might be too early to test, but Simon was an evil vampire so anything was possible.

Mel noticed my fidgeting and tried to take my mind off the two sticks busy changing to either one line or two. The tests she had run on the poison revealed they were comprised of similar strands of the same stuff. So, we were right in assuming it was the same serum Billy had used on Lance. She categorized her findings but destroyed the samples. It was bad stuff, and she didn't want anyone to find them, replicate them and use them ever again.

The sound of her voice had managed to calm me and ease my tension. But it was short lived. When she rose, my stomach dropped, and my feet were heavy.

I needed to know, but, at the same time, I didn't want to know. But what if I was pregnant? What if there was a slight chance it was Sebastian's? Could I get rid of his child? But what if it was Simon's? Argh. I wanted to throw up.

Mel grabbed the tests and stared at me. "Do you want the good news or bad news first?"

"Please don't do that to me. Just say it." I squeezed my eyes tight.

"Not pregnant."

I exhaled a sigh of relief. "Thank fuck. But you'll still draw blood to make doubly sure?"

"Yep. We can do that here quickly." She knew my fear

of needles and gently pushed my face to one side while she drew blood. It was the second time I didn't feel pain. Perhaps I was over my fear. Here's hoping.

With one less thing to worry about, I could concentrate on more important things.

Chapter Twenty-Six

Billy was dead. Simon was dead. Kasdeya was dead.

No more deaths had been reported in the shifter community, but Sebastian was still missing. Most had presumed he was dead, except a handful of us.

Léon believed he was alive after Anne and I spoke with him, but the overwhelming sense of grief was still in him and me.

Against his wishes, I'd arranged for a visit to Chicago, so I could meet with the oracle. From what Lance had said, she knew me and needed to speak with me face to face, and soon.

With much convincing and reassurance, I went alone. Léon argued that I needed Sawyer or Marc with me. I argued against it. I managed to calm his overprotective nerves by telling him that Lance would personally fetch me from the airport and take me to the oracle. I would be there for a day at the most, and, if I was sleeping over, Lance would arrange my accommodation. I would be safe. I would be cared for. He didn't have to worry.

Léon loaned me his private plane, so I was traveling in style. As we touched down at Chicago airport, I recognized the black SUV and the tall blond standing beside it. I had only brought a small carry on with a change of clothing just in case, which Lance grabbed from my hands when I reached him. He hugged me and squeezed a second longer than necessary.

Once I could breathe again, he greeted me with a scrutinizing eye, like I was about to crack. "How are you doing?"

"Fine."

I was fine, but also not so fine. I was in limbo, that space between sanity and psychosis, somewhere between being sensitive and numb. I wanted to be out there searching for Sebastian, but I also wanted to know what the oracle knew.

"I can see you aren't fine, Blaire." He narrowed his eyes at me.

"Then why did you ask?"

"Hmm, stubborn."

"Always."

"I hope Marc is being the best were-rat possible."

"Marc is great. Thanks for letting me borrow him."

"No. He's yours to do with as you please."

I frowned at him. "Marc isn't a toy to possess. He's a human."

"I know, but he's yours, all the same." He opened the car door for me, threw my bag on the back seat and climbed in to start the engine. "Let me know when you need more of my men. I only have the best."

I glanced at him, his cold blue eyes piercing mine. "Thanks," was all I could say. I didn't like his choice of words to describe the men who worked for him, and he seemed like the type of person who wouldn't stop describing them the way he wanted to. I left it at that. However, I did want to know more about the mysterious oracle and why she wanted to see me so badly.

We merged into traffic on the freeway. "You were very cryptic about this oracle, Lance. Who is she, and what does she know?"

"She didn't tell me, just that she can help."

"Do you trust her?"

"With my life."

"Who is she to you then?"

He sighed. "My mother."

I was too stunned by that revelation to say anything else. We drove the rest of the way in silence. No wonder he had been pushing me to see her. He knew what she had to say must be important. She was his mother, after all. He trusted her judgement, or whatever she knew. But I had no idea how she knew me. I guessed it wouldn't hurt to find out. Perhaps she could enlighten me on my past.

Lance parked the SUV outside an apartment building. He cut the engine and faced me. "She doesn't want me to escort you inside. Go to the sixth floor, apartment six thirty-eight. She's expecting you."

"Thanks," I said and exited.

A doorman dressed in a long coat and top hat opened the door to the apartment building. "Morning, ma'am," he said while tipping his hat to me.

"Morning," I said and entered. Inside, I was greeted by warm air and a red carpet to guide me to the elevators. Mailboxes lined either side of the foyer that led to two elevators next to a small round table with two chairs—for those who wished to read their mail, I supposed.

I thumbed the up button and waited for the elevator. The doors opened with a swish, and I entered, hitting the button for the sixth floor. The ride up was efficient and quiet. When I reached the sixth floor, the same color red carpet greeted me and then split in two directions. The plaque on the wall up ahead informed me that I needed to go left. I passed the various apartment doors until I reached apartment 638; the smell of peanut butter cookies assaulted my nose and made my mouth water, transporting me to a childhood I no longer remembered.

As I lifted my fist to knock, the door opened. A woman my height with soft blond curls and crystal blue eyes very similar to Lance's smiled at me. "Blaire, you're just in time."

I closed my mouth and smiled. "Ah, Lance didn't tell me your name. He only refers to you as the oracle."

She chuckled sweetly. "He's such a goofball. My name is Vivian."

It was strange to hear her talk about her son—the were-rat king—as a *goofball*. I smiled at Vivian, giggling on the inside. Could I tease Lance without getting killed?

She opened the door wide enough for me to enter. I followed her through a narrow hallway into the kitchen where fresh cookies were cooling on racks.

"Let's sit and chat until the kettle boils for tea."

I nodded, following her into an empty living room sans two double-seater couches facing each other. The walls were medically white, and, even though the room was right next door to the kitchen, I couldn't smell the cookies anymore. There was nothing, just air.

"You are frowning," she said as she sat, motioning me to

sit across from her. "Is it because you can't smell the cookies in here?"

My frown deepened. "Yeah. That's exactly what I was thinking. But—"

"There are a lot of things I know, Blaire. But first, before I get into all that, tell me. Do you remember me at all?"

I studied her—her blue eyes, blond curls, oval face. I shook my head. "No, can't say that I do."

"I didn't think you would remember me, but I had to ask. You were only a baby when your parents brought you to me."

My frown was back, and my head throbbed. "Why would they bring me to you?" I asked curiously and intrigued—lethal combinations for someone who might not like what she was about to hear.

"You were about a year old, and even at that tender young age they knew you were special." Her smile was delicate and seemed rehearsed for all her clients.

I kept quiet. I wanted her to carry on. This was the most anyone knew of my parents.

"You started exhibiting behavior around the house that alerted your parents that you could do certain ... *things*."

"Like what?"

"Things would move. The hair on your parents' body would rise every time they touched you or picked you up. When a dog approached you, before it could get near, it went whimpering in the other direction. Your gran was a witch. She tried to put a spell on you, but it backfired and hit her instead. Apparently, it took her a year to regrow the purple hair." She chuckled. "I could just image what that looked like. Anyway, they came to me, so I could see exactly what you were. They had an idea, but they needed more information, as you can imagine. Even before they rode up the elevator, I felt your presence."

I rubbed my arms as chills ran down my spine.

"I opened the door, much like I did for you today. For such a small bean, you masked your power well, but I still *felt* you. I asked your parents to stay outside while I took you in my arms. I remember looking down at you, your green eyes staring into mine. You had the world of knowledge, but no one could understand you." She paused, not having blinked yet. "Tell me, Blaire, have you discovered your saber yet?"

I swallowed hard, and it hurt. "Yes. It happened a few days ago."

"Through your rage?"

I nodded, unable to blink. My heart raced. My blood rushed in my ears.

"An explosion of white light?"

I nodded again; I didn't trust my voice. She was good. And she knew so much. My palms sweated.

"And your healing powers but I guess everyone knows about that now, don't they? And how you can syphon powers from others."

Another nod. "But I haven't figured out how to keep it yet."

"Ah, your treasure chest, your box of tricks—it's there. It's still inside you. You just need to find your hiding spot. I'm sure it's full of all sorts of naughty things." She tucked her one leg under the other and leaned back, utterly relaxed. "Your shielding needs improvement though. That white light of yours is still sprinkling around me like confetti."

I froze, staring at her with wide eyes. "I thought I was improving."

"Just a couple minutes of thoughtful practice every day should do the trick, and you'll be as good as you were before your accident. But don't worry about it now. Not everyone is as perceptive as me." She winked. "Do you know of the other thing you can do?"

I cocked an eyebrow, shrugging. "What other thing? I can't do anything else. Well, anything I can remember. I've been collecting lycanthropy strains." I shrugged.

"That's due to you being able to syphon powers, it's only your saber you can shift into." I nodded again, listening, absorbing. "You certainly are one of a kind. This other thing is only a small part of you though, but it's there. I didn't say it earlier, but that was one of the real reasons why your parents came to me. Remember I said a dog had approached you?" I nodded again; it felt like that was the only thing I was doing —listening and nodding. "Well, the dog wasn't exactly alive."

"What?" My eyes widened.

"Somehow, you managed to raise your dog that had died the day before. But, like I say, it's not your main talent, but I'm sure if you practiced enough and homed in on it, you could do it as naturally as breathing. But, if I were you, I wouldn't. Vampires don't appreciate it when specials can control the dead—and, ultimately, control *them*. Those who possess that skill are heavily guarded, and even then, they don't raise zombies as often. Any zombie raising is done with a very good reason and by someone who's well protected. Be careful who you mention this to—"

Vivian said something else, but I couldn't hear her. I saw her lips move and then not much of anything else. Minutes or hours must have passed, I wasn't sure. All I could do was just stare at her. My mind was trying to process this information, trying to understand what exactly I was capable of doing. It was too much. It was all too much for me to understand what I was.

My skin felt like it was peeling away from my muscles. My fingers and toes were ice cold. I heard a snap and felt a tug in my chest. I glanced down to see myself sitting on the couch. Me, my soul, floated from my body. I was light as air and drifting near the ceiling.

So this is what they described as an out-of-body experience.

Still entirely numb, I steadied my breathing like Seraphine had taught me. I needed to control my thoughts, so I didn't spiral out of control and leave my mind and body completely. It was too much.

First, it was the grief from losing Sebastian. Then everything I had endured with the witch, the vampire, the voodoo priest, and now *this*. That I could raise the dead. That I had power over the dead. It sounded almost impossible that I could do all these things. Surely, she was wrong. A thought crossed my mind; it could explain why most vampires didn't like me, and that it wasn't just jealousy. And why I could make Léon's heart beat. No ...

"Are you okay?" Vivian asked, her voice dreamlike inside my head. Slowly, I reemerged through the darkness and into the room. She brought me from my trance and into reality, into the now.

"Uh-huh, I think so. It's just ..." I licked my lips. "A lot to take in, you know? Even though I already knew about most of it, everything is catching up to me."

"Yes, I'm sure. When Lance came to me asking about this girl who could do all these things, I knew he meant *you*, and it was imperative that I spoke with you. But only face to face. To give someone information over the phone is so impersonal. I hope I've helped to shed *some* light on how special you truly are."

"You have. One more thing, can you remember anything about my parents?"

"Only that they were very private people. I couldn't read them, and felt your mother was special, but she shielded very well. As I said before, I was more interested in you."

"Thank you, Vivian. Is there anything else?" I checked my phone, surprised that three hours had passed.

A smile splashed across her face. "Time does fly here, doesn't it?"

"But—"

"No buts. You were processing all this information. I left you alone for a while. You needed time to understand what I had said. Lance is still outside waiting for you. Don't worry, he won't leave you."

I sat for another moment before I joined Vivian in the kitchen. The smell of cookies was long gone. She handed me a tin wrapped in a ribbon filled with cookies.

"Thanks."

"My pleasure, and tell Lance he must see me if he wants his own tin." Her grin was contagious, but I wasn't in the mood. I knew my smile was forced, but she didn't call me on it. She was certainly kind enough for the both of us.

Just as I reached the hallway that led to the elevator, she paused before closing her front door. "And, Blaire ... He isn't dead."

"What?"

"Sebastian isn't dead," she whispered, another smile playing on her face. "When you see Scout, *everything* will fall into place."

Before I could say anything else, she closed the door in

my face, dead bolting it. I was stunned—happy, sad, elated, angry—a plethora of emotions hit me at once, and I didn't know which way to go. I heard the elevator chime its arrival, snapping me from my emotional hurricane, and walked toward my ride down.

Once I was outside, the cool air slapped hard against my face, waking me from what I could only describe as a trance.

"Where's mine?" Lance asked when I approached. He was already pulling me toward the parked SUV.

"Your mommy said that if you want some, you have to visit her."

He grunted when he opened the door for me. "And trippy inside, wasn't it?"

"You could say that. I still can't feel my body."

"Yeah. She has a way of numbing you. It goes away, don't worry."

I rubbed my index and thumb over the bridge of my nose.

"Hope you don't mind. I've arranged a room at my place."

"Won't Mandy have an issue?"

"Yeah, probably." He grinned. "But I'm King."

Epilogue

I instructed John, the pilot of Léon's private plane, to return to Sterling Meadow without me. He scrutinized my decision with hard brown eyes and shook his head. "Léon won't like this."

"Please don't tell him anything until after you've landed," I said as I handed him my earrings—the ones Sebastian had given me with the built-in GPS tracker.

John pocketed them. "Fine, but you do realize he'll kill me for not bringing you home."

"I'm sorry." I handed over the tin of cookies as a consolation for getting him into trouble.

"Where are you going?"

"To see my daughter. I can't go when people are breathing down my neck or tracking me. Her safety comes first." I turned on my heels without waiting for his response and reentered O'Hare Airport to find the nearest Starbucks.

When the oracle had told me that everything would snap into place once I saw my daughter, I knew I had to see her, and soon. And to hear confirmation that Sebastian was still alive, I didn't feel guilty about leaving for an extra day or two to see my daughter.

I bought the first flight to Portland, Oregon. I'd memorized their address when I had opened my safety deposit box a few weeks ago.

Once I landed and rented a vehicle, I drove straight to their address. I parked across their street and waited. It was after 3pm when I saw kids walk home from school.

When one of the kids broke away from a group and entered the house I was watching, I knew it was her.

I climbed out my rental, crossed the road and walked up the footpath.

As I was about to knock on the door, a man's voice sounded behind me "Blaire?"

I turned around to see who it belonged to. "Mason?"

Next in the Blaire Thorne Series

vinci-books.com/salvation

The truth is closer than ever and it will change everything.

Children are disappearing in Sterling Meadow, and Ralph and I are digging deep. But when the call I've dreaded arrives—Scout is in danger—I must make an impossible choice. To save her, I'll face the man who destroyed my past. The truth will shatter everything.

Turn the page for a free preview…

Salvation: Chapter One

TEN YEARS AGO

I drove while Ralph leafed through documents in one of his yellow folders. I was sure he bought them in bulk, because he always had at least ten on hand. He seemed to collect them like others collected stamps. I giggled to myself imagining him hunched over his worktable, separating them by the different shades of yellow. He kept paging forward then backward then forward again, flapping loose pages then placing them back in the folder.

"What are you looking for?" I asked with irritation laced in my voice.

"I just want to make sure we have the right guy. That's all."

I sighed. "It's a vampire, Ralph. I can feel it in my bones. Now stop paging through that damn folder. You're messing with my Zen."

"Pfft, whatever!"

"We're here anyway, so shove it somewhere out of sight."

We arrived at Lake Hills Institute for Children. The sinister-looking building was three and a half stories high; the half was for the creepy attic at the top with broken crescent windows that looked like a mouth missing some teeth. The building was once white, about a hundred years ago. Now it was grey with some areas near the ground rotting away with black mold. I wouldn't want to be near the place when it crumbled to the ground, but I felt sorry for the kids who wouldn't grow up. The only parking bays taken were cars that belonged to the medical staff, which weren't that many. I parked beside an old sun-kissed box BMW near the entrance.

A gust of wind blew through the trees, and a chime sounded from somewhere inside the institute. A cold shiver ran down my spine. I stood on one spot and stared at the trees.

"Come on, princess. I'm not getting any younger." Ralph moaned as he climbed the stairs to the entrance.

An eerie feeling washed over me. I ran my fingers over the gun in my shoulder holster. Touching the cool metal was soothing and eased my fight-or-flight instinct. Now I was ready. Well, kind of.

"Someone's out there." I rubbed my arms and headed toward him.

"You know what to do if the boogeyman jumps out of the forest?" He chuckled.

"Yeah, I'll use you as a shield as I test drive our new bullets."

Ralph continued chuckling as he ascended the steps.

"Glad I'm still amusing." I elbowed him in his side.

"Come, partner. Your favorite doc waits." He wrapped

his meaty arm around my shoulders and dragged me to the front door.

I groaned as we reached the entrance. The smell of urine assaulted my nose first, stealing my breath. I stopped breathing to avoid the stench. On the other side of the locked metal gate, a naked young boy sat on the floor busy mixing a yellow substance into the dirt that had gathered in the corner.

I widened my eyes at Ralph.

"Please, Blaire, just don't piss off the doctor again," he chastised me even before I could say anything.

"Well, well, well. Look what the cat dragged in," the nurse chimed from behind her glass cage.

"Nurse ... whatever your name is, can you not see the little boy urgently needs your help?" I pointed to the dirty, naked child.

"Not my duty, monster killer." The nurse folded her arms and pursed her lips.

"It's not only monsters I kill." I glared at her then added quickly, "Is the doctor in? He's expecting us." I shot her my best fake smile.

"Wait here. Let me check." She rose from her torn chair and exited the glass cage, disappearing somewhere in the institute.

"I fucking hate this place." I felt I needed a hot bath and to scrub my skin with a body brush until I bled.

"What did I just say?" Ralph grumbled.

Shrugging, I added, "I didn't piss off the doctor."

"No, but that nurse will tell him and piss him off all the same."

"They hired us, Ralph. They should be glad we're even here."

"Let me do the talking, please." His shoulders sagged, and he gave me his best blue puppy-dog eyes.

"Fine. But only because you looked so cute when you asked, and you said the magic word." I grinned while he groaned. He hated it when I called him cute, but it's hard to resist his charm.

On the right-hand side of the entrance hung a plaque with a large picture frame. It read that the school had opened in 1889 and housed talented children. I wasn't sure if they meant the kids had some form of disability or were mystical or magical. But the kid on the floor didn't seem the latter. Twenty staff members adorned the photo, all dressed in white, comprising of nurses, orderlies, and the man in the middle who ran the place—Curtis Hilling. Underneath the frame hung more plaques stating which of the Hilling sons had taken over and from which year. Arthur took over from his father in 1901. Isaac ran the place from 1946, Charles from 1983, and, lastly, Lu from 1999.

The buzzer sounded, and the gate clicked open.

"Dr. Hilling can see you now. Go straight to his office. If you don't remember where it is, just walk down the hallway. You can't miss it. It has his name on his door, if you aren't sure. If you can't read, just look inside the office. He's sitting at his desk."

Ralph pushed open the gate.

I followed him and closed the gate behind me. I started walking toward the door where the nurse sat in her little glass safety office, but Ralph pulled me away to walk beside him. I would not do anything that hurt too much. I was just going to tell the nurse we remembered where the doctor's office was. Maybe slap her. Instead, I stared at her with murderous intent.

The smell of feces wafted in the air as we passed the

boy. He was now pushing brown mushy stuff through circles of yellow mud.

I covered my mouth with both hands and gagged—yuck.

A cockroach scurried past me and met up with its buddies on the other side of the corridor. I shuddered. This place was not sanitary and should definitely not be housing any children, no matter their age. I didn't think it was safe for adults, unless a cleaning crew made the place sparkle, which I doubted. The institute had years and years of grime stuck everywhere that needed to be burned, not just cleaned. And I would gladly light the match.

As we approached the doctor's office, one side of the corridor wall displayed brown finger marks about hip high in a wavy pattern, as if the child had run dirty fingers against the wall as he or she went along. I hoped it was mud. I wasn't confident it was and wouldn't stick my tongue there to test it either.

Ralph entered the office first to find Dr. Lu Hilling sitting behind his desk, as the nurse had said. He ignored us until Ralph cleared his throat.

Dr. Hilling glanced up; for a moment he just stared as if he didn't recognize us, then eventually, he smiled, rising from his chair. "Ralph, Blaire. So good to see you again. Please, won't you come in?" He walked to a trolley and picked up a jug. "Can I offer you something to drink?"

"No, thank you, Dr. Hilling," I said, eyeing the suspicious liquid.

"I'm good," Ralph replied quickly.

I was sure he would rather lick the wall than drink what Dr. Hilling offered us in that jug.

"Are you sure?" Dr. Hilling confirmed, pouring the liquid half-way into a glass then another glass. "The water comes fresh from our well." He picked up both glasses and placed them on his table, each opposite a chair. "Please sit."

We sat, and I eyed the brown-yellow substance. Water my ass.

"Thank you for coming. Hopefully, it won't be a waste of your time again." Dr. Hilling sat in his soft, comfortable chair while we sat on hard wooden ones.

"How old is the child who went missing this time?" I asked, wanting to get straight to the reason why we were there. Again.

Ralph widened his eyes at me. Apparently, I forgot I couldn't speak to the doctor.

I shrugged.

Dr. Hilling cleared his throat. "Eight." He leaned back in his chair, threading his fingers and placing them on his large stomach.

"When was she taken?" Ralph asked.

"Sometime last night."

"Does anyone check on the kids during the night?" I asked, ignoring Ralph's fierce glare.

"Only after lights out, thereafter, once again after five hours."

"So—"

Ralph kicked my shin.

I bit my bottom lip, trying to ignore the sharp pain shooting up my shin. This was partner wars, and he just threw the first kick. I ignored him like any good partner would and continued my questioning. "All these children you look after, are they only supervised when somebody is around?"

Dr. Hilling nodded, the hair framing his face showing signs of grey. His deep-set brown eyes seeming to burn a hole into my forehead. If he had knives, I was sure he would throw them at me. He bounced upright in his chair and hit his hands on the desk, making me flinch. The yellow water rippled in the glasses.

"With the limited resources they give us, we care for these children to the best of our abilities, Miss Thorne. Without us, where would they go? And we rely heavily on donations ever since the government stopped funding us." He rose, towering over us. Shadows played on his face, leaving him with sinister features. "Let me take you to the room from which they took her. Perhaps you can pick up on clues we may have missed."

Ralph stood. "That would be great."

Dr. Hilling exited his office with us following. The good doctor was around my height and had a round, supple ass that bounced with each step. From the front, his hair was short and neat; from the back, a tight ponytail secured the bottom half of his hair. His shoulders were as broad as mine, while his front showed signs of small round breasts where, I assumed, he would strap them close to his body.

Dr. Lu Hilling, as we had suspected the first time we had visited, was actually Louise Hilling—born female. We didn't mind what our client's sexual orientation was; the job always came first. It was, however, how he performed his job that made us suspicious.

Ralph elbowed me, I lost my footing and crashed onto the first step, knocking my shin. I was sure it would leave a bruise, especially since this was the second time I had hurt myself. I cried out in pain.

"Are you all right?" Dr. Hilling asked, bending to help me up.

I waved him away. "I'm fine, thank you. Just knocked my leg. Perhaps take Ralph up while I rest on the steps?"

"Fine. Come, Ralph."

I watched Ralph and Dr. Hilling disappear up the stairs, then I ran back to his office. I had about a minute. I rifled through the papers on his desk and opened the drawers to find invoices and folders for food orders and purchases. On the right was a metal filing cabinet I hadn't tried yet. I opened the bottom drawer first and found bank statements. What caught my attention was the wire transfers from the institute into Dr. Hilling's personal bank account.

Voices echoed down the hallway; they were on their way back. I rose from his chair and ran to the stairs as quietly as my shoes would allow. I sat on the step as I saw Ralph.

He winked.

"See anything interesting?" I asked, steadying my breath.

"Nope, but I suggested we look around outside. Last time, they cut our visit short, but today, we have all the time in the world." Ralph beamed at me as he walked past.

Dr. Hilling offered me his hand. When I grabbed it, I felt a hint of magic behind his grip; hot pinpricks fluttered across my palm.

I'd had enough practice not to show signs I held any power nor did I reveal I could register power. It's safer that way for me and anyone who knew me.

Dr. Hilling blinked, and, for the first time, I noticed a nictitating membrane; a transparent third eyelid moved across each eye, similar to that of a crocodile or lizard. He was not even human. How had I not seen that coming?

I revealed nothing as I stood and followed Dr. Hilling and Ralph outside.

"As I've said before, this isn't the first child to have gone missing, Miss Thorne. This vile monster has taken five of our precious children already."

I nodded in disgust. "We will catch them, Dr. Hilling. Whoever the monster is will pay for what they have done."

Once outside, I saw a handful of kids skipping rope, another drawing with chalk on the cement, and one girl laying under a tree. I did a double take at the girl under the tree. "Is she clothed?" I asked, shocked they would allow a young girl to be naked outside. Older men worked here. I said a silent prayer, asking that they weren't hurting any other kids.

"There are"—Dr. Hilling cleared his throat—"some who do not listen to us." He waved over an orderly. "Please arrange for Miss Bayle to be dressed, and give her Diazepam if she resists you."

"Do you medicate them often, Dr. Hilling?"

"I fail to see how your questions are relevant to the case at hand, Miss Thorne. You need to find the beast who's kidnapping my children and doing who knows what with them, not question how I run my facility."

Sucking in air and patience, I responded as calmly as I could. "I need to understand what's happening at your institute, Dr. Hilling. Maybe these children are choosing to leave your institution at their own free will, or, as you suggest, someone's stealing them from right under your nose. I only ask these questions so we know exactly what is happening here. And, if it is a monster taking the children, we need to stop them sooner rather than later."

Dr. Hilling blinked, and again, I saw that third membrane slide across each eye, and he fidgeted with his sleeve.

Ralph cleared his throat, slicing through the uncomfortable silence. "I suggest we widen our search and go farther into the forest. Is that gate always open?" He pointed to a weathered gate that had seen better days. Even if it was always locked, monsters could break it with a sneeze. Or jump over it. Some monsters could fly, no matter the size of the lock or gate.

"No. It's supposed to be locked," Dr. Hilling said, rushing in the gate's direction.

The lock was broken and laying on the ground. I guess someone sneezed after all.

"You stay here, Dr. Hilling. Ralph and I will be back. And please take all the kids inside. It's not safe for anyone to be outside until we catch this monster." I pushed passed him with Ralph behind me.

Dr. Hilling didn't answer me. Instead, he turned and ushered the kids inside like a good doctor following orders.

Grab your copy...
vinci-books.com/salvation

About the Author

A Multi-genre author writing twisted endings...

N Gray is a USA Today Bestselling Author who lives in Cape Town, South Africa, with her daughter and adopted cat named Miss Beans.

During the day, she's an analyst and provider profiler for a medical insurance company. At night, she types on her curved keyboard, creating fictional characters some may love and others you want to kill yourself.

She writes in four genres: urban fantasy, thriller, horror, and paranormal romance.

She now writes under Natalie Michaels for her new thrillers and SD Syns for her new horrors.

Acknowledgments

Thank you to my readers, old and new, for taking a chance on my books.

You are the reason I write the stories I do. As long as you keep reading, I'll keep writing.

I'm truly humbled by your support and encouragement.

I write in as many genres as I love reading in. There are so many stories swarming inside my head that I could never just choose one.

Horror is my guilty pleasure. I love writing short stories filled with dark humour and the occult with a twist ending.

Urban fantasy and paranormal romance are where I love to spend my time, and I have so many books planned that I don't have enough time (*but I'll get there*).

And lastly, my thrillers. Who doesn't love sitting on the edge of their seat while reading about what goes on inside the antagonist's mind? Well, I love writing about them.

www.ingramcontent.com/pod-product-compliance
Ingram Content Group UK Ltd.
Pitfield, Milton Keynes, MK11 3LW, UK
UKHW040247291225
466476UK00003B/9